THE NIGHT
VOYAGERS

THE NIGHT VOYAGERS

DONN KUSHNER

Lester Publishing

Canadian Cataloguing in Publication Data

Kushner, Donn, 1927–
    The night voyagers

ISBN 1-895555-69-8 (bound)   ISBN 1-895555-79-5 (pbk.)

I. Title.

PS8571.U75N54 1995 jC813'.54 C95-931420-2
PZ7.K87Ni 1995

Lester Publishing Limited
56 The Esplanade
Toronto, Ontario
Canada M5E 1A7

Printed and bound in Canada

95 96 97 98 5 4 3 2 1

for Paul and Catherine

Acknowledgements

I am indebted to Kathy Lowinger and Gena Gorrell for patient and thorough editing of different versions of this story, and for trying to control the complexities of my imagination. Nancy Pocock, Rodolfo Arenas and others provided valuable discussions of the situation of Latin-American refugees. Lesley Krueger read an earlier version of the book and provided very valuable information on Spanish phrases and, especially, on the state of human rights in Central America. Naturally, I bear the responsibility for any errors.

Contents

Foreword

In the Spanish-speaking area known as Central America — south of Mexico — a number of small countries have suffered terrible civil wars. The wars are usually between the governments, which control the money and power, and "leftist" or "socialist" rebels who want the people to have a more equal share. The governments say the rebels are Communists; the rebels say the governments are dictatorships.

In the course of these civil wars, thousands of innocent people have been killed, mainly by the governments' armies or by their unofficial "death squads." Often people just disappear, and their families don't know whether they'll be back or whether they're gone for ever.

Many people have tried to escape this violence by fleeing to North America, especially the United States. But the American government posts immigration officers (called *migras* by the fugitives) along the U.S.–Mexico border to try to keep them out. This is partly because the refugees are suspected of being Communists — long seen as enemies — and partly because there's a long list of people waiting to enter the country legally, and the government feels it's not fair to let others slip in ahead of them. Many refugees have been turned back at the border; others were caught inside the United States, and sent back to the countries they came from.

Yet others managed to stay, sometimes with the aid of the sanctuary movement. This was a secret network of people who believed that, if refugees were in danger of torture and death, they should be allowed to remain. The members of the sanctuary movement helped refugees by hiding them, feeding and clothing them, and secretly moving them farther into the country. People who were caught helping refugees could be fined or sent to prison.

This is a story about one family and their desperate flight to safety. The time is about 1985.

A glossary of terms and a list of sources of information on the sanctuary movement and ancient Mayan mythology can be found at the end of the book.   D.K.

ONE

In the Ball Court

The ball court was no bigger than the weed-choked one in Chilichepango, where they had slept one night. It was certainly much smaller than the great court in Chichén Itzá, in the Yucatán region of Mexico, far to the north of their own country. Manuel's father had seen pictures of that one, and he had described it using his own carefully shaded drawings: it was a Mayan place of great palaces and pyramids, with a sacred ball court where the penalty for losing a game could be death.

But even though they had crossed a river and passed through a tunnel of barbed wire to reach it, *this* ball court was surely not meant for anything so important. It was shut off from the sky by a high roof, but the plaster had cracked and fallen. Chunks of plaster lay scattered across the rotten wooden floor, so that Manuel had to kick the ball very cleverly to keep it from striking them. On each side of the court was a high row of three hoops, horizontal metal ones. The court at Chiliche-pango was different — it had vertical stone circles sticking out from the walls, and Manuel's father had once told him that the

Mayan Indians who played there hundreds of years ago had to get a heavy rubber ball through the circles using their knees, shoulders or thighs — never their hands.

Those were like the rules for the light black-and-white ball his older brother, Pepe, had found on their journey, that he always kept with him now. Except this ball wasn't solid, it was filled with air; and you were allowed to use your feet. You could kick it here and there, down the wide open field into the goal; only the player guarding the goal could use his hands.

If you were skillful enough at this game of *futbol*, his father had said, smiling at the thought, you could be rich and famous. You could travel in airplanes all over the world, and eat in the finest restaurants. On the way to the stadium the police would surround your car on all sides, but only out of respect, and to protect you, to keep away the crowds of fans who wanted to tear off your clothes as souvenirs. Once you arrived at the stadium, the police would go away and the people in the stands would cheer for you and call out your name.

Manuel looked around this small court again. There were the stands for the spectators, just as there must have been for the royal games in Chichén Itzá long ago. In the seats at either side, past the diagonal slashes of light from the late afternoon sun, he could just make out the spectators. His father, of course, sat in the highest row, in the center of the right-hand stands, where he could get the best view. So far, there were no players but Manuel himself. None of the Lords of Xibalba had shown up yet for the game — but then, his father had explained that they only came when you least expected them.

But Manuel saw that there were other spectators too, down in the first row of the stands, where they could easily slip behind the seats and out of sight: the boy with his flute; the beggar-girl with her drum and castanets. Though she had become so lively lately, so keen to explore this completely new world, she was sitting very still now. She had been no more than eight, Manuel guessed, and small for her age. The flute boy must have been at least twelve, a year older than Manuel himself, though at times he looked much more than that. Sometimes he even looked older than Pepe, who was fifteen. Now he was keeping his hand on the girl's shoulder, lest she move. They had heard the others coming before he did. Even though they knew the others couldn't see them, they still kept the caution of their former life.

Light, discreet footsteps sounded by the door at one end of the ball court. Manuel slipped behind a broken partition that ran down one row of seats, just before his mother entered, followed by the man Pepe mockingly called "the Gray Coyote." Pepe had given him this name because the man had been covered with desert dust, so that he looked as gray as a real coyote. The other "coyotes" who hung around the border stood out from the travelers by their new clothes, their clean skins, their gold watches and chains, their red bandanas, their air of daring. These were the guides, and they worked in pairs, charging the highest prices they could get. One of them took half your money before you crossed the border; his partner took the other half after he led you across and set you on the way to a new life in the promised land. If the *migras* caught you after that, too bad — your guide was gone, and so was your money.

But the Gray Coyote had no partner. He was someone you would never notice at all, Pepe said with scorn. Manuel agreed silently that you wouldn't notice him at a distance: a short, thin, gray man. Closer, he had seen that the Gray Coyote had large eyes, wary and gentle, which were always on the lookout for danger. Manuel admired the man. Wherever he went, no one would know such a person was there, he thought. You could learn a lot from him. He had suddenly appeared beside their mother, from nowhere, as they neared the American border. He was the one who told them to cross it this way, over the shallow river to the ball court.

Now he stood in the doorway with Manuel's mother. "You see," he said, "no one is here. Only your younger son, hiding behind those boards — his shadow trembled just now. There's no one else."

Manuel glanced quickly at the flute boy and the beggar-girl. The boy smiled grimly and touched the girl's arm so that her castanets jingled, but only Manuel could hear them.

"What is this place?" Manuel's mother asked the Gray Coyote.

"The district school."

His mother turned around slowly, looking at the ball court. Her shoes swept out a circle in the dust. "*This* is a school?"

"We're in the old gymnasium. You can see the hoops for basketball."

"I know what a gymnasium is. Why do they keep it in such a state?"

"It's deserted, of course. This was the poorest section of town, and it's so near the border. The river is shallow here, and a lot of people crossed here before the immigration authorities set up the barbed wire and extra guards. The district got a bad name, so they built a new school and closed this one. Now everyone crosses the river farther west, on the other side of the city."

"That's where we were going when we met you. Why have you led us this way? With such a crowd, we wouldn't have been noticed."

"You can't count on that!" The Gray Coyote seemed shocked at the thought. "The *migras*, the border patrol, are swarming like flies there, and many will be caught. And I had the feeling that your older son would march across with banners waving, that he'd be sure to attract trouble."

His mother looked through the door, and Manuel realized

that Pepe must still be standing out there, almost at attention, as Manuel had seen him do when he kept watch. "He might," she admitted.

"So they'd learn that you're OTMs."

"That we're *what*?"

"OTMs," repeated the Gray Coyote. "It's English — '*other than Mexicans*'. They just send the Mexicans back across the border; some of them try to cross again in a few hours. But you, they'd fly you back down south to your own country. And even if you were lucky enough to get out alive a second time, you'd have to make the whole journey again. All those thousands of miles."

"Back to our own country," she said bitterly.

"Or Pepe might have thrown a rock at the border patrol," the Gray Coyote continued. "I've been watching him, he's ready for action. They wouldn't like that *at all*! They'd be sure to send you all back home. You mustn't do anything to give yourselves away."

"I know."

"If you're sent back, you'll be called traitors. They say anyone who escapes is a traitor. And you know what they do with traitors."

"Of course we know."

"Good. So you see why it's best to cross here. Now listen," he added seriously. "From here you go on alone. The road behind this building leads to another road, in good repair, but it's sometimes watched. When you see the pavement become smooth, don't follow it. Cross the stream — it's dry now, this late in the summer; it fills up in the spring when the snow melts in the mountains. You'll see a path that ends behind a church with a plain wooden cross. A Protestant church, and in a wealthy district. You'll see grass all around it — they have enough water to keep the lawn green. There are ladies in the basement room there who speak Spanish."

"I can speak English," Manuel's mother said.

"That will make it even easier." The Gray Coyote smiled. "They're good people," he added quickly. "They know how bad things are for us back home, and they want to help us."

"I hope they can. And you? Won't you come too?"

"Oh no!" he said firmly. Then he explained, "You see, I'm waiting here for my wife and daughter. Somehow we were separated on the journey. But they know — rather, my wife knows, since my daughter is so young — the way to the border. If I wait by the river I'm sure to see them pass by, or to hear word of them. You didn't see them, by any chance?"

The Gray Coyote had slipped a worn photograph from his shirt pocket. "My daughter's name is Esmeralda," he added.

Manuel's mother shook her head gently. "I'm sure we haven't seen them. But if we do, if by any chance they cross here, how can we let you know?"

"Leave word at the church," he said. "They know me there. They get many such messages. And you and your sons can find shelter there for a time."

Manuel and his mother watched the Gray Coyote walk with easy steps toward the door of the ball court. He looked back sadly; then suddenly he was gone. The flute boy and the beggar-girl stood at a broken window, whispering together and pointing. Manuel followed them to the window.

The landscape outside was ragged; rusty swings and a broken seesaw stood among sparse weeds. But where was the Gray Coyote? Surely the weeds weren't thick enough to hide anyone, even someone so thin! The coils of barbed wire they had passed through glittered in the bright sun, but didn't stir — no one was crossing the river there now.

Pepe was crouching behind a small shed in the school-yard. He had already seen the gymnasium, and a classroom beside it, with an American flag painted on the wall and a dirty model of the solar system hanging from the ceiling. He had said nothing about the flag but had noted scornfully that Neptune and Uranus were mounted in the wrong order. Then he had gone to the shed to keep watch. Pepe's lean, dark face, grown thinner during their trip through the desert, turned eagerly northward to the distant hills, searching for danger everywhere. From his brother's stance, Manuel was sure that Pepe had caught no glimpse of the Gray Coyote either.

He looked back to his father for guidance, but his father only clapped his hands together silently, in honor of the Gray Coyote's ability to disappear so quickly and easily. Such a person must be right at home in lands where you always had to keep moving, Manuel agreed. He noticed that he was becoming more and more able to understand his father's meaning without the need for words.

Then Manuel caught sight of the *migra*'s hat beside the river, below the barbed wire — the wide, broad hat with the tall crown. The Gray Coyote had warned them about such hats, which fortunately could be seen at a distance. This *migra* was walking along the riverbed, looking carefully at the banks and the row of stones that made an easy path. The Gray Coyote had made them walk in the water so they wouldn't leave any trace of their passage on these stones. But there were marks on the grass where they had jumped up on the bank. The *migras* were said to be very good at tracking their human prey. When this *migra* turned around, he would surely know they'd been there.

Then Manuel saw the barbed wire shake by the riverbank, off to the left. It must be the Gray Coyote passing through. Why did he show himself now? Of course: so that the *migra* would follow him. He had seen the wire move and in a moment he had run up the bank. He was looking along the river with binoculars; he was speaking into a black instrument; he was watching the sky.

"He's not looking for us," Manuel's mother said behind

him. "But he must have called for a helicopter. We have to go quickly. Pepe was well hidden. You should have stayed outside with him instead of moping in here alone. But come on — now we know where to go."

The *migra* had disappeared behind the barbed wire, and the sky was still empty. Pepe had left his watching post and had slung on his pack, ready to set off.

"You were right, we've already crossed the border," their mother told him. "We are in the United States now — in a state called Arizona."

"Are we? Are we really in the great and wonderful United States?" Pepe sneered at the deserted schoolyard and the broken buildings. "What did you find there?" he asked Manuel in a softer tone, but he knew Manuel wouldn't answer.

"He was dreaming," their mother whispered.

"He's always dreaming. What do we do now — stay here?"

"No. Señor López told me of a road to a church."

"Where is he? Will he take us there?"

"He had others to wait for; he had to return."

"He's welcome to go." Though Manuel thought, watching his brother's thin lips droop, that Pepe was disappointed to have missed the Gray Coyote's departure. "So long as he doesn't come back and send the *migras* after us," Pepe continued.

"He's not that sort," their mother said firmly. "He's an honest man and he's as frightened of them as we are. They won't even see him. There's the road to the church, just past the fence."

Pepe saw the road then, full of weeds as it was, and began to lead the way to town; but soon their mother called him back. "You're marching in there as if you want to capture the Hill of the Jaguars," she told him. "Let Manuel go ahead. We'll know if he smells danger, even if he still won't talk."

"And he used to talk so much!" Pepe looked at his little

brother and shrugged. "Doubtless this great, free country will restore his tongue!" he added, sarcastically.

"Just keep your eyes on him," their mother said. "Remember what happened outside San Cristóbal."

"I remember," Pepe said in a low voice. He fixed his eyes on Manuel's back as his brother glided ahead of them down the path, scarcely disturbing the weeds.

Manuel watched his footsteps carefully, and each stone and clod of earth, so he wouldn't leave any traces — as his father had told him to do. All the while, he was thinking about what had happened in the hills outside San Cristóbal, before they had entered Mexico from the south.

Manuel had seen one of the Lords of Xibalba there, this one dressed as a border policeman with a long rifle and binoculars round his neck. The lord was looking far into the valley in case anyone passed by, so that he could send them to his own place, Xibalba, the Land of Death.

That time it was his father and the flute boy who had saved them. His father, who kept the best watch, had spotted the lord first. He had whispered to the flute boy, who had set his straight wooden pipe to his mouth and played a beautiful, sleepy tune. Not enough to put the lord to sleep, of course, or to make him forget his duty — the Lords of Xibalba would never do that. But this one was so enchanted by the music that he raised his eyes and looked for victims and enemies far away, and ignored the bushes just a few yards from his feet. The flute boy pointed out their way with his bare toes and with the end of his pipe, and Manuel led his mother and Pepe below the bushes and past the crest of the hill, so that the lord's most powerful binoculars couldn't reach them.

And sure enough, now the flute boy — whose name was Ricardo — led the way again, away from the deserted school with its ball court. From the way the boy skipped ahead, Manuel was sure none of the lords could be lurking about.

And soon Ricardo was no longer alone. Elena, the beggar-girl, danced beside him, clicking her castanets in rhythm to his tune — a light, teasing melody that only Manuel could hear. The children were no longer so tired, he thought. At times they had drooped, as if the journey was too much for them. Perhaps they would keep their new energy in this new country.

Ricardo and Elena led the way down the old broken road, and when it became smooth they walked along the dry streambed. Here Manuel drew back, and his mother stopped behind him, watching him closely. He thought he saw a log lying in the streambed. It was resting quietly on the cracked mud surface, but it wouldn't stay there when the spring waters came. Should he try to save it?

"Why are you stopping?" his mother asked.

Then, as he slowly approached the stream, Manuel realized that this was no dead log from the forest but only the center of a drooping tree branch. It was attached to the main trunk across the stream, a foot from the ground, but the join was masked by weeds. The branch lay across the stream, and by his feet it produced cluster on cluster of strong, dusty leaves.

Now nothing stopped them from following the path beside the stream. The children laughed at Manuel's mistake and led the way. Even though they knew others couldn't see them, they waved when a tractor drew a hay wagon along the road; they waved at an automobile filled with shouting young men, one of whom raised a brown bottle in the air. Manuel saw that his young friends had no fear, and he had none either. His mother and brother trembled when these strangers passed, but he knew there was no danger.

Meanwhile his father stood apart from the others and silently watched the tail of their procession, ready to give instant warning in case any of those wicked lords caught their scent.

TWO

The Disappeared

"You certainly speak English well," Mrs. Fisher said. "Yes, you do," agreed Mrs. Pearl.

"I used to practice it with my husband." Manuel's mother spoke slowly, trying to make each word correct. "He loved languages; he read English books when he could find them. He said we might all travel one day. The boys too."

"And you *have* traveled," said Mrs. Fisher. She was a large, gray-haired woman in a black skirt and an embroidered blouse that showed two sweat spots under her arms. Chains of turquoise, set with silver, hung around her neck.

"I imagine he didn't mean like this." Mrs. Pearl was thin and dry, in faded orange slacks and jacket.

Both women also spoke slowly, and Manuel found he could understand them easily. Perhaps his father *had* meant this kind of travel, he thought. He looked around; there was no sign of his father now, so he couldn't ask him. But before, in that other life, his father had spoken of their future "travels" lightly, as if they could never go in the ways pictured in the shiny magazines on the newsstands.

He himself was hidden behind some stacks of cardboard boxes on the cement floor of the big office in the church basement. The air was very dry, but the floor was cool and smelled damp and new. His skin felt cool and new too, though he had dried off from the shower he had taken an hour ago. Mrs. Fisher had been waiting in this basement office when his mother rang the doorbell. She had given them thick towels and had shown them where to shower after their trip through the desert. That cold, delicious shower had made him forget for a moment all the terrible things that water could do. As he thought of the shower, his skin began to itch again in memory, though all the dried salt and dirt were gone now. His mother had watched him wash, as if he were a little baby. She said she wanted to be sure that he wasn't too bitten by flies and ticks, and that he hadn't picked up any lice. She had to see for herself, she told him, since he had decided not to speak.

She hadn't even taken the first shower herself, Manuel remembered. She must have been really worried about him! They had had little chance to wash during the long, hot, crowded bus rides up through Mexico: one bus after another, some smelling of gasoline fumes, others with the windows sealed shut. Being dirty had bothered her more than any of them, even more than Pepe, who was ready to tear off his clothes and jump into any river they passed. Pepe would even have swum in the river they had crossed on the border, if the Gray Coyote hadn't stopped him. Their mother had shaken her head too, but whispered, "I wish we all could, but there'll be water on the other side."

While they were washing, Mrs. Fisher had telephoned for Mrs. Pearl, who lived nearby, to join her; then she had asked Penelope, the college student who was helping them this term, to show the Cárdenas family how to put their clothes through the washing machine and dryer.

Penelope was kind, Manuel thought. In their old life his

mother would have thrown most of the clothes away, they were so filthy, so torn by desert thorns. Penelope had only said something about coming through the desert in "rags and tatters," and then "We'll get you some fresh clothes, too." She had found him clean, worn jeans in a back room, and a shirt covered with smiling cat faces. What would Pepe say about these?

But Pepe was asleep, no longer forcing himself to keep watch. His calm breathing sounded from behind the bedroom door, blending with the motor of the refrigerator in the corner, which never seemed to stop.

It was the first time since they had left their village in the hills back home, Manuel realized, that his mother seemed ready to let events happen by themselves. In the desert, her long, dark hair had been braided and coiled in a bun under a black scarf. Now it hung loose and shining over her shoulders, and over the dress the ladies had found for her — a yellow, blue-dotted dress with a wide collar that made her look almost as young as Penelope. But even when she smiled slightly, mockingly, at the cheerful dress, her face was serious. She was as watchful as ever, saying less than she thought; but she no longer seemed to be always looking for a way to escape.

Manuel was supposed to be asleep too, but he had slipped out of the bedroom while the two ladies were taking seats opposite his mother at a long table. He wanted to see what was going on.

From an open box on the floor near him a man's face looked out. His father? No, it was an older man — stouter, less lively. He lifted the sheet of paper quietly. There was a whole family on the page: the father, two sons, a daughter, a mother too. The caption beneath read, in English, "One of Our Success Stories!"

"And your husband was a schoolteacher?" Mrs. Pearl was asking the questions, writing down each answer in a spiral notebook. Mrs. Fisher was knitting a thick blue sweater, using wide white needles that clicked regularly.

"Yes, a schoolteacher," Manuel's mother said. "A man who always loved to teach and learn."

"And you were teaching in the city? Both of you?"

"My husband was teaching in a big high school. I was studying to be a teacher, a teacher of business methods, until the government closed down the university."

"What excuse did they give for that?"

"They said the university was full of Communists."

"I'm sure it wasn't!" Mrs. Fisher exclaimed.

"I wouldn't know," Manuel's mother said carefully. "Many people in the university didn't like the government. The government says that the rebels, and everyone else who doesn't like it, are Communists."

"It's just what they would say." Mrs. Fisher's needles sounded more strongly, but in the same rhythm.

"My husband was not so concerned with politics," Manuel's mother said. "He thought ——" Her eyes turned in Manuel's direction; she must have seen him. "He thinks everyone should learn."

"He *thinks*?" asked Mrs. Pearl.

"Of course he does," Mrs. Fisher said quickly.

"But his school was next to the university, and the government must have decided that the teachers there sympathized with the rebels. One day an army tank drove through his school's front door. A colonel came to apologize the next day. He said it was an accident; but he was laughing."

Mrs. Pearl turned over a page of her notebook. "Did they attack the school again?"

"Later. The tank had cracked the roof. Rain was coming through. My husband organized teams of students to patch the roof, but one morning it was full of machine-gun bullet holes."

"They shot it full of holes during the night?"

"Yes. The school was between the university and the European embassies. All the embassies could see the school. The government didn't want to be accused of destroying a school, so they said the bullet holes had been made by vandals, by rebels."

"That follows the pattern." Mrs. Pearl wrote down several sentences, it seemed, and frowned at them. "Your government is still concerned about its international image."

"Then," Manuel's mother said, "one of the teachers — went away."

"Frightened away, of course," Mrs. Fisher said. Her knitting needles clicked strongly.

"That's what must have happened," Manuel's mother said, smiling slightly. "*Entonces perdió sus temores*," she added, translating her words in a low, clear voice into English — "Then he lost his fear" — in case the two ladies hadn't understood. They continued to question her, while Manuel's thoughts wandered to the teacher who had disappeared.

———

He was a mathematics teacher, and he had come to Manuel's father's school for a meeting one night. He and some other teachers wanted to talk about how they could teach arithmetic to children who had never handled money or learned to count past ten. He had stayed behind, after the others left, to explain some teaching methods to a village teacher. The village teacher had returned to his home, they learned later, but the mathematics teacher was never seen again.

He had "disappeared," Manuel's parents agreed. Many people disappeared these days. One instant they were where they should be: at work, or in their gardens, or walking down the street to buy a newspaper. And then suddenly they weren't anywhere. No one had seen them; sometimes no one had heard anything about them. The stories of their lives just stopped, and remained unfinished. The way they vanished seemed worse than death itself.

Death was not so frightening, Manuel thought. His parents had taken him to the hospital to see his grandmother in her last days, and he had followed her coffin to the cemetery. At least they knew what had happened to her: that was how life ended when you were very old.

Not like what happened to the mathematics teacher — or to that young doctor, a family friend, who had often worked in the barrio at a clinic for the poor. He had been at the hospital when Manuel visited his grandmother.

Sometimes this Doctor Luis came to play chess in the evening with Manuel's father. They played in the kitchen, where his father was supposed (but often forgot) to light the oven at seven o'clock for their supper, on the evenings when his mother had late classes in accounting. Manuel remembered the last time very well. While the game went on, the doctor spoke to him in English. He was hoping to study abroad and was trying to improve his skill in that language. Also, he said, the main medical journals were in English.

Doctor Luis had asked Manuel to read to him in English from a storybook he had given him for his eleventh birthday. Manuel chose the story of Snow-white, even though he thought the Disney movie was pretty corny. He read about the evil Queen who was jealous of her beautiful stepdaughter, and told a huntsman to kill the child in the forest and bring back her lung and liver to show that she was dead. "The huntsman obeyed, and took her away; but when he had drawn his knife and was about to pierce Snow-white's innocent heart, she began to weep and said: 'Ah, dear huntsman, leave me my life! I will run away into the wild forest and never come home again.'

"And as she was so beautiful the huntsman had pity on

her and said: 'Run away then, you poor child.' 'The wild beasts will soon have devoured you,' thought he, and yet it seemed as if a stone had been rolled from his heart since it was no longer needful for him to kill her. And as a young boar just then came running by he stabbed it, and cut out its lung and liver and took them to the Queen as proof that the child was dead. The cook had to salt them, and the wicked Queen ate them, and thought she had eaten the lung and liver of Snow-white."

"What are 'lung and liver'?" Manuel asked the doctor.

"*El pulmón y el hígado,*" Doctor Luis said, looking up from the chessboard.

"*Qué feo!*" Manuel said. "How gross!"

"Check," said Manuel's father.

"In other, somewhat less gross versions, the huntsman brings back the heart of a deer," the doctor told Manuel.

"It's your move," said Manuel's father. While the young doctor looked, puzzled, at the board, Manuel's father said, "There is another version of the Snow-white story in the *Popul Vuh*. A more vegetarian version."

"You still keep your fondness for the old Mayan legends?" Doctor Luis asked, moving a piece on the board.

"I have to. They were our ancestors too." His father winked at Manuel.

He had told his sons what he knew of their own family. They were descended mostly from the Spaniards who had invaded the region over four hundred years ago, but some of their blood came from the Mayans, who had been there first. The Spaniards had burned most of the Mayan books as heretical. Almost by chance, some of the Spanish friars had saved the *Popul Vuh* and one or two other books.

"Aha! Checkmate," his father said. "I win again. But why didn't you use your pawns more? You gave up too much strength there."

"I don't like to put the little pawns in danger," said Doctor Luis, laughing ruefully.

"Ah. You're as fanciful as the old legends."

As Manuel listened, the two stories connected in his mind like parts of a jigsaw puzzle. "That hunter in Snow-white is like the owls who saved Ixquic, isn't he?"

Doctor Luis smiled at him as he set the chess pieces back on the board. Manuel continued, "Papá told me. The owls saved a girl from the wicked Lords of Xibalba, the Land of Death."

"I wish other wicked lords were as easy to fool," said Doctor Luis.

"Another game?"

"No, I must get back to the clinic."

"Go carefully," Manuel's father told the young doctor.

But perhaps Doctor Luis didn't go carefully enough, for Manuel never got to tell him the rest of the story. At the beginning of the next week the doctor didn't show up for the chess game. Nor had he appeared at the clinic. And when his fiancée, a nurse at the clinic, very bravely went to report his absence at the police station, they said they knew nothing about him. They kept her at the station a long time, asking questions about the clinic in the barrio, asking why there should be a clinic there at all when there were already such good hospitals in the city. It was no wonder, they said, that a quack like this Doctor Luis, or whatever he was called, had decided to sneak away before he was caught. Good riddance to him! they said. Don't bother us again!

———

His mother must have been telling the church ladies about things like this, because he heard Mrs. Fisher say, "So you and your husband thought you would be safer in the country?"

"Safer?" His mother looked up in surprise. The refrigerator's motor suddenly stopped, as if it were surprised too.

Surely everyone knew that the country was more dangerous than the city! His mother pursed her lips. "He *had* to leave his school in the city."

He did have to leave, Manuel remembered; the threats had become quite open. One morning all the blackboards had been smashed in and the back pages of the calendars in the different teachers' rooms had been torn away, to show each teacher how much time he or she had left. In his father's room, only a month was left on the calendar. He didn't think he could teach safely anywhere in the city.

"He had heard of this school in the hills, for the children of coffee workers," Manuel's mother said. "It was in a simple, isolated village. He said our presence would bother no one there." She shrugged. "He convinced himself. He couldn't imagine life without teaching."

"Yes, I see," said Mrs. Pearl. The refrigerator started again, as if it agreed with her.

———

His father had been very happy in that small village, thought Manuel. The children soaked up knowledge, he said, the way a man in the desert would gulp water.

These children had been surprised that the school-teacher's son, a boy with his head full of books, wanted to play *futbol* too. At first they and the ball had run circles around Manuel in the dusty playing field behind the church. But then his feet and eyes had learned to keep up with the others. When he scored his first goal against the team from the next village, his teammates carried him around the field on their shoulders.

Pepe didn't want to leave the city, so he slept there during the week, in a tiny room in his uncle's house, and only joined the family on the weekends. What did they expect him to learn in the hills? At home there was the library and the science club, and computers in the principal's office of his school — computers they hadn't let him touch. If people in the village saw a computer, they'd think it came from outer space. When Pepe walked to their house from the bus stop every Friday evening, he looked with contempt at the village streets — all three of them, as he said — with their tan adobe houses roofed with tiles or sheet metal, and at the church below, beside the pond. "The center of progress," he called it, in a mocking but puzzled voice, as if he still couldn't understand how any of them had come here.

But the rest of them had found a place in the village, Manuel thought. His parents had brought his schoolbooks along. They would help him continue his courses, and they would arrange for him to write the examinations for his old school in the capital. But his studies took only part of the day, and his father recruited him to help teach the beginning students in the village school. His mother taught there too, helping the children learn to read and write.

Busy as he was with the village school, his father found time to look around at his new world. "Think how they'd envy us this view back in the city!" he said. "This is how it must have been in the time of the old Mayan stories."

They were standing together by a window of their small adobe house, which still smelled of good earth. The village was on a hillside, and their house was on the highest street. It was at the same level as the square with the bus stop, where the road from the nearest town ended — for of course there wasn't room for the bus to pass between the village houses. Below them was a pond that Manuel considered his own private place. It was fed by a stream that ran past the bus stop, then turned downhill past the church until it was stopped by a dam. A bamboo grove hid the pond from the rest of the village. From the walkway along the top of the dam you could look back across the calm green water to a mirrored double image of the top of the church steeple; if you turned, you could watch the stream trickling down over the stones of its old course, which fell away steeply here, between the broad leaves and the bamboo fronds that hung over it.

Coffee trees grew on the other side of a wide ravine, and above their red berries the hill became drier and rockier. Behind the crest of the hill rose the perfect cone of an extinct volcano. Its rocks were so sharp and black that when the air was clear it seemed that, if you stood on top of the coffee hill, you could reach over and touch it.

Manuel always pointed out the volcano to Pepe when he came home on weekends. But his brother only shrugged. "It's a big lump of dead rock," he said. "If it was still active, *that* would be interesting." He grinned. "It could blow this rotten country to hell!"

Then, as Manuel stared at him, Pepe realized how dangerous such words were, and began to talk about a book on geology he had read, and how long ago the volcano had been formed. He had thought of studying geology once, to learn all about the forces that had shaped the earth. But now he'd decided that such forces were too slow: who could wait a million years to find out if the books were correct? Lately he'd become more interested in chemistry, where some really exciting reactions took place in a fraction of a second. He'd long outgrown the chemistry set he'd had when he was Manuel's age, and had persuaded a teacher in a rich private school to let him help in the laboratory so he could get some practical experience.

Pepe snorted. "Practical experience for what? In this country? In this dump of a village?"

Things did happen in the village, Manuel kept telling him. One weekend Manuel was so eager to see his brother that he waited for him at the bus stop. Only the growing darkness stopped him from dragging Pepe to see his great discovery that evening. "A red man in the woods; a stone statue! There's no path to it. I saw it when I took a shortcut. I bet no one else knows about it!" He had only told his parents, who hadn't yet been able to go and see for themselves.

His brother smiled skeptically, but he wasn't angry when Manuel woke him next morning. He followed him around the head of the ravine and into the forest on the other side of the coffee groves. Manuel led the way between bamboo thickets and plants with wide, drooping leaves. They passed beneath a high ridge of black rock from whose cracks a dead tree still protruded, its branches brought to life by two gloomy, silent, red-and-green parrots. They walked on to a secluded grove of pine trees ringing with the calls of invisible insects. There the statue stood.

It was a man with a very ornate hat, hair cut straight across his forehead, and pouting lips. Along the lower edge of his coat were a number of oval objects, which they both thought might be hearts. The man was carved out of soft, reddish stone, and there were deep chisel marks around his feet. Someone had hacked him so that the stones had crumbled and little of the feet remained.

"The work of amateurs," Pepe remarked scornfully. "They meant to steal it, but they destroyed its commercial value by their clumsy hacking. Look." He pointed to a thick limb above their heads, where a weathered wooden pulley was fastened with a yellow rope. "They planned to lift it off and haul it away. And sell it to some rich gringos. 'Pre-Columbian art,'" he added in English. "But they messed it up so much that it wasn't worth going on. And how could they bring a cart here?" Pepe pointed down the narrow trail that switched back and forth along the steep hillside. "No," he said sarcastically, "they were going to be big robbers, but they got tired. They would have needed a helicopter to lift the statue out safely —

and where could they get a helicopter? The army's using them all to fight the nasty rebels."

There he went again, Manuel thought. Pepe's mind was so full of politics that it sometimes had no room for anything else.

The next day Manuel led his parents — who needed no coaxing — to the statue. "I found him!" he said proudly. "No one else knows — except Pepe."

His mother smiled. "Why, he looks just like Professor Sánchez at the university!"

Then Manuel noticed his father's glance and saw traces of a path under the pine needles. Of course the village would know about a statue that was this close. But his father wasn't concerned with who had discovered the statue, or who it resembled. He shook his head at the stone man's wounded feet. Then he walked around the statue, looking at its carved ornaments from every angle, raising his hand to brush the moss from some of them. "We must go back now," he said "A student is coming to see me."

His father was silent until they passed beneath the dead branches with the parrots, who raised their heads to watch them all critically. "I'm not sure," he said, "but I think that was a statue of a True Man."

The parrots squawked in agreement, and Manuel asked, "A True Man? Was that in the *Popul Vuh* too?"

"The name was there." His father gave the parrots a friendly look; they stared back at him. "I've been thinking of those old stories since we left the city." He chuckled sadly. "The ones about the creation of humans. The old gods, the ones they called the Creators, didn't do such a good job when they made people."

As his father went on with the story, he turned around to look at Manuel, so that twice he nearly stumbled on the rough path. He shook his head at his carelessness. "We'll finish at home."

"I should think so!" said his mother. "We don't need a broken leg too." His father was so thoughtful that Manuel was almost sure he had forgotten the story. But after supper that evening, while his wife corrected lessons in the bedroom, he went on with the tale.

The first men, Manuel's father told the boys, were made of clay and had minds as dull and muddy as clay. They could move but not speak. The next ones were made of wood; they quarreled with other forms of matter, and this matter struck back at them. They were hacked and cut, and later transformed into monkeys.

Their father rose to add more oil to the lamp, then changed his mind and continued the story in the dark main room. "What about the next ones?" he asked. "The ones alive today? What materials were they made of, what are *we* made of? The old stories say we were made from corn, that corn was the final, perfect material. Our old red friend in the forest may have been a statue of one of these True Men." He rose to look out the window at the moonlit palm leaves. "Isn't it more likely, though — with no offense to the statue you discovered, Manuel — that there is *still* something gravely wrong with the construction of people? Could this account for their present behavior?"

At this point Pepe, who was proud of being a realist and didn't believe in "fairy tales," rose, took another lamp to the inner room where both boys slept, and settled down with a thick book. His father watched him go with a smile. Later, when they were both in bed, Pepe explained to Manuel that he preferred books that taught a proper, scientific view of society. He had made some new friends — people he'd met in the hills behind the village — and they all agreed that human societies could be analyzed scientifically. It was just like the laws of chemistry: by using the right principles, you could figure out exactly how societies should be governed.

There was no need to talk of these forgotten stories, hundreds of years old.

As for Manuel, he never left his father's side when he was telling the old stories. His father's voice grew happier as he spoke of the divine twins, Hunahpu and Ixbalanque, who went to Xibalba, the underworld, the Land of Death. "Their father had been murdered there," he said. "But even after death he was able to bring his seed to life in the world above. His sons went down below to avenge him." And there, he told Manuel, after many adventures and much sorrow, these sons overcame the wicked lords of that place.

Remembering these stories, Manuel thought he could have listened to his father forever.

The telephone rang in the small office. Pretty Penelope opened the door and put out her head, its swinging pigtails tied with a red ribbon and a blue ribbon. "Dr. Silas called; he's still on the phone. He says he has a load of provisions." She giggled. "I know what that means! He says, can we pick them up in Deadwood Gulch? Where *is* Deadwood Gulch? I've never heard of it."

"You wouldn't have," said Mrs. Pearl. "There's no such place. But I know where he means. Yes, tell him Deadwood Gulch is fine." Penelope closed the door. "Our phone's tapped, of course." Mrs. Pearl lowered her voice, though no one could hear her. "But they don't seem to have learned our code words yet."

"Were your phones tapped in the village?" Mrs. Fisher asked. Mrs. Pearl clicked her tongue.

"We had no telephones," Manuel's mother said. "They had other ways of watching people they suspected. And they suspected everyone."

There must have been other ways of watching, and his father's presence must have bothered someone, for one evening he didn't come home. None of the neighbors had seen him. Some became nervous when his mother asked about him. Manuel went running up and down the alleys and paths of the village, questioning everyone. Soon Pepe joined him; he had left his school in the city to ask questions too. How long had his father been away? Manuel wasn't sure; time had grown so confused in his mind that, thinking back over those days, he wasn't sure in what order things happened. He remembered that Pepe had wanted to talk to the army sergeant who lived by the bus stop and spied on all the travelers, but that their mother had stopped him. Manuel was with her when she asked the sergeant herself, but he claimed to know nothing.

"Never heard of him. How long do you say he's been here? Six months? I'd have seen him in that time, if he really lived here. Why did he come so secretly?" The sergeant had a wide face; sweat drops kept gathering above his mustache and he blotted them with a red handkerchief. "A school-teacher? I bet he was! What did he teach?" The sergeant laughed. "How all those ignorant children should be faithful to the government, eh?"

Two days later, after a night of hard rain had washed the sky to a clear blue, Manuel's thoughts became clearer too. He was suddenly sure that his father had just gone to another school without telling any of them. Father was so absent-minded about leaving messages! Manuel didn't understand why his mother was still so worried. She even skipped her classes at the school to ask questions everywhere. She didn't tell him what answers she received — which was only fair, he realized, since by this time Manuel had decided to stop speaking. But she talked to Pepe.

Manuel heard these questions, and the answers to them, when they spoke off to the side in low voices. Perhaps they thought that, because he didn't speak, he couldn't hear. He had to keep from laughing at that — it would have given the secret away.

He learned that their mother had traveled by bus to the army post in the market town five miles away, but that the young man at the desk there had said he knew nothing about her husband. "He probably doesn't want to be found," he'd sneered. "I bet he thought he was too good for the simple village life. He must have gone back to his girlfriend in the big city. Why don't you pack up and go look for him there?"

For a time it seemed that their mother was always traveling to the army post to ask questions. Pepe explained to Manuel what was really going on. "Of course they know where he is," he told Manuel. "They have him shut up somewhere; they must want him to 'confess' to being a rebel or a Communist, or I don't know what. They think they can hide him. But Mamá is sure that, if she keeps asking, she'll find out one day." He looked hard at Manuel, though he had been told not to try to make him speak. "I bet *you* know something. Won't you tell? Tell *me*, at least." But Manuel didn't answer, and in a moment Pepe started to speak again. Manuel nodded then, to show that he understood every word.

Their mother, Pepe explained, was meeting with other women whose husbands had disappeared. These women were acting together now; that was the way to get things done. If enough of them kept going to the army post, to the mayor, to the governor, always demanding answers, never satisfied, there was a chance that someone would get some information. Or the foreign newspapers might report all the disappearances, and embarrass the government into telling the truth.

Meanwhile, Pepe was carrying out a search too, in his own way. It was no use asking people in their village or even in the market town; those who were innocent didn't want to know anything, and the others wouldn't tell. But in the forests and hills there were people who knew what was happening. They weren't fooled by the government's lies. And they would tell the truth.

For a time, Manuel saw Pepe eagerly talking to boys and young men he hadn't seen before. There was also a tall, beautiful girl who wore flowers in her hair. Though she was two years older than Pepe, she seemed to want to be his special friend. She listened hungrily to every word he uttered. These young people must have had access to office machines, because soon there were hundreds of sheets of paper with their father's face on them. The face was darker than the photograph it had been copied from, but the face and eyes were unmistakable. Each sheet had the word "*Desaparecido*" — "Disappeared" — printed across the bottom.

Manuel met these pictures on walls and in alleys, on shop windows beneath government decrees or advertisements of fortune tellers and pills for all sicknesses. Sometimes the pictures only stayed on the shops for an hour before the shopkeepers found them and tore them off. Those in back alleys lasted longer, one as much as two weeks. His father's eyes in these pictures seemed to look directly at him, and to follow him as he finally walked away. He saw the face again at night, in his dreams.

Then one evening one of the pictures winked at him. When Manuel leaped back, the picture took on its usual appearance, with wide-open eyes and a faint smile.

That was the beginning. Afterward, Manuel noticed that his father's pictures often winked or smiled at him as he passed. It seemed that his father didn't like to be looked at directly, for he could only see such changes sideways, out of the corner of his eye.

One day all the pictures kept their serious, motionless gaze, but then Manuel saw his father himself, standing at some distance among the trees. When Manuel approached, though, his father backed away until the forest hid him. This happened a second time, too. Manuel had always admired his father's ability to move quickly and quietly. When he was teaching, he could circle to the back of the classroom without the most mischievous student being aware of him; now he could move more smoothly and secretly than ever. Manuel tried to follow him, but it didn't matter what obstacle his father encountered; he still kept his distance. If it was a wall, he sprang over it. If it was a large boulder, he somehow passed around it and appeared on the other side.

Manuel knew, without his father telling him, that he shouldn't speak to anyone about this. If he told no one what he saw now, and what he had seen earlier, his father would be safe — he would come back to them. But what if Manuel said something by accident? What would happen to Father then? That was when Manuel resolved never to speak again, to keep his father safe.

Late one evening María, a woman their mother had met in the market town, scratched at their door. She had walked all the way to their village in the rain, she said, and would walk back before dawn. The buses were often watched, and she didn't want the soldiers to learn that she had come to warn them.

"Both you and your older son are suspected of sympathizing with the rebels," Manuel heard her whisper. The wicked rain whispered too, outside the window.

"I know they don't like me asking questions," his mother said. "But why are they after my son?"

"He's been seen associating with the rebels."

"Who says so?"

"Inmaculada, his so-called friend. The girl who wears the flowers in her hair. The one who always talks revolution. A friend who cleans the army post says that girl is an informer; she reports everything to the government. My friend says that some gentlemen will come for you — all of you. You must leave while you still can."

"When are they coming?"

"When the roads are drier. Today even their jeeps would sink in the mire." María pointed to her shoes, and Manuel saw that they were caked with mud. "Maybe tomorrow, or the next day," she said. "It seems that they are coming for other people too, and they want to do it all at once."

"But they won't come tonight?"

"No. Tonight would be a good time to leave. I must be back home by morning, but I have a friend who would hide you in the forest for a few days, and then send you on your way north."

His mother didn't answer immediately. "But to leave the country, with no word from my husband! And no word *for* him," she said at last.

"What can you do for him now?" María asked. "Besides," she added kindly, "when he returns we'll tell him where you went, so he won't worry. My friend in the forest can pass on messages. Your husband would want you to be safe."

"Perhaps. Yes, he would." Manuel's mother nodded.

"Do you have any friends in the north? In the United States?" María asked.

"A cousin. She's a doctor but she entered the United States secretly, she has no green card so she has to work wherever she can. I think she has a job in a restaurant in California, but we don't have her address."

"She has to keep out of sight herself. I don't think she can do anything for you. But there are people who will help you once you cross the border into Mexico. They have no money, but at least they'll send you on your way. And there are people in the American churches, when you cross *that* border. They know what happens here." Then her voice fell to a whisper, as she repeated some names in their mother's ear.

That was how they began their journey. Pepe came home soon after María left. When their mother told him they had to get away, for once he didn't argue. He asked her what to bring and what to leave. But first he fetched some books and papers from under his mattress and burned them on the cooking fire. He took out some money he had hidden under a brick, as did his mother. Very little, she said, but she had kept aside as much as she could, in case they had to run. She packed all the money in a kind of belt strapped around her waist, under her blouse. They took some clothes in plastic bags: two black ones, not the orange ones that were easily seen. And they left the lantern burning as they walked into the rain. "That way," their mother said, "people may think we're coming back."

"And you," she added to Manuel, "stay close to Pepe. Come instantly if he calls you." Manuel nodded.

Pepe had cut a hole in another black plastic bag and put it over his head as a raincoat. He placed a straw hat over his tangled hair. "What if we lose sight of him?" he asked. "How will we find him?"

"He won't let us go on without him," their mother said, as if she believed it. "He'll have to speak then."

Because of the rain and darkness, Manuel didn't see his father that night, as they walked through the forest to the home of María's friend. But he was there the next morning, waiting in the thick, leafy trees nearby. And that evening, when they set off for a farmhouse in the hills — still in a light sprinkling of rain — he was close behind them.

The others joined them later, first one and then the other. Ricardo, the flute boy, had been sleeping in the sun, under a cloud of flies, beside the market square in a large town they passed through a week later. He stood up and yawned when Manuel's father whispered to him, and came along with them, though he kept looking back to his sleeping place. Two days later Elena, the girl with the castanets and the drum that hung at her belt, rose from a pile of old clothes beside the road, smiled, and danced along too. She tired easily, Manuel thought. She kept looking down at the ground as if she wanted to rest again. He thought that if the flute boy hadn't been along she would have dropped out and gone back.

But as they traveled Elena's spirits seemed to rise. She marched forward bravely, and soon began to keep close time to Ricardo's music with her drum or castanets, as they all headed north.

THREE

A Place to Stop Running

The sound of Mrs. Fisher's knitting needles had stopped, Manuel realized. Now they started again, but on a narrower piece of blue wool. "And your husband also disappeared?" Mrs. Pearl said.

"I don't like that word," Manuel's mother objected.

"Of course you don't!" Mrs. Fisher said firmly, and her needles clicked more firmly too.

"Why don't you like the word?" Mrs. Pearl asked.

"Because he must be somewhere. I would rather know where he is, and whether he is all right."

"Oh!" Mrs. Fisher drew in her breath. She stopped knitting, then looked down and silently began to count the stitches on a needle.

"I understand," Mrs. Pearl said. "You want to know the truth, whatever it is. But now let's talk about what you must do to try to stay in the United States."

And then the two ladies talked quickly, interrupting each other, and the talk became very complicated: all about "G-28 forms" and "VDF forms" and "refugee status" and "judicial hearings." Penelope flushed the toilet, and water flowed in the bathroom on the other side of the wall. There was plenty of water here, Manuel thought, even though the soil outside was so hot and dry, almost like the desert.

His mind hadn't really left the desert: the spiny plants whose roots could suck water even from dry, sandy soil; the waves of heat-distorted air, so that sometimes he wasn't sure if his father and his other companions were really with him.

They had been with him back when they crossed the border into Mexico, from the south. But they had seemed to leave him for a time, when he, Pepe, and their mother had to travel north through Mexico on the dirty, crowded buses. That was such a long way! Thousands of miles, Pepe said. They had to keep moving; their money was almost gone, and there were few people who could help them — and so many who needed help. Pepe himself would have stayed in Mexico; it was their mother who wanted them to make a new life farther north, in "America." For the time being, Pepe thought he had better go along, and Manuel too.

Though very worried at his companions' absence, Manuel had almost been relieved not to find them on the bus. They had better sense than that, he thought. He remembered one bus, with the seats all taken, and the filthy aisles crowded with chicken crates and smelly, drunken people. His companions probably had their own ways of traveling. And sure enough, they were with him again in the last part of the journey, when Manuel's mother decided to leave the roads, which would be watched by the immigration police, and cross the desert. That clean, dry land was the right place for them.

Now Penelope was washing her hands, with the water flowing freely. This must be a very rich land, Manuel thought. Would they be able to stay here?

While the ladies went on talking, a slim, elegant black cat appeared behind the box of pictures, looking at the smiling cat faces on Manuel's shirt with great disdain. Manuel clicked his tongue and smiled at it; it was just like the cat in the village, the one that his father had said could sniff out stupidity. If the cat let you pet it, his father said, it had a good opinion of you. But if it decided you were stupid, it might spit and scratch.

Manuel lifted the sheet with "One of Our Success Stories!" from the box and crumpled it silently into a ball. "*Hola*, Diablo!" he whispered, He held out the ball on his palm to the cat, which arched its back, much as that other Diablo had done in the village, and flipped the ball away with its paw. He stroked the cat with his other hand. "Did you come as we did?" The cat — might it really be Diablo? — purred darkly.

The ladies' ears were sharper than Manuel had thought. Mrs. Pearl's chair legs scraped as she turned. Mrs. Fisher dropped her ball of blue wool. It rolled under the table and the cat scornfully watched it roll past. Mrs. Fisher cried, "Oh! Your son is talking! He was so quiet before that I didn't even know he was here."

Manuel's mother looked under the table. "He was talking to the cat. Manuel! Go to bed now, and be quiet. Don't wake Pepe."

Manuel rose quickly and stepped quietly into the bedroom, leaving the door slightly open. There was no danger of waking Pepe, he saw. But he himself wasn't going to sleep! He could still hear the voices in the next room, and in a moment he slipped down to the floor by the wall, where he could see the ladies. He didn't think his mother objected to his listening, only to the ladies knowing he was doing so.

His mother said, "You were telling me about the forms I must sign."

"Were we going too fast for you?" Mrs. Fisher asked. "The G-28 form means they can't send you back until a judge decides if you can stay in this country. That's the one you have to sign. The VDF — that's a Voluntary Departure Form — means you agree to be sent back immediately. That's the one you must *not* sign."

"I understand."

Mrs. Fisher must have retrieved her ball of wool, for the knitting needles clicked as regularly as ever. "Of course, we go with our clients to the immigration office now. But the authorities have caught a few of them. They're holding two now at the police station, and bringing back some others who had gotten farther north, to be deported back to your country. We hope they'll be the last ones. We're very afraid of what will happen to those who are sent back. We're putting up all the legal obstacles we can, and we're planning a big demonstration by the jail."

"That should be very useful." Mrs. Pearl took up a separate sheet of paper and studied it. After a time, she said, "At least in legal matters we know our enemy. We keep close track of everyone they catch. Our observers go round to the jails regularly, and some of the ordinary prisoners are on our side — we have to pay them, of course. They let us know if anyone needs our attention in a hurry."

"Oh, really?" Mrs. Fisher asked eagerly. "How?"

"They have their signals," Mrs. Pearl said briefly.

"So you see," said Mrs. Fisher, smiling at Manuel's mother, "we do have an organization. And eventually you'll come up before a judge and explain why you want to stay here." She nodded at the knitting she had completed, folded it, and placed it in a flowered cloth bag.

"What do you think the judge will decide?" Manuel's mother asked.

"That's the problem," said Mrs. Pearl. "If we want to make a case for you, we'll have to convince the judge that you really were in danger, convince him officially, that is."

"But surely they *were* in danger!" Mrs. Fisher broke in.

"We were in great danger," Manuel's mother said. "The gentlemen of the night were coming to call on us. We had to run."

"Of course you were in danger," Mrs. Pearl said. "We know that. But the judge will say, Why didn't you wait to be sure? Judge Winter said that, in another case. He said, 'Where's the *documentary* evidence? The *written* evidence?'"

"Written evidence?" Manuel's mother asked. "Do you mean an official statement: 'This woman's husband, who never existed, has disappeared'?"

"I admire your spirit," Mrs. Pearl said. "But the judge will say, Why didn't you wait?"

"If we had waited we wouldn't be here."

"In that case the judge wouldn't have to deal with you." Mrs. Pearl turned to Mrs. Fisher. "Apparently the last judge was complaining in public, at a concert intermission, about all the problems we raise."

"Well, I should hope so!" Mrs. Fisher stood up and straightened her back. "I sit too much in this work." She sat down again. "We've really had no luck with our courts so far. And the people in town aren't sympathetic either. They've grown so used to hearing the same horror stories. Frankly, some of them are bored. Of course, it's new for you," she added kindly to Manuel's mother.

"Not as new as it once was."

Mrs. Pearl nodded. "I don't want to hold out too much hope for when you do see the judge. But sometimes we're lucky. What angle did the Blue Mesa group use? Was that with Judge Kerwin?"

"Yes! Wilson Kerwin. But hasn't he retired?"

"I remember now — he was due to retire soon and he could afford to stretch the rules. Also, there was the golfing aspect."

"Golfing?" Mrs. Fisher asked eagerly. "My poor George was something of a golf nut. Did one of our people meet the judge on the golf links and win him over? Or was one of the refugee claimants working out there?"

"Hardly. But one man whose case came up before Judge Kerwin had had his thumbs removed by his torturers. His advisor at the Blue Mesa church had played golf with Judge Kerwin. He took his client around all eighteen holes of the course. Then he primed him with information about golfers past and present, including two famous golfers in his own country, until you would have thought he was a first-rank player himself. And how could anyone test him? He couldn't play golf without thumbs!"

"I did hear something about it. Wasn't the judge so sympathetic that he approved the application immediately?"

"After his afternoon nap. But that was Judge Kerwin at Blue Mesa. What about our Judge Winter? Is he still refusing to let anyone stay?"

"I'm afraid so."

Mrs. Pearl shook her head. "We don't want you turned back here, especially since there seems to be such a convenient transport system back to your own country. Likely we'll send you on to one of the northern groups. Yes, we'll do that." She lifted a blue cloth briefcase from the floor, collected the papers on the table, and stored them neatly away. "Meanwhile," she said to Mrs. Fisher, "what arrangements have you made for Mrs. Cárdenas and her sons?"

"We have a nice room for them. I think Mrs. Cárdenas understands that they have to keep out of sight until she files the G-28 form."

"I understand. And do we stay here? Is this the nice room?" Manuel's mother looked around the low basement.

Mrs. Pearl said, "In any case, it's a safe room. We've declared this church a sanctuary, and no one has invaded it yet."

"A sanctuary?"

Mrs. Pearl noticed a pencil at the edge of the table and put it in her briefcase too. "The term is much used in the Bible. There were cities of sanctuary where people were safe from persecution. There is a long tradition of sanctuary in churches — that means that if people come into a church and claim sanctuary, nobody is supposed to take them out by force. So we use our church as a sanctuary, and there are others like it all over the country."

"The police and the immigration authorities don't dare come in," Mrs. Fisher said proudly. "People like you are quite safe here."

"Suppose we say, rather, that the police haven't chosen to come in yet; there's no law saying they can't, but I think they won't, here. But we don't want to press our luck; we certainly don't want to press yours. And you can stop running for a time. For now, we've booked you a house-keeping room in a motel. We'll take you there when it's dark. We'll stock the refrigerator so you won't have to shop for a couple of days. I'm sure you'll be careful. Try to keep out of sight. If you *are* picked up, call the number on this piece of paper. The immigration agents, the *migras*, proba-bly won't notice your boys as long as they keep quiet. But they may wonder about *you*."

"Yes, isn't she pretty!" Mrs. Fisher exclaimed.

Manuel's mother looked down. "Thank you."

"And you seem so calm! I'm sure I couldn't be so brave."

Mrs. Pearl opened her briefcase and looked through the papers in it. Then, satisfied, she closed it again. "You never know how you'll act until the time comes," she said.

"That's what I've learned." Manuel's mother's voice was as detached as if she were speaking about someone else.

"But you can all rest now," Mrs. Fisher said. "And I'm sure Manuel will talk again. He's started already. He only needed to stop running."

"Not quite," said Manuel's mother. "He was talking to the

cat. He talks to animals. Also to himself, often; and perhaps to others that he thinks he sees."

"But he's sure to begin speaking to you again soon," Mrs. Fisher assured her.

"He may. I think he will. But I wonder what he'll say."

"Please don't be offended," Mrs. Fisher said, and then her voice dropped so low that Manuel could hardly hear it. "But isn't it a — a psychological problem? We have some very good doctors, even in our small town. Our Dr. Silas is especially interested in cases of — well — *troubled* children."

Manuel's mother was silent. Manuel could imagine the expression on her face, which was turned to the floor. Then she raised her head. "Excuse me, but not now. How long will we be here, do you know?" She looked at Mrs. Fisher, who dropped her eyes. "It may be only a short time," his mother continued. "Besides, Manuel eats and sleeps well enough, when he can. He obeys orders. He still has a voice, though not for us. When we have a real home again, I think he'll speak." She added, "Perhaps he's wise. After all, what good has all our talking done so far?"

"I do see what you mean!" Mrs. Fisher said brightly.

"Do you?" Mrs. Pearl asked.

"Yes, I do, appearances to the contrary." In a moment, Mrs. Fisher added, "My goodness, I have to go now. I'll let Mrs. Pearl look after you, Sonia. May I call you Sonia?"

Manuel's mother nodded shyly.

"I'm Elizabeth and this is Greta," Mrs. Fisher said. "We don't want to be too formal. Once you're settled in, I'll invite you all for supper."

FOUR

The Lords of Death

f his mother was so calm in the presence of the church ladies, Manuel knew, it was because she felt she must always appear to be in control. Even when the family had still been together, she had been reserved with strangers, though not unfriendly. The women in the village had found her very formal, but had thought this was only natural in a schoolteacher's wife, who was a teacher herself. She had kept her reserve even when she marched with the women in the market town, demanding information about her husband. As if, Manuel thought, she could make their life as orderly as it had once been, by controlling her own feelings.

But during their journey he had sometimes heard her crying at night, when she thought he and Pepe were both asleep. Even after she stopped crying, she stayed long awake. The last time this happened — when they slept on the bare ground behind a billboard near the bus station in Mexico, just before they started across the desert — Manuel looked around for his father. Finally he saw him watching them sadly from a distance. He remembered that once, when he was really a baby, he had woken crying from a bad dream. His mother had entered his room and leaned over him, her hair hanging over her smooth cheeks. As she whispered something that made the dream go away, he had seen his father, in bright green pajamas, standing in the door but coming no closer.

Why had his father held back on that night so long ago? Because he'd seen that Manuel was almost asleep again? Was he sorry to remember that time, now that he had to keep his distance? That night behind the billboard, Manuel opened his mouth to call him, but his father shook his head. Manuel understood that, if he called, his father would go away forever.

By daylight their mother was quite composed. She spent much time in the church basement. She had volunteered to help there, first as a translator, later with the office work. She told her sons that, though this branch of the sanctuary organization handled a good deal of money, the accounts were in terrible shape. This didn't surprise her. She had been able to straighten them out a little, she said. Mrs. Pearl had watched her, nodding approval, while Mrs. Fisher shook her head in amazement.

From her conversation with Pepe, Manuel learned that she had filled out one of the G-28 forms in the presence of the immigration officials and Mrs. Pearl. It had all gone quite smoothly. The official had been very polite, their mother said, even smiling; but she thought such smiles were worth very little.

Now that they had submitted this application to live in the United States, the family could not be forced out until they went to court and a judge decided for or against them. This meant that they no longer had to hide in their motel room. It was one of some twenty-two rooms in an H-shaped, low building with a sign, "Elite Motel." The motel was just two blocks from the church, and it was the place where the church usually reserved space for "sojourners" like themselves. All the rooms opened out onto a gravel parking lot. A red and green automobile was always there; it often had the hood open and a thin, cursing man working on the engine.

The Cárdenas family's room faced the side of a long stucco building. A sign on its front read, "A. Wemyss, Greengrocer. Fine Produce." The same words, in dignified black letters, appeared on the side of a long blue van, which was often parked beside the building.

Sometimes other children, American children, played in the yard. At first a few kicked the *futbol* around with Manuel. They spoke to him in English, then in their school Spanish; but when he never answered they stared at him, and stopped playing with him. One boy, Gregory, had even gotten into a good game with him; then Gregory's mother called her son back and, when he didn't come, dragged him away. "You don't know *what's* wrong with him!" she yelled.

Pepe, who had been watching this, said, "Never mind; with a mother like that he has more troubles than you do." Pepe brought out his black-and-white ball and played with Manuel for a while.

Of course, Pepe didn't spend all his time looking after his little brother. He quickly tired of watching television in their motel room — though not before he'd told his mother just what he thought of the programs. The only ones he liked were the science and nature shows, and there were few of these — none during the daytime. Manuel thought Pepe liked the old cowboy movies too, though he wouldn't admit it; besides, all the advertisements spoiled the action.

Mrs. Fisher had helped Pepe get a library card, "What about Manuel?" Pepe asked. Mrs. Fisher looked flustered, had a long talk in a low voice with Penelope, then said it would be simpler if Pepe took out books for Manuel on *his* card.

As he walked with Pepe toward the town library, Manuel saw that Ricardo and Elena had come too. He had hardly missed them in the last few days, but he was very glad to see them now. He didn't see his father yet, but knew he would follow.

The library was a wide pink and green concrete building between their motel and the main shopping street. It stood on a dry yellow lawn, between houses with dry yellow lawns and vacant lots of dry brown earth. Weeds trembled and blew over these lots; on a pile of rocks in one lot, little brown lizards raised their heads to watch them walk past. Whenever Manuel started to chase these lizards, they managed to disappear under the rocks. Elena joined in too; the lizards ran from her as well, though she cast no shadow. Once they managed to get a lizard cornered between two rocks; it looked up indignantly as if to say, "What are *you* doing chasing *me?*" That made them pause for a second, and the lizard scooted into a hole.

Few children used the library during the day, and Pepe roamed around the stacks in a restless way that made the young librarian raise her eyebrows, until she got used to him.

Pepe could find none of the "political" books he was looking for. "They probably ban them here too," he told his brother, who suspected that Pepe was just glad to find something to complain about. Pepe had been almost disappointed by the good treatment they'd received from most of the Americans they'd met. He had explained to Manuel often enough that the United States was the main supporter of their evil government back home. "They think the rebels are all Communists," he told Manuel, "and Americans are afraid of Communists. So they always support the other side."

Now Pepe found their own country in a large atlas that even showed the route they had taken from their home to the Mexican border, and then north. He asked the librarian for paper and made a rough map of their journey as far as this dry town in southern Arizona, which, he was surprised to find, appeared in the atlas too.

In the background of the quiet library was the steady hum of a central air conditioner. Everyone who came in said, "Isn't it *hot* outside?" The inside air was certainly cool, Manuel thought. It was clear, too, and the rooms were well lit with fluorescent bulbs in the ceiling. Here, he thought, you knew that everything you saw was real — not like outside, where the air was distorted by waves of heat. In the library, people you approached wouldn't suddenly vanish; nor would they appear out of nowhere, as his companions sometimes did.

Manuel wasn't sure which he preferred. He began to roam around the shelves, looking through the section labeled "Fairy Tales." What was this? Yes, it was the same edition of old stories that Dr. Luis had given him so long ago. He settled down to read it, in a chair facing the window, more at ease now. He started to read a new story, about a murdered man's bone that was made into a flute and brought his murderer to justice. Then he was brought back into his other world by the sound of a flute, a wooden flute, outside the window.

Ricardo and Elena were sitting on a stone bench that faced another stone bench beneath a grove of dusty pines. Elena was keeping time with her castanets, accompanied by the drum. Their music may have reached farther than the children thought. They had said that only Manuel could hear them, but the girl at the library desk frowned at a small radio on a shelf and turned down the dial. "I didn't think it was on," she said.

But Manuel could still hear the music. He looked around for Pepe. His brother was whispering to a tall young man who, earlier, had been showing a stack of pamphlets to the librarian. This man now sat at a reading table, more pamphlets spread out before him, his feet resting on a guitar case. Manuel touched Pepe's arm and showed him the book; his brother nodded. The tall young man slapped Pepe's shoulder in a friendly fashion as Pepe led Manuel to the library desk.

"So this is your brother, Pepe!" the librarian said. Pepe shook his head and put his finger to his lips. "Oh, it's all right for him to talk if he keeps his voice down," the librarian assured him. Pepe shook his head again. "Never mind," she told Pepe, "he'll speak English soon." Pepe didn't correct her. She looked at the big book Pepe had taken from Manuel's hand and said, "He can read *that*?"

"He can read whatever he wants," Pepe said.

"Oh, I didn't mean there was anything *wrong* with him," the librarian said, dropping her voice at the end. She blushed and quickly stamped the book.

Pepe said, "*Aquí no saben nada.*" (They know nothing here.)

The librarian winked. "*Saben más que piensas.*" (They know more than you think.)

"Sorry," muttered Pepe, "I have to be more careful."

The young man with the guitar called him over to his table. They began to talk together, very earnestly. In a moment the librarian joined them, keeping an eye on her desk. Manuel touched Pepe's arm and pointed out the window to the benches. Pepe looked and nodded; he went on talking to the others as Manuel left the library.

In the dusty grove, Ricardo set down his flute. "What's that, another book? I thought you left all those behind."

"I got it from the library," Manuel told him. "I can't take it with me when we travel again, but I can read it here, in this town."

"Why would you want to take it with you?" Ricardo sniffed. "What good have books ever done you?"

Manuel couldn't answer this question. He had never asked himself what "good" books and reading had done him, any more than he had asked what "good" were eating and breathing.

But Ricardo wasn't finished yet. "Your father had thousands of books. That didn't stop him from disappearing."

"What do you mean?" Manuel demanded. "He disappeared *there*, but he's here now." He looked around, as if his father might appear out of the dry world around them, say from behind the ragged sphere of desert tumbleweed that had somehow got this far into town and was now struggling against the wrought-iron fence at the back of the library. The more distant landscape, especially the range of hills to the north, was blurred by heat waves. Manuel wondered how hard it would be to cross those hills, if they had to escape the *migras* or the evil Lords of Xibalba.

There was no sign of his father, but he said confidently, "He's somewhere. You'll see him soon." Then, as a new thought struck him, he added, "You both followed him, didn't you?"

"How could he be *anywhere* if he disappeared?" Ricardo demanded stubbornly.

"You're wrong. If he disappeared, he can be anywhere at all."

Ricardo smiled skeptically. "So you see him sometimes; we do too. But where is he when we don't see him?"

Manuel certainly wasn't going to answer that question! Besides, he really didn't know where his father had gone when he didn't return to his home in the village that day. His father must have known they'd all have to leave. Probably he had simply left first.

Manuel was relieved, though, when Elena, who had stopped trying to follow this strange talk, said, "What's that book?"

"Books!" Ricardo muttered. He was just angry, Manuel thought, because he couldn't read. Neither could Elena, or most of the homeless children who lived in the streets in his country. This journey was the first time he had really spoken to such children. He had seen others, of course — beggars on the city streets, sometimes gangs of them at a distance, running at the sight of a soldier or a policeman. He had been

glad these gangs hadn't found him alone. His parents sometimes gave money to street children, and once his mother had
sent him and Pepe to a house that provided shelter for many
of them, to give them outgrown clothes.

Now these two were always around, and he still wasn't
sure how to handle them. Often they seemed to regret coming
along on the journey. In some ways, Manuel reminded
himself, they knew much less than he did. The new countries
were stranger to them than to him, because he had read books
about Mexico and the United States. But what did they know?
They had seen nothing of the wide world before: just the dirt
of the marketplace and the legs of the adults going by, and the
few coins they tossed down. He really would have to take
their education in hand.

Still, he couldn't treat them as if they were completely
ignorant. They had their own knowledge and their own experience. Now Ricardo was looking scornfully at the wide pink
library building with its green trim. Elena followed the flute
boy's gaze. "It's pretty," she said timidly.

"No it's not," Ricardo said firmly. "It's somebody's stupid
idea of a watermelon. It's the wrong color for its shape."

He was probably right, Manuel decided, though he hadn't
thought about the library building before, only about the
books it contained. But this scowling, difficult flute boy had
a sure feeling for beauty. Even his father listened respectfully
when Ricardo spoke — though not as respectfully as when
he played his flute.

Still, he said to Ricardo, "If you don't like anything, why
did you come? Why didn't you just go on sleeping?" But had
Ricardo only been sleeping that day? If so, why didn't he cast
any shadow now? Why couldn't other people see him? Still,
let it be called "sleeping."

Ricardo glared at him, but said at last, "There was no one
to hear my music. I needed someone to hear it."

"Who can hear it now?"

"*You* can. And other people hear it a bit, even if they're not sure."

This might be true, Manuel admitted to himself, remembering the librarian reaching for the radio. The flute could sometimes be heard in the air, like a breeze or an echo. People raised their heads as if they heard something. Ricardo's music should be heard, he thought. It would be a pity if it was lost forever.

"What about you — why did you come along with us?" he asked Elena, more gently.

"Oh, I was lonely. I'd given my food money to Lydia, to give to the doorman of the Hotel Columbus so he'd let us beg from the gringos. But Lydia ran away with the money."

"What did you expect?" Ricardo muttered.

"But I thought Lydia was my friend. Then I was too tired to beg, but I was too hungry to sleep. *So* hungry, and cold and dizzy. So I just lay down beside the road. Someone was calling me, but I didn't like his voice; he tried to make it so sweet! He said, "Come down below, my dear little child. We have such games for you. Don't go wandering off into the cold, empty air." Elena shivered. "I was afraid of those games, and of the empty air, too. I didn't know what to do. Then I heard Ricardo's flute. Did they call you from down below too?" she asked the flute boy timidly.

Ricardo sniffed. "Someone called, but they can't catch me like that! I wanted to stay up here."

"I'm glad you stayed," Elena said. She smiled at Ricardo. He didn't exactly smile back, Manuel noticed, but his hard mouth softened. This dirty beggar-girl was probably the only being, in this or any world, that the flute boy liked. And why not? They were each other's only true companions.

On their journey, Ricardo had first watched Elena with scornful pity as she danced with her castanets, the way she had once done for pennies in the markets. Then he'd found a small drum for her, and they'd started to make music together. He had nodded approvingly. "Back there we could have made a good team, with gringos all around to watch us and throw money. The pickpockets would have had such good luck with our audience that *they'd* have paid us to play too!"

Elena had been looking at Manuel's book of stories with special interest. "Look, it has a red cover," she said. "There was a storyteller in the marketplace who had a red book. She read a story about a beautiful girl. A bad queen sent a soldier to kill her, but the soldier set her free in the forest. Then she found a home in a cave with seven little men. And later she came back and killed the bad queen."

"That's the story of Snow-white!" Manuel said. "It's in this book too." He looked it up in the table of contents, and turned to the right page.

"Why didn't the soldier kill her?" Ricardo asked.

"Because he felt sorry for her."

Ricardo shook his head scornfully. "He couldn't have been a real soldier, then."

"Read us the story," Elena pleaded.

"In a minute," Manuel told her, and turned to Ricardo. "Sometimes soldiers don't obey orders. The owls were soldiers of the Lords of Xibalba, but they saved Ixquic."

"Which lords?" Elena asked.

Ricardo poked her in the ribs. "*You* know which lords. You saw them on our way. Who do you think was calling you down below before I came along?"

"Oh, *those* lords. Were they following us?"

"They follow everyone," Ricardo said, a new tone of respect in his voice. "They don't want anyone to escape." He turned to Manuel. "You said some of their soldiers disobeyed? And got away with it?"

"That's right." Manuel looked around. His father couldn't be far away; he'd be there to correct him if he made any mistakes in the story. Yes, there he was; he had just freed the tumbleweed by the fence, so that it flew off and tumbled out of sight between two houses.

"It's a story from our own people," he told the children. "The book is called the *Popul Vuh*. My father knows it best, but he told it to me." Then he told them the story, and they listened open-mouthed.

Two divine beings, Hun Hunahpu and Vucub Hunahpu, Manuel said, had disturbed the Lords of Xibalba, the Land of Death, by playing ball above their heads, up on earth. These lords summoned the ball-playing brothers for a game down below. But there they tricked them, made them follow the wrong roads, hid their true names from them, and set tests for them that they failed, so that these heroes were completely under the power of the Lords of Death.

Manuel stopped to explain that, in the old days, someone who knew your name had power over you. It was important to keep your name secret.

Ricardo sniffed. "I know that! Do you think I gave my right name to the soldiers when I ran errands for them? How could I hide from them if they knew who I was? I don't know what made me tell *you* my name!"

Manuel thought of assuring Ricardo that he didn't want power over him, but decided to go on with the story.

And what a terrible world it was down there! he said. It was a place of torture, of hot stone benches that burned the flesh, with a house of razor-sharp obsidian knives, a house of freezing cold, and a house of savage jaguars. There the brothers were put to death. They were beheaded, as sometimes happened to the losers in the games in the old ball courts.

"Was there a house of electricity too?" Ricardo asked.

"No! It was too long ago," Manuel informed him.

Ricardo sniffed. "They should've had electricity. Those Lords sound like Sergeant Duarte of the Seguridad, the Security Police. He sometimes used hot stones in his 'gymnasium' in the basement, to torture the poor people he called his 'clients.' But he thought electricity was more modern. Sometimes he used too much. We could tell that out in the square, because the lights in the upstairs offices went all dim. We'd say the sergeant was celebrating someone's birthday down there."

Manuel didn't want to hear about what happened in the basement of the Security Police. He went on with his own story. Those wicked lords didn't do the job well enough, he said. After they cut off Hun Hunahpu's head, they threw it into a barren jicaro tree, where it flowered into the yellow gourds that are the tree's fruit now. The Lords of Death hadn't expected that. They were afraid of the tree, and told everyone to keep away from it. But the maiden Ixquic — the daughter of Gathered Blood, one of the lords — passed under the tree and spoke with the skull in the branch, asking for one of the magic fruits.

The skull told her to reach out her hand, and it spat into it. Then it told her that this had made her pregnant, and that it had given her its descendants. Said the skull, "The lord or wise man or orator leaves his image to his son or daughter, and I have left my image to you. Now go to the surface of the world, and save your life and that within you. Believe in my words, and they will be true."

Naturally, all the Lords of Xibalba, including the girl's father, were outraged at her behavior. They called their four owls, their messengers to the upper world, and told them to take Ixquic away and bring back her heart.

But the owls felt sorry for the girl. When she pleaded with them, they agreed to spare her life — if they could somehow fool the Lords of Xibalba. They took the red sap of the Blood Tree and poured it into a bowl, where it clotted into the shape of a heart. They brought this back to the foolish Lords of Death, who burned it, sniffed its smoke, and were satisfied. Then the owls rose and flew to the world above, where Ixquic had gone, to serve her. Their descendants are still with us.

Ixquic bore two children, Hunahpu and Ixbalanque, in the world above, and they later avenged their father and their uncle. But before Manuel could tell the others how they had done this, Elena said, "Your brother's calling you." Manuel looked up and saw Pepe beckoning from the window. Had he seen him telling the story? But he must have seen him talking to the others before. As for speaking to regular people — Pepe had never tried to make him do that, after the first few days. Perhaps his mother had told him not to.

As Manuel rose to go inside, the beggar-girl said, "When will you tell the rest of the story?"

"Soon."

"Oh, please!"

Manuel saw Ricardo looking to one side, to where his father was still standing. "You're right," Ricardo admitted. "There he is. He hasn't really disappeared. Anyway, Sergeant Duarte didn't get him, or he wouldn't look so strong and free."

"He always was," Manuel said.

The young librarian watched Manuel curiously and intently as he entered the library again. "You certainly were reading the Grimms' stories; and out loud, too. Were you telling the stories to yourself? I saw you were hardly looking at the book. Which stories do you like best?" The air of the library was so clear that Manuel could see specks of lipstick on her teeth, and the hungry gleam of her eyes. "He'd be perfect!" she told Pepe. "Our congregation would be so interested! It would get some of them moving again."

"No." Pepe shook his head. After a time, he said, "Maybe

my mother will talk to your congregation. You can ask her. She'll wonder where we are now." He picked up his books and told Manuel to follow him.

Pepe was silent at first as they walked back toward the motel. "That girl," he said at last. "Her name's Beatrice. She's the same age as Inmaculada." He grimaced, then shook his head as he remembered the beautiful army informer from the village. "No, Beatrice is all right."

They were walking by the pile of rocks, and a lizard calmly watched them go past. "They're planning a big protest demonstration tomorrow, did you know that?" Pepe said. Manuel nodded; he had heard the ladies talking about it in the church on their first day. "The *migras* are bringing this family in from a little jail in the country, and some other people too. They're taking them to the airport to fly them back home. To *our* home," Pepe added, his mouth twisting. "One of the men used to be a political candidate for the wrong party. You know what'll happen to him when they get hold of him; to the rest of them too, probably. The guys in the police aren't particular about how they stamp out 'rebels.' If they even suspect you, that's enough for them." He sighed. "It's just as well Mamá got those papers signed, so they can't throw us out of here until we tell our story to a judge." He sniffed. "It won't do any good, but at least we can wait a little before we start running again." He looked sternly at his brother. "Why were you sitting out there in the heat? You need to get some rest. You'll have to be in better shape when we're on the road again. They have some kind of secret network, Beatrice says, for moving people around so the *migras* don't catch them. But I bet you it's not going to be any fun. Just more running and hiding, all the time." He sighed again.

Manuel nodded. Whatever happened, he promised himself, he would keep practicing his *futbol*.

———

He was waiting for the cool of the evening to begin practicing that same day, in the shade of the blue dumpster in the
motel parking lot. The dust was thick there, once he had
swept the gravel away. He had decided to make a little village,
with stones and dirt — a village like the one in the hills, as
he so clearly remembered it. A mound of dust and gravel was
the hill on which most of the houses stood. Larger stones rep-
resented the houses, and a small matchbox beside a flattened
space was the row of three shops by the bus stop. There were
no stones large enough for the church, but he set up a dry
stick with two thorns, for the cross on the steeple.

His mother saw him at work there. He thought she would
laugh at him for playing such a baby game, but she said,
"Why, that's our village, isn't it?"

There was no harm in nodding, so he nodded.

"And here is our house." She pointed to the stone that
stood where their house had stood, and was the same color.
"And the church, too." She frowned. "But the ground is flat
here, just past the church. Where's your special little pond?"

Manuel put his hand down hard over the spot beside the
church. "That's right, it was there," said his mother. "Why
don't you dig it out?" She rose, walked to the motel, and
returned. "Look, the caretaker left a little spade with his gar-
dening tools."

"No!" Manuel cried. He pressed his hand to his mouth.
His heart beat so quickly, as he tried to call the word back, that
he felt the blood throbbing under his hand. Then he realized
that he had done no harm by speaking. He hadn't told any
secrets. Maybe she would stop worrying about him now.

But she *mustn't* be allowed to dig a pond. He swept his
hand across his village, knocking the little stone houses here
and there. He flattened the hill, then seized the spade from
her and began to spread gravel over everything, so that soon
the village would never have existed at all.

His mother had stepped back. "Now, why did you do that?" Her voice was cool, as if she were speaking of a stranger. Manuel busied himself with making the village site perfectly smooth. His mother laid her hand on his shoulder. "Yes, you do that," she said. "Wipe it all out. Wipe it out of your mind, too, if you can."

She rose to watch someone approaching from the motel parking lot. "Who's this?"

"Mrs. Cárdenas?" Manuel recognized the voice of Beatrice the librarian. The young man with the guitar, whose name was Andrew, walked behind her.

His mother walked away from the dumpster. "Yes."

"Is your son here? I mean Manuel."

His mother looked around the courtyard. "I don't see him." She looked down at Manuel, who backed around a corner of the dumpster, behind some cardboard boxes. It was always best to wait before showing yourself; he knew that as well as his mother.

"That's all right," Beatrice said. "I really wanted to talk to you. Maybe it's just as well that Manuel isn't here."

His mother nodded. "Won't you come inside?"

"We'll be glad to. Isn't it *hot*? Here it is, almost the end of September, and it's like the middle of summer. Thank God for air conditioning!"

All three of them entered the motel room. Still hiding behind the dumpster, Manuel wondered why they had come. He remembered the hungry way Beatrice had looked at him in the library. After a moment, he left his hiding place and crept beneath the window. Beatrice was sitting right beside it. Fortunately the air conditioning unit was at the other end of the room, so its hum didn't drown out their voices. Perhaps Beatrice was speaking extra loudly, Manuel thought, so that his mother could understand her. Andrew spoke in a normal, almost soft voice, but his words were quite clear.

His mother said, "I've heard about the demonstration."

"I'm sure you have," Beatrice said. "I wasn't going to ask you to take part in it; that might not be safe. All the newspapers will be there, and we hope the television reporters will come too. We may even make the national networks! But we're having a meeting in our church the night before — tonight, that is. You have no visible marks, do you?"

"Marks?"

"Marks of torture, I mean," Beatrice said brightly. Then she added, "No, your body doesn't seem to have been damaged at all. Besides, we've had enough cases with scars and deformities. In fact, they sometimes do more harm than good. They put some members of the congregation right off."

"I don't see how they can harden their hearts so!" Andrew said. "I know I couldn't."

"They don't really harden their hearts," Beatrice assured him. "But when it gets too painful for them to listen, they tune out."

"I can't tune out! The U.S. government is going to fly those poor people back to their own country, after they suffered so much to get away. And you know what'll happen to them there, at least to the adults. They'll all be killed!"

A hollow thump sounded; Andrew must have kicked his guitar case. "Sorry," he muttered.

"We can't be sure they'll be killed," said Beatrice. "It is quite a collection, though," she added. "There were OTMs in three separate jails. OTMs are 'Other Than Mexicans,'" she added helpfully.

"I know that," Manuel's mother said.

"The immigration agents are collecting them here so that they can all be returned on one plane. There's so much paperwork, and some of the airlines don't want to be involved. We can't stop this flight legally, but we need support for the next time. That's why I'm calling on you and Manuel."

"I have no visible marks, as you said. Neither has Manuel. Also, he doesn't speak."

"We understand that. I couldn't believe it at first, but now I realize it's true. But you know, his silence would be so much more eloquent than anything he might say. It would have such an impact!"

"Yes, it would be a real spectacle."

"Oh, I didn't mean that!"

"Didn't you?" said his mother. "No, I really don't think we'll put him on display."

"Well, I should think not!" Andrew exclaimed. "I never knew you were planning that, Bea. I wouldn't have come with you. Please excuse us, Mrs. Cárdenas. You've all been through so much already, we shouldn't subject you or your son to any more stresses. We *don't* want to make a spectacle of you, no matter what the cause is."

"Thank you," said his mother. Then she added, "In fact, I don't think it would hurt him. It might even interest him to see what a whole crowd made of such a private thing. You see, it is very strange. How can a boy who was once such a talker, almost a chatterbox — is that the word in English? — now refuse to speak?" She spoke in a high, clear voice. She probably guessed that he was listening, Manuel realized. "But still, I think I have to respect his silence. He must have a good reason for it, and one day I'll learn the reason."

There was a brief silence. His mother was right, Manuel thought, it *would* be interesting: to stand before all the people at the church, who would stare at him and smile kindly and make encouraging motions, as if these would get him to open his mouth! Maybe the two musical children would stand there with him. He could wait to speak until they did. And would his father be with them? No, his father was too serious to play such kids' games; he would only watch, smiling, from the back of the audience. He would know his son could keep a secret well.

But it was no use thinking of this; his mother had said no, and so had Pepe, in his own way.

Beatrice said, "Well, it was just an idea."

"Yes. Did you want me to speak to the congregation myself? But what could I tell them that they don't already know?"

"Maybe you're right," Beatrice said. "You're so calm, so reasonable. Some of us think the time for reason is past."

"It may have passed long ago," Manuel's mother said. But she didn't offer to speak again, nor did Beatrice ask her. When the librarian and her friend left, a few minutes later, Manuel was again hidden behind the blue dumpster.

FIVE

The Wolverhampton Wanderer

Some of the heat had passed by next morning. There was a high-pressure wave from the north, the television said, one that cleaned the air at last. Now Manuel saw the distant red hills very clearly. They were not just flat ridges, but jagged, with low, sharp, bare peaks like giants keeping guard. Would they have to cross these peaks? Would his companions be able to make the journey too? And would any of those evil Lords of Xibalba follow? So far, he hadn't seen them since he'd crossed into the United States. But maybe he'd been too busy looking out for the *migras*.

He was going to be very close to some of the *migras* that morning, because of his mother's work in the church basement. A new couple had crossed the border — a very frightened couple, Manuel thought. How had they managed to come even this far? They wouldn't say a word to the church ladies, but they spoke with his mother. Today she was going to the immigration office with them and Mrs. Fisher, as their interpreter, to help them apply for the G-28 forms that would make them safe for a time.

This was a good day to do it, Mrs. Fisher said. As far as she knew, there would be no other applicants, so the immigration office would have less excuse for delays. Also, she hoped the big demonstration taking place outside the office and the jail would distract the office staff, and make them less likely to try any tricks.

Still, if the immigration authorities thought up new obstacles, they might have to send out for legal help. At such times, they had found, the telephones in the immigration office always seemed to be tied up. The pay phones down the street were often vandalized, so it was best to have someone on hand to carry messages. The immigration office could hardly object to the interpreter bringing her young son along. Manuel's mother had already told Mrs. Fisher that she didn't have to worry; Manuel could be relied on to run back to the church, where Penelope would be waiting to pass on any written message. No one would ask him questions, Manuel's mother had told him. He hoped there *would* be a message to carry, so he could get away from the immigration office more quickly.

They were supposed to go to the office at eleven, which gave Manuel plenty of time to practice his *futbol*. But as he kicked the ball out toward the parking lot, he found his two young companions waiting for him by the dumpster.

"You're supposed to tell us how Ixquic's sons got even with the bad lords," Elena said.

Ricardo nodded shortly. "Yes, what did they do?"

Manuel settled down to tell them how the sons of Ixquic found revenge through a ball game — or rather three ball games. The games were played a few days apart, down in Xibalba, and Hunahpu and Ixbalanque had to overcome the skill, malice, and trickery of the Lords of Death. The twins won the first two games without much difficulty. The hard part came in the nights, which they had to pass in the evil houses of the lords: the House of Cold, the House of Knives, and the House of Jaguars — even though, he added, there was no House of Electricity. Through the help of their animal friends, the twins overcame all the perils of these houses. But at last, in the House of Bats, Hunahpu made a careless movement and one of those great fierce creatures snapped off his head. The triumphant Lords of Xibalba hung his head over the court for the last ball game. Now, they thought, Ixbalanque would have to play alone — and he was sure to lose.

But Ixbalanque and the animals who were his friends fooled the lords. The turtle made himself into a mock head for Hunahpu, so that Hunahpu could still take part in the game. Then, when the ball was rolling, the rabbit made the lords believe *he* was the ball, and ran away into the forest. While the lords were following the rabbit, Ixbalanque was able to put his brother's real head back on his body, and the two parts joined themselves again. Together, the twins won that game too.

"How could they put his head back on?" Ricardo asked skeptically.

"They were gods," Manuel said. "You could only kill them for a little while."

"Oh, gods," and Ricardo shrugged. "I guess they had their own kinds of ball games and their own rules. I wondered why the lords didn't use that head for a *futbol*. I'll bet that's what Sergeant Duarte would have done."

He paused to think. "Well, maybe Sergeant Duarte didn't play *futbol*. But Corporal Barrios did. He was so good that later they let him out of the Seguridad to play for the Panthers in the national league. Ricardo's face softened. "How he could play, that corporal! When he touched the ball, it seemed to be just waiting for his foot. It would spin any way he wanted, as if it followed his thoughts. He could make it dance and sing. In the parade ground he once asked me to play the flute while he made the ball dance. Those were his words."

Ricardo looked at Manuel coldly. "*You* can't play *futbol* the way he does. You'll never be able to make the ball follow your thoughts. I've watched you."

"I think he's good," Elena said loyally. "Especially for a city boy."

Ricardo looked at her, almost angrily. "So what? I can see what his feet do. He can learn to do better, but only a little. Do you think you could play a ball game with the Lords of Xibalba?"

"If I had to," Manuel said.

"Huh!" snorted Ricardo. After a moment, he admitted, "You're not that bad, really. Just don't think of anything else while you're playing. That's what Corporal Barrios told me."

Then Ricardo turned away so decisively that Manuel had nothing to do but take his *futbol* out in the gravel courtyard. He resolved not to let the flute boy's words disturb him. Ricardo knew about music, all right, but he didn't know everything. Still, Ricardo's advice made sense. If he was going to play at all, he should play his very best.

He scratched out a square in the gravel in front of the dumpster. Then he kicked the ball with enough sideways spin that it bounced back from the dumpster with a different angle each time. He thought about his foot movements at first, trying to put just the right spin on the ball, but soon his foot seemed to be moving by itself. The ball shot away and bounced back, as if it were attached to his foot by an invisible string.

The exercise was really easy; there was no one but him and the ball. But a real game, with teammates and opponents, wouldn't work this way. With steady pushes of his foot, Manuel dribbled the ball over the gravel to a patch of bare brown earth. Elena and Ricardo sat on top of the dumpster, watching him. The beggar-girl shook her castanets in applause from time to time. The flute boy played softly to himself, but the melody didn't interfere with Manuel's rhythm.

Now he began to drive the ball toward another side of the dumpster, with deft inner and outer instep kicks. As it bounced back to him, as if from a teammate, he began to return it, imagining that he was facing an opponent. He feinted to the left, then dribbled to the right; he dodged a tackle and spun around to drive the ball into the dumpster's wall with a smart heel kick.

Then it happened. One of the Lords of Xibalba stepped in. Manuel saw him almost with relief; he had always known they would follow him. Now he didn't have to wait any more. This wasn't one of the great lords, whose names his father had told him. It certainly wasn't One Death or Seven Death. It wasn't even a second-rank lord, such as the Filth-Maker or the Bringer of Misery — or the Wayside Watcher, who seized unwary travelers by their throats and carried them off. This was some lesser lord. Manuel would have to be very careful, he thought. If you spoke to them at all, it was important to call these lords by their right names. Otherwise they might gain control over you, as they had over Hun Hunahpu and Vucub Hunahpu. Those two had mistaken wooden images for the real lords, and thus had lost the power you obtained by calling someone by his proper name. Manuel decided not to answer at all if this lord spoke to him — or to answer only after the lord had revealed his name.

The nameless one was as tall as a man and was dressed in what he must think was the latest fashion. He wore a *migra*'s tall hat, but he was certainly no *migra*. At his neck was a shawl of red embroidered feathers, and serpents writhed around his throat and his bare feet. They were very agile serpents indeed. Whenever the lord kicked at the ball, trying to gain control of it, the snakes moved neatly aside.

The lord was obviously not at ease in the upper world. Sweat drops kept gathering above his mustache, and he blotted them with a green handkerchief. His eyes stared hungrily at the ball, as if he would like to catch it and keep it. But he didn't do this, nor did he knock the ball out of the field — either action would have revealed his presence to people who couldn't see him. He just touched the ball sideways, altering its spin so that its movement became more erratic. Sometimes his foot didn't touch the ball at all, but the serpents brushed it with their noses and subtly changed its direction. Ricardo and Elena giggled at this; Manuel hoped they wouldn't come down from their dumpster and join in the game.

He kept his temper. He knew he mustn't lose his concentration on the ball. But he was just getting it under control again when he heard a voice from outside. A big voice, with a new accent.

"Aha!" it said, "it's young Pelé himself! With such sly, clever moves, you'll soon be with Tottenham Hotspur." A big foot reached out and trapped the ball easily, then passed it on to Manuel, who also trapped it, and kept it while he decided if this man was on his team. It was the grocer, in his clean white apron. Manuel had seen him before, at a distance: a stocky, solid man, a little older than his father, his hair touched with gray.

With a malicious scowl, the nameless lord drew back. Manuel's father appeared between two of the parked cars in the Elite Motel lot, and Manuel saw, from the look in his father's eyes, that he had been watching for some time. His father looked in a friendly way at the grocer, who of course couldn't see him.

"How are you at headers?" the grocer asked. Without waiting for Manuel to answer, he nodded to him for the ball. He lofted it to the wall with a sharp stroke of his instep, caught the rebound on his forehead, and drove the ball back to the wall again. For a few minutes he kept the ball in play against the dumpster like a perfect machine, with alternating strokes of foot and forehead.

"That was my specialty," he told Manuel. "An educated forehead. Only I wasn't able to pass so well when my mates had a clear field. I thought too much about all the possibilities. Otherwise I might have made the Wolverhampton Wanderers! They were our local team. That was my home — Wolverhampton, in England. A scout was watching our team behind the factory. My mates told me afterward that he said, 'If that lad's feet were as educated as his head, we might have given him a tryout.'" He chuckled. "That was always my problem: my head was more educated than my feet. But I did wander here and there, so you might still say I'm a Wolverhampton Wanderer.

"Now, you just stand over there as if you were on my team, and I'll show you."

When Manuel had taken his place, the grocer sent the ball right within his range, with a cunning kick. It seemed to be calling to his feet, so easy was it to reach out and capture it. He kicked it back to the grocer, just where he wanted it to go. The ball went back and forth between them. Then the grocer called, "Watch this, now!" Somehow, the next ball spun just where Manuel thought it couldn't go. He had to turn and chase it. He returned it to the grocer, who again sent it back out of his reach. This happened twice more. The third time, Manuel understood the ball's new direction and kicked it back.

"That's the way!" the grocer called. He flipped the ball up into his arms. "Let's take a break while I catch my breath. I'm not as young as I was." The grocer rolled the *futbol* in his hands, looking at it critically. "You must direct the ball so that your friends can touch it as they want, but your enemies can't reach it," he said. "It's all in the force and the angle, and the spin you put on it. And you must guide it through a crowd, with your enemies racing all around you, when you've got no protection at all. You mustn't think of all the huge two-hundred pound louts leaping round you, or the fans scream-ing in the stands." Here he made a wry face. "Just concentrate on the ball itself, and where it must go.

"And practice handling the ball all the ways you're allowed," he added. "Use your head, chest, and knees. A good exercise is to bounce it from knee to head." He pro-ceeded to do so. "Palmquist kept the ball in the air like this for ten solid hours. A record. Very impressive, everyone said. Still, what use are such tricks in a real game?" But he went on keeping the ball in the air.

Manuel heard the van drive up and its door slam. The nameless lord stood beside it, grinning. A young blond man leaned against the back of the van, grinning too. Now he straightened up and applauded.

The grocer caught the ball and laid it carefully on the ground. He pulled a large watch from his pocket. "Are all the deliveries done, Hubert?" he called.

"Sure, boss. To all the people who were at home."

"All who were at home! You had time for twice as many customers as the list I gave you."

Hubert yawned. "I had to wait till they came to the door, didn't I?" He winked. "You seem to take your time with your own deliveries, I notice."

"Never mind my deliveries." The grocer opened the back of the van and stuck his head inside. "You let the fruit wait in the sun. It's starting to go!"

Hubert joined him. "Smells all right to me."

"All those lovely oranges!" said the grocer. "I should never have trusted you with them. Come on, we'll take them inside and salvage what we can."

"Sure," the blond young man said, moving very slowly. He yawned again. "I see you're playing with the dummy there. Has he said anything yet?"

"Never you mind. Some people talk too much. Just get on with your work."

Hubert shrugged, took up a crate of oranges, and began to walk very slowly toward the store. The nameless lord walked along beside him, lovingly sniffing the spoiled fruit.

The grocer seized three boxes, stacked them together, and carried them into the store. He had taken too many, but he wouldn't put them down. The lord from Xibalba watched eagerly. Was he hoping the grocer would drop the boxes, or fall? The lord looked disappointed when the grocer managed to open the side door and enter the shop.

The thin man came around the corner, opened the hood of the red and green car, and began to bang something inside with a hammer. The Lord of Xibalba drew nearer to the open hood of the car. He was just about to touch the engine when the flute boy, who had been watching him closely, began to play a soft, sleepy tune — the same one he had used to lull the Lord of Xibalba who'd been guarding the border outside San Cristóbal. The nameless lord listened and nodded drowsily, and the snakes at his neck swung around eagerly to hear the music.

Then the lord swayed forward and grazed his forehead on the car's open hood. He jerked back just as the thin man slammed the hood down angrily, but two of the snakes disappeared with a metallic screech. The lord, greatly embarrassed, stepped back and arranged the other snakes around his neck to cover up for the missing ones.

Ricardo began to applaud, and said, very politely, "Congratulations, sir. You got away just in time!" Elena started to giggle, but he silenced her with a poke to her arm.

"We have to be quick on our feet down in Xibalba," the lord said loftily. So he hadn't noticed the mockery in Ricardo's voice, Manuel thought. Just how dumb could he be?

"I can see that, colonel," Ricardo said, even more politely.

"Why do you call me 'colonel'?" the lord asked sharply. "What?" he snapped to one of the snakes, who was whispering in his ear. Then he spoke more tolerantly to Ricardo. "Ah — before you reached your present condition, when you were in your native town in this upper world, you ran errands for the soldiers." The snake whispered again in his ear and the lord smirked. "Very naughty errands, sometimes. Well, *we* don't mind. So many soldiers are our servants now in Xibalba; why shouldn't they have had their fun? Why shouldn't a boy like you sneak liquor to them, and carry notes to their girlfriends?"

So that was how Ricardo had made his living, Manuel thought. He had seemed too well fed for a beggar, even one who was such a skilled musician.

"I only wanted to help, major,"

The lord shook his head. "I'm not a major. You're clearly a very simple young man."

"I can't help that, lieutenant. I never had the chance for an education. I only know about life in the streets. Not important things like officers' ranks."

"That's what the High Command told me when they sent me up here." Then the lord's tone became severe. "You didn't come when we called you earlier."

"As you say, sir, I'm very simple," Ricardo said humbly. "I didn't understand. I asked myself why you'd want someone as worthless as me."

"We want everyone! There is a saying up in this world: 'If you save one soul, you save the universe.' We want *just the reverse.*"

Ricardo shook his head. "I'm sure I'm not worth your trouble. But please tell me what your rank really is. I don't want to make you angry."

"To be exact, then," the lord said rather huffily, "I am a sergeant."

"A sergeant! That's wonderful! I really admired Sergeant Duarte of the Seguridad. Are you related to him?"

The lord shook his head. "We all know Sergeant Duarte of the Seguridad, but I am Confusión."

"Sergeant Confusión!" said Ricardo in apparent awe, turning aside to wink at Elena. How easily he had gotten the lord's name out of him!

"That's my work — to confuse," the lord explained proudly.

"And you're good at it, too," Ricardo told him. "I don't understand you at all."

"You will understand it fully when you become my assistant."

"Your assistant? Really? What an honor! What do you want me to do?"

"You must help me confuse the minds of our enemies," Sergeant Confusión told him.

"But I don't know who our enemies are."

"Our enemies," said the lord loftily, "are all those who want to escape us. In the end, everyone must come to us."

"No kidding? Do they really have to?"

"In time they'll have to. But you should know better than to ask such questions. Stick to the task at hand. Our duty is to confound our enemies' hopes, to see that their ways are lost, their paths hidden, that nothing works for them. That way they'll leave this world sooner, and come to us. That boy —" Sergeant Confusión nodded toward Manuel — "has some foolish ideas about the importance of a ball game. You saw how I interfered with his play."

"Yes sir, you sure had him fooled!" Ricardo said this with a completely straight face, but this time Sergeant Confusión caught the mockery. "My little friends were watching his technique closely," he assured Ricardo, looking down at the serpents that peered from his neck. "They'll pass the word on, and the information will be useful when he comes down to us. Our Private Basher and Corporal Crusher know how to play ball with little boys of this world."

Suddenly the lord from Xibalba wasn't so funny, Manuel thought. He'd keep up his *futbol*, sure, but he'd take care to avoid any games with those champions of Xibalba!

"But we have bigger work now," Sergeant Confusión said. "The High Command is irritated that so many of our enemies are getting those immigration forms, and escaping their proper fate. We'll soon put an end to that! Come with me to the immigration office and learn how it's done." And with these words he vanished.

For a moment Ricardo didn't speak. "What a dope!" he said finally. "Were you really worried about him?" he asked Manuel. "What about you?" he asked Manuel's father, who had walked up behind his son. The schoolteacher looked very serious and shook his head. "You think we should still watch out?" Ricardo asked. The schoolteacher nodded gravely. "Well, we'll see."

His father was too worried, Manuel thought. Surely there was no danger from a boasting fool like this Sergeant Confusión. Surely they would reach safety despite anything he could do, at the immigration office or anywhere else.

SIX

The Cage

Mrs. Fisher was driving the car, and the new couple, Juan and Clara Milla, were sitting so low in the back that their heads barely showed in the window. Manuel realized that they were afraid of being stopped and sent home before they got a G-28 form. His mother came out of their room just as Mr. Wemyss walked toward them from his shop. He was carrying a basket of beautiful apples which he presented to Mrs. Fisher. "Thank you," she said, and smiled at him. "We'll eat them after the interview."

Manuel's mother had taken his *futbol* from him. "I'll hold that if you like, ma'am, and give it back to him later," Mr. Wemyss told her. "The immigration officials wouldn't understand such games. They have games of their own." His mother nodded her thanks.

As Manuel walked toward the other side of the car, he saw the grocer's young assistant pointing a camera at them from behind a corner of the van. What was going on? Mr. Wemyss and Hubert didn't like each other, so why did Hubert want a secret picture of his employer?

As their car approached the immigration building, a policeman directed them to a parking lot on the side. They could see a line of people with signs walking in a circle in front of the building. A second policeman told them to enter the building by a side door. Ricardo and Elena were waiting by that door, and followed them in.

The office they had to visit was one of several that opened off a long corridor lined with benches. Manuel and the two children sat on a bench. Manuel could see both the desks in the office. A gray-faced woman sat at one of them, before high piles of paper. A painted sign on her desk read, "Miss Merilee Griffin."

"Well, here you are again, Mrs. Fisher," she said, and sighed.

"Always busy in a good cause," Mrs. Fisher said cheerfully.

The woman looked up wearily. Did her ashen color come from some sickness? Manuel wondered. "And these are?"

"Mr. and Mrs. Milla. And Mrs. Cárdenas, who is our interpreter."

"An interpreter," the woman said, as if she didn't know the word. "Oh, hello Fred," she added as a man walked in and sat down at the other desk.

"Yes, an interpreter," a thin voice said. Manuel looked up quickly and saw that "Fred" was really the Lord of Xibalba, Sergeant Confusión. No one else had noticed this; only Manuel had recognized the sergeant's face. He thought he spotted a serpent looking out at his collar, too, but he was sure nobody else had seen it. The lord said, "They have to bring an interpreter now! You've gone to all that trouble to learn Spanish; remember how long it took you to pass the examination that got you *this* lousy job. Now they bring in people who can't even understand your Spanish."

Miss Griffin gave no sign that she had heard, though Manuel was sure the words had somehow reached her. "An interpreter?" she repeated. "Well, I don't know. What are her credentials?"

"My credentials, madame, are that I can speak both their language and yours," Manuel's mother said.

The woman looked up in surprise. "Well, I suppose it's all right," she said finally.

"We have to make an application on a G-28," Mrs. Fisher said, "as we have done before."

"As they certainly *have* done before!" the lord hissed. He hadn't raised his head from the stack of papers in front of him. Someone who hadn't heard him speak would have thought him an ordinary *migra*, studying these papers and making notes with a blunt pencil. His serpents were well hidden now, Manuel saw, but the bright green epaulets and chevrons on his shirt were certainly not those of a *migra*.

"As they've done before!" the lord whispered again across the room to the woman at the desk. "Why do you let yourself be a rubber stamp for processing such trash?"

"Yes, as you say, there have been quite a few requests," Miss Griffin said to Mrs. Fisher. "I don't believe we have any of the proper forms left. Some are expected soon."

"Tell them the forms have all been changed," "Fred" said. "Tell them you don't know when they'll be here. They'll have to go away and wait. And they might so easily be picked up while they're waiting." He giggled. "*We* can help arrange that."

Miss Griffin began sifting through her piles of paper. "In fact," she said, "there *have* been some changes. I've had a circular about some quite new G-28 forms. Now, where is it? I may have to ask you to come back."

"What's this about new forms?" Mrs. Fisher asked. "I hadn't heard about them."

Clara Milla whispered in Manuel's mother's ear, "Did we do something wrong? Should we go away?" But her husband shook his head sternly. He wouldn't be so easy to fool, Manuel thought; he seemed like a gloomy, suspicious man. Perhaps that was why they had got this far.

His mother said, "No, don't move." Then she said to Miss Griffin, "These new forms, madame. When did they come into effect?"

The woman looked up in surprise. "Why . . . two weeks ago."

Manuel's mother shook her head. "I received my own form last week." Aha! thought Manuel, Miss Griffin was trying to fool them. "So you must have had them at that time."

"That's right, you did," Mrs. Fisher exclaimed. "Oh, hello, Dr. Silas!" she called to a white-headed man who had just looked into the room. "I'm sure it's all settled now," she assured Manuel's mother. "Excuse me a moment." She took Dr. Silas's arm and drew him into the corridor.

The lord at the next desk made the smallest possible movement with one finger, to attract Ricardo's attention. Anyone else would still have seen a normal *migra* busy with the papers on his desk, but Manuel heard him whisper, "Now watch this, you beggar-boy. See how it must be done." He called to Miss Griffin, who again showed no sign of hearing him but frowned at the papers in a desk drawer she had just opened. "If you give them the G-28 form, you'll have to see them again, many times. Do you want to see them? Doesn't the man look like the one who spilled garbage on your driveway when they came to collect it this morning? And doesn't the woman look like your last maid, the one you had to let go when she broke your dishes? She has the same insolent face. Get rid of them now, for good!"

Then he rose, carefully arranged some papers in a folder, smiled at Miss Griffin, and walked out. Manuel saw his shadow pass, and realized that the lord had somehow borrowed the body of the real Fred. Miss Griffin nodded as if she had heard all this, and also rose. "*Now* I remember where we put the forms," she told the Millas, with a little laugh. She stepped to a filing cabinet.

"What did the señora say?" Clara Milla asked Manuel's mother.

"That she has found the papers." Both Millas smiled in relief. "Wait," Manuel's mother told them.

"Here you are, then." Miss Griffin laid a form on the desk and held out a pen. "You must sign here. Or make an X if you can't write. I'll print your name and witness it. No, you don't have to translate it," she told Manuel's mother, "they understand me quite well. Here, sir, take the pen."

Juan Milla smiled in relief and stepped forward, reaching for the pen. Manuel's mother laid a hand on his arm and stepped forward beside him.

"He is to sign, not you!" Miss Griffin said sharply. "Here's the place." She pointed to the paper.

Manuel's mother tightened her hand on Juan Milla's arm. "Stand still! Sign nothing! Do you understand?"

Juan Milla looked puzzled at first, then nodded. "*Claro.*"

"Wait until I return!" Manuel's mother walked to the door. "Mrs. Fisher!" she called.

"You must sign here," Miss Griffin repeated, in Spanish. Clara Milla looked at her husband, who shook his head. "Señora Cárdenas said no," he reminded her. Manuel's mother entered the room again almost at once, and Miss Griffin looked up, surprised. Mrs. Fisher followed her in. "What is it?" she asked.

Miss Griffin tried to pull the form back, but Manuel's mother was holding it firmly on the desk. "Look at this," she told Mrs. Fisher. "Is this the G-28 form?"

Mrs. Fisher stood beside her. "It certainly isn't! What were you trying here? This is one of your VDFs. You tried to trick them into signing a Voluntary Departure Form!"

"It was a mistake," Miss Griffin said hastily. "We have so much paperwork these days."

"We know your mistakes!" Mrs. Fisher spluttered. "You thought you could just ship them out of the country!"

Manuel's mother had gone to the desk. She pointed to some papers in one corner. "Isn't this the form you want, Mrs. Fisher? The G-28 form?"

"Of course it is!" Mrs. Fisher seized the form before Miss Griffin could move.

"It was a mistake," she repeated.

"Well, let's just make sure there are no more mistakes." Mrs. Fisher and Manuel's mother helped the Millas fill out the form while Miss Griffin turned wearily away, not protesting. Manuel's mother whispered to him that there would be no need for special messengers. "But don't go far. Wait near the door." She nodded toward the corridor.

Before Manuel could move away, Fred came in again. But could this be the same person? Now he looked like an ordinary *migra*. There were no serpents around his neck, and his uniform was plain. "Hi, kid," he said as he passed Manuel. "Morning, Mrs. Fisher." He nodded affably to the Millas and Manuel's mother. "Did you get the case sorted out?" he asked Miss Griffin.

"Oh yes," she said brightly. "There was almost a clerical error, but we caught it in time."

"That's good. We don't want any of those clerical errors." Then Fred's voice dropped. Manuel's mother and the others were halfway to the outside door, but Manuel heard what Fred said: "They're really stirring up trouble by the police station. Some of the protesters were here, but they're moving to where they figure the action is. They have the newspaper and TV people there too. They'd just love to get wind of some 'clerical error.'"

"Manuel," his mother called to him.

Fred spun around and looked at Manuel. "Run along, kid," he said. "What are you doing here, anyway?"

Outside the door, Ricardo stood beside Sergeant Confusión. The Lord of Xibalba, who had so cleverly entered the body of Fred, was now back in his own body. Manuel was quite sure this was so since the lord no longer cast a shadow. The lord was sourly watching Mrs. Fisher and Manuel's mother talking to the Millas. They were all eating Mr. Wemyss's apples, and his mother handed one to Manuel.

"I'll go back to the church now," she told him. "You can go back to your ball practice. You can eat your apple on the way."

At first Manuel wondered why she was in such a hurry to see him go. But then he heard a confused sound of voices a few blocks away. Three women and a man with signs over their shoulders were walking away from the immigration office, while an immigration official who had just come out of the office watched them. They must be going toward the demonstration. His mother would probably rather he didn't go there. But she wouldn't say so directly — not to Pepe, and not even to him, since he wasn't a baby any more. Manuel turned back to Ricardo and Sergeant Confusión.

Ricardo's eyes were shining with amusement but he tried to appear impressed. "You sure had them confused in there, sergeant!"

"I think so," the lord said smugly.

"The lady at the desk was so confused that she almost made a mistake. Did you want her to do that?"

"Sometimes a 'mistake' may be intentional. In the land of Xibalba, paths are made to mislead travelers. Those who think they are going in one direction are really going in another."

"Gee, it must be a mixed-up place," Ricardo said.

"Not at all, once you understand it. You'll love it down there. You both will." The lord nodded toward Elena, who was watching them from a distance with her thumb in her mouth.

"Sure," Ricardo said. "But tell me, sir, I still don't understand. The people in there got the papers they came for. Was that what you wanted too?" His tone was innocent, but the question made the lord furious.

"Yes, they got the papers they wanted, and a futile gesture it was! It will gain them nothing in the end, just a longer time of fear and uncertainty. If they had just signed when they were told to, their fate would be properly settled, like the fates of those who came before them and those who will come after. Follow me to see how such affairs *should* be managed. They are over there, at the police station." He nodded down the street, where many cars were drawing up and parking. "Can't you hear them squeaking and howling? I don't mean the forces of the law, or even those who have accepted their destiny calmly. I mean the filth and scum who collect around them."

Sure enough, new sounds reached them: many separate voices, then a mixing of these voices into a muddled chant.

"You can hear the noise they make, the useless noise," said the lord. "Come, we'll enjoy the sight of it! And you can come too," he added to Manuel and Manuel's father, who had followed them to the immigration office but waited outside the door. "You can see how things are done in your new, civilized land."

"I know already, Sergeant Confusión," Manuel's father told him.

The lord made a very sour face, realizing he had given his name away. Then he was gone, and Manuel's father too. But Manuel understood now where they had gone, and he followed them. He could practice his *futbol* later.

The police station, a yellow adobe building, was set back from the main street behind a wide gate and an orderly row of tall palm trees. Dusty police cars were parked neatly between the trees, and inside the gate a high black jeep faced the street. A policeman stood on either side of the jeep, holding a long club diagonally across his chest. One photographer was taking pictures of the policemen; all the others were watching the lines of demonstrators.

Manuel had often heard Pepe sneer at such people. "In this country they're in no danger! All they do is walk around waving signs, and getting their faces on television. Or signing stupid petitions. And it makes them feel like heroes!"

But Manuel thought Pepe was too harsh. These looked like good, serious people. The older ones were soberly dressed. The young men and women wore bright clothes; some had yellow T-shirts showing hands gripping black bars over the word "LIBERTAD" — Freedom. Almost all the demonstrators held up signs. "Let Them Go," read one sign. "Sanctuary Is Sacred," read another. "No More Meat for the Butcher," said a third. Other people carried flat wooden crosses, like cemetery markers, with names and numbers written on the cross-pieces: Carlos Centeno Gonzáles, 26; Oracio Gomes Miranal, 53; Oscar Sotelo Fletes, 70; Ramón Cepedo García, 8; Miranda María Cardenal, 27. Manuel realized that the numbers must be the ages of the people named.

Then he saw his father standing at the end of a line of demonstrators. His face was very sad and he held up a cross that read, "Dr. Luis Álvarez, 34." No one else noticed this except Sergeant Confusión, who had been smiling at the other crosses but scowled angrily at this one.

Their father looked uneasy, and when Manuel followed his gaze he was surprised to see that, whatever his past opinions, Pepe was taking part in the demonstration too. He wore one of the yellow T-shirts and a wide straw hat with a red band. Beatrice the librarian and another girl had laid their arms fondly on his shoulders. They were smiling, but not Pepe. He looked stiffly at the crosses, his face as dark with anger as if he knew each of the people named there.

No one else was so angry. Even the oldest demonstrators

smiled in the fine fresh northern breeze. At one end of the line Penelope and three young men stood around Andrew and his guitar, singing, "Let my people go!"

Ricardo, who was sitting on one of the police cars, listened to the music more critically. Once he picked up his flute to join in, then set it down with a scornful expression. Manuel listened closely too. Yes, the singers were sometimes a little off key, and their rhythm was ragged. They would never pass the test of Ricardo's harsh judgment. Every note Ricardo played was perfect, and his music flowed like a clear, sparkling stream. But now Elena had joined Ricardo. Manuel saw them whispering together, watching Sergeant Confusión, who was walking behind the line of demonstrators. Then they followed him.

Other people were less critical of the music than Ricardo. One of the policemen beside the jeep began to nod happily in time to the beat, and Penelope left the singers and tossed a wreath of small white flowers over his club. "Thank you!" said the policeman, raising his hand to sniff at the flowers. "They smell sweet!" he remarked. Shyly, Penelope smiled back.

Another policeman came out of the police station and stood beside the jeep. "We're always glad to see you folks," he said comfortably. "Expressing your views. That's what democracy is all about. But you really have come to the wrong place. All we have in our jail right now are common criminals. No one you'd be interested in."

Some of the demonstrators laughed; others jeered. "Let's see!" someone shouted.

"Now, if you went in and walked from cell to cell, you *would* see," the policeman told them.

More of the young men and women laughed. "I positively swear to you that the people you are talking about are not in this station," the policeman insisted. He spoke so solemnly that some of the older demonstrators seemed convinced. The younger ones looked at each other. A small group began to whisper together.

A clicking caught Manuel's attention. Elena was snapping her castanets at him from the street. "Come on!" she called. "Ricardo says it's really something to see! That stupid Sergeant Confusión showed him where the prisoners are." She raised her hands above her head, twirled around, and danced farther away. In a moment Manuel had followed her. He saw his father watching him, motioning him to return, but he paid no attention. Pepe saw him go too, and started to follow.

Elena danced and clicked her way down the sidewalk, slipping merrily aside from the cameras and cables and the thick crowd of spectators. Manuel slipped between them too, though some people shouted at him. He looked back for an instant and saw Pepe still following him.

Now Elena had turned down a very narrow alley — just a space between two buildings, hardly wider than the staggered garbage cans that lined its sides. Manuel followed her to the end of the alley and stopped by a high, solid wooden door, topped with barbed wire, that seemed closed with a heavy padlock. Then Elena pointed slyly at the padlock and Manuel saw that it was open. He lifted it off and slipped past the door.

He found himself in a bare, dusty yard with a wide pile of white bricks and coils of fencing wire. The beggar-girl danced past these coils but nodded to Manuel to hide. He crouched behind the bricks and looked through the wire. Some thirty feet away was a tall wooden structure. One side was fenced in with strong, shiny wire, and so was the top. A wide piece of striped canvas over the wire on the roof shaded the floor of the enclosure. The boards were new and the grass beneath the canvas was as high as the grass outside, except along the edges, where the people sat.

They sat there patiently, looking at their hands or at the

grass. Sometimes one of them glanced up at a policeman who sat on a wide bench with two *migras* in their tall hats, only partly shaded by the dusty crown of a palm tree.

"That sun's a killer!" said one of the *migras*, a red-faced, redheaded man. "You folks are lucky to be sitting in the shade." His face and voice were so friendly that several of the people sitting on the ground smiled timidly. A woman with a small girl sleeping on her lap smiled. An older woman sitting behind her, against the fence, frowned but then quickly smiled in turn, as did an old man facing her, a younger man at his side, and a very squat man who sat apart. A slim man, who had been scowling, smiled thinly and asked in clear English, "Would you like to change places, señor?"

"Well, I'm afraid we can't do that, sir," the *migra* told him. "Those aren't our orders. We're supposed to look after you here while they arrange for transportation. We hope it won't be too long."

"It can be as long as you like." The English-speaking man looked quickly around at the others, who watched him hopefully as he spoke in this strange language.

"You're quite a joker," the policeman said. "But it really won't be long. How long would you say?" he asked the red-headed *migra*.

"Well, they're bringing the van around by the back road, to keep it out of sight of those folks in front. Of course, they keep a pretty sharp lookout. It's not as easy to fool them as it used to be."

"Pardon, señor," said the English-speaking man, "but why have you put us here, apart from the other prisoners?" He nodded toward the back of the police station. Two windows on one side were barred; a man was looking out of one and two men out of the other.

"Because you aren't prisoners," the redheaded *migra* said. "Not exactly."

The policeman added, "That's right. There's no charges against you, except for being illegal aliens, and we're not going to prosecute you for that."

The other *migra*, a sour, gray-haired man who had been silent till now, said, "Since you all agreed to be sent back home of your own free will."

"Those are some pretty nasty fellows back in the jail cells," the policeman added. "You sure don't want to mix with them!"

Now the sleeping girl opened her eyes, and stared in a different direction from the others: at the beggar-girl, who had been standing ever so quietly by the fence, and who now smiled at her and clapped her hands. "She'll play with me!" Elena called across to Manuel. No one else seemed to hear her. The girl in the cage blinked as if she couldn't believe anyone was there. Then she looked across at the opposite wall, where Ricardo stood beside Sergeant Confusión. She blinked and closed her eyes again.

"You see," Sergeant Confusión said, "everything is in good order. They are going back to their own place. Observe how calm they are!"

"They sure are," Ricardo said. He grinned. "I guess they didn't manage to sign those G-28 forms."

The sergeant started to clap Ricardo on the back, then saw the warning look in his eyes and stopped. "You're starting to learn, youngster!" He snickered. "Some of them *thought* they were signing G-28s, but they really signed Voluntary Departure Forms, VDFs. The officials knew their business better than that Griffin woman we just saw. In one family only the oldest man, the grandfather, signed the VDF."

"The old man there?" Ricardo asked, nodding at the cage. "Why did he ever leave home?"

"He didn't know how tiring it would be to travel. When I whispered in his ear how much better it was to go home, he signed like a good boy."

"And did that one sign like a good boy too?" Ricardo nodded at the English-speaking man.

Sergeant Confusión laughed, and the serpents around his neck hissed. "He's in the old man's family. He didn't want to leave the rest of them. If we lose some, we win some too. Don't be so cocky, youngster. I can see that look in your eyes. Our motto is, never give up. We never do. Now watch; none of them will have to wait long."

As he spoke, the policeman and the two *migras* had risen to their feet. A van with small dark round windows, its body painted with a desert scene of Joshua trees and low cacti on a background of yellow sand and blue sky, had just turned down the gravel road from the side street. The windshield was also of dark glass, and it was only when the van drew nearer that Manuel could see two more *migras* in the front seat.

"Is *that* a government van?" the policeman asked the red-headed *migra*.

"It is right now," the *migra* assured him. "We've rented it from a country music group, because we needed a van that didn't look too official. But we had to take their sign off the top, or they wouldn't have let us have it." The van turned toward the coils of wire, then backed around beside the cage. "Let's go, folks," said the redheaded *migra*. He waited until the two other *migras* in the van had joined them, then unlocked and opened a corner door. Sergeant Confusión joined the line of *migras*, moving close behind them, so that it was hard to tell just how many there were. He motioned to Ricardo to join him, but the flute boy stayed by the front of the cage, grinning stupidly and clapping his hands.

"Come on, folks! Just a little ride before your flight home!" the redheaded *migra* called. The people in the cage had started to enter the van, moving between the fence and the line of *migras*.

"What a homecoming they'll have!" the van driver said, drawing back a little.

Sergeant Confusión said, "Don't let them go! Your buddies will just have to catch them all over again."

The driver looked round, puzzled, and Manuel wondered if he'd heard. The driver stiffened his shoulders and stepped forward.

Then the policeman, who was standing at the rear of this line, called softly, "Uh-oh, we've got company!"

The door from the alley had opened. Pepe stuck his head through, then drew back. At the same time, a line of demonstrators appeared on the side street at the end of the gravel road. They began to march forward, side by side, completely blocking the road. The policeman began to speak rapidly into his hand radio, still keeping his place in the line.

The grandfather and grandmother had meekly entered the van. As the *migras* drew closer to the van door, three more policemen came out of the station. The policeman at the end of the line called, "We'll need a little help in getting through." He waved at the demonstrators, who were within sixty feet of the van and were standing arm in arm, blocking the gravel road.

Now there were new arrivals from the open alley door: Andrew with his guitar, which he held over his head; two more young men; and Penelope. Pepe came last of all, almost shoving the others in his haste. He stepped around them, started to run forward, then looked back and saw Manuel. He waved his hand fiercely, warning him to stay down. Then he paused, clenching his fists and shuffling his feet up and down. Their father had followed Pepe out of the alley. He stood watching him with great concern.

The four others who had come through the passage formed a line again and approached the van. One of the *migras* had just climbed into the driver's seat.

"Let them go!" Penelope cried. Two of the men called, "Let them go!" and Andrew called, "Free them all!"

"I'll clear the road pretty quick!" a policeman called. He walked past the van, swinging his club, but another policeman called him back. "We just have to move the van out. We don't want to hit anyone."

"You lied to us!" Penelope cried indignantly.

"Come on," the second policeman said to the *migras*. "Just get the van packed up. You can get a clear run through the field there," he said to the first policeman in a low voice. "You can outflank 'em."

"Now, just move along there, please," the redheaded *migra* said to the last of the people from the cage. The gray-haired *migra* seized the arm of the English-speaking man and propelled him into the van.

Whose voice was that calling, "Pepe, no!"? Could it be their father? Why was he speaking?

Just as the redheaded *migra* reached out to close the van door, a white brick shattered the rear window, spraying glass in his face. He leaped back, wiped at his face, and looked with amazement at his bloody fingers. The *migras*, the police, and the four demonstrators from the alley stared at Pepe, who had just picked up a second brick. Manuel's father waved his arms frantically, but Pepe threw the brick. It dented the side of the van.

Andrew had picked up a brick too. Now he threw it. It bounced off the top of the van.

Then the police were running toward the alley. One blew a whistle as he ran. Manuel slipped around a corner of the pile of bricks, out of sight.

But they were after his brother and Andrew, not him. Pepe, scooting among the garbage cans, had reached the far end of the alley. Andrew was just behind him, carrying his guitar carefully in the narrow passage. A photographer aimed a camera at the back of Pepe's yellow T-shirt, which showed black bars but no hands or words. Pepe dodged into the mass of spectators just as a policeman forced his way through. Then Pepe doubled back, away from his grasp, and disappeared. The policeman ran forward toward Andrew just as another policeman seized him from behind. His guitar rang out sadly as it fell, then one of the policemen shoved his foot through it. Sergeant Confusión, who had been watching these events closely, applauded the guitar's destruction.

"Come back here, you little bitch!" the redheaded *migra* called. He was standing by the back of the van, motioning to the small girl. Somehow, during the excitement with the broken window, she had slipped out of the van again. Was her father the English-speaking one? Had he sent her out? "You come back, do you hear!" the redheaded *migra* cried, his voice partly muffled by the bloody handkerchief he had pressed to his chin. He began to walk toward the girl, who backed off into the weeds. But he wasn't watching his feet. Suddenly he tripped on a loose brick and, arms flailing, fell forward, his head and shoulder striking the brick pile.

The gray-haired *migra* slammed the van door shut. "Look after Harold!" he called to one of the policemen. Two demonstrators who had come to the other *migra*'s aid backed off. The policeman raised the injured *migra* to his feet and, very gently, led him toward the station.

The gray-haired *migra* was watching the girl who had escaped. He began to saunter in a wide circle to cut her off. "Come on, darling," he told her in Spanish. "You don't want your folks to go off without you now, do you?"

The girl looked at him without understanding. Elena drew near her and danced around, smiling and winking at Manuel. "Get my playmate for me!" she called. Manuel stood up, caught the young girl's eye, and motioned to her.

How she could run! Elena clapped her hands and clacked

her castanets together to speed her on her way. The gray-haired *migra* tried to catch her but tripped over his own feet. Sergeant Confusión ran too, spreading out his arms, but, if the girl saw him, it only made her run faster. Then she was clear, running behind the demonstrators and following Manuel into the weedy lot. He looked back at her, waving at her frantically to hurry. He had reached a dip in the ground so he couldn't be seen from the cage or the van. The girl would be out of sight there.

But when she lost sight of the van the girl stopped running and put her finger in her mouth. Manuel waved again for her to come on, and crouched in the weeds to show her how easy it was to hide. Elena beckoned to her fiercely; the clicking of her castanets filled the air. The girl looked around, afraid to move. "Crickets?" she asked.

Now the gray-haired *migra* stood beside the girl. His movements were calm and deliberate. He beckoned to the van, which was inching toward him through the weeds. Very smoothly, the *migra* opened the front door of the van. "Come on, darling. You can ride in front with us. You see your folks in the back there. They're all waiting for you."

He offered the girl his arm in a courtly gesture. She took it politely and was escorted to the front seat. Sergeant Confusión watched her, rubbing his hands together in satisfaction.

"Let's move, now!" the gray-haired *migra* told the driver. "The plane leaves in an hour. We don't want any more trouble." He climbed into the front seat and the van drove off. It was a block away by the time the main group of demonstrators reached the side street. Some followed after it, calling, but most scattered. Penelope was crying; Andrew tried to approach her, but the policemen who were holding him pulled him away. Many people were crowded around the empty cage. Manuel mixed with a group of children, none of whom spoke to him.

But the flute boy did. "The soldiers didn't even shoot! This really is a different country." He shook his head, made as if to place his flute in his mouth, then set it down again. "They're lucky they didn't meet Sergeant Duarte. He talked about the 'demonstrators' up here and what *he'd* do to them if he had the chance. That bunch in the van better hope he's not waiting for them when they get home. He used to brag about the welcoming parties he arranged for people who ran away and were sent back."

"Did he *talk* to you about that?" Manuel asked. Surely Ricardo hadn't been a friend of the terrible Sergeant Duarte!

"He talked to all of us kids on the street, especially when he was drunk. Then he was our great big pal. He even pretended to like my music. But you had to watch out for him. I wasn't careful enough once, when he was getting over a hangover. He kicked me in the head because my flute 'disturbed his rest.' I should go back and disturb his rest again, but he's not worth bothering about."

But Manuel couldn't keep his mind on what would happen back home. He was thinking about Pepe. Why had he thrown the brick? Sure, he had been brave, but also foolish. The Gray Coyote had been right when he'd told their mother that Pepe would march with banners waving. That was just what he'd done, and what had come of it? Now the people in the cage were on the way home, and Sergeant Duarte or someone like him would be waiting for them. And the American police would be coming after Pepe. How could they persuade a judge to let them stay?

He remembered how his father had cried, "No!" It was the first word from him on all their journey, but Pepe hadn't been able to hear it. And how the Lord of Xibalba, Sergeant Confusión, had smiled and applauded the results of Pepe's action. Maybe these lords weren't so easy to fool after all.

SEVEN

Logs in the Stream

Mrs. Fisher thought there would be no danger if Manuel practiced with his ball behind her house. There was enough room for him to play between the garage and a high board fence. To see over the fence, any watchers would first have to walk through a quarter-mile of dry land — her "great cactus garden," Mrs. Fisher said fondly. They would have to pass between the Joshua trees that stood there like guardians. The space between these tall, strong cacti was full of spiny bushes and sudden outcroppings of rock. It would be hard to walk or even crawl through such country.

Besides, before an intruder came that close, her fuzzy black dog, Castro — part poodle, part cocker spaniel — would sound the alarm. Then Manuel could hide behind Castro's house until the strangers left. And what if they did see him — a young boy kicking a soccer ball around the back yard? They'd mistake him for Mexican, and think he was the son of the cook, or the gardener.

Their presence in her house was quite legal, of course,

Mrs. Fisher said. But it seemed wisest now, while Pepe was being sheltered in the church, for Manuel and his mother to move out of the motel and live with her. Otherwise, those who noticed that Pepe was no longer with them would ask too many questions. They should try to attract as little attention as possible.

He would know about an intruder even without the dog, Manuel thought. Lizards ran all over the "cactus garden," looking knowingly through the fence, as if their cousins by the library had passed on word of him. Their rustling flight would tell him someone was coming, even if that lazy dog Castro didn't wake up.

Mrs. Fisher liked to watch Manuel practicing his soccer. "That's the way!" she would call out. "Show us what you can do! Some things are more important than talking! I know you'll talk when you're ready!"

Manuel was grateful that, after the first attempts, she had stopped trying to make him talk. She was slow to learn, but she'd finally gotten the idea. He had heard her whisper to his mother, "It's just a question of keeping him in the right environment for a time."

"That would be a change," his mother had said.

Mrs. Fisher put him in the room of her younger daughter, who was away at college. She carefully pronounced the names of the rock stars whose pictures hung on the wall, many of them wearing dark glasses. She also carefully explained how to use the stereo set, and the earphones, if he didn't want anyone else to hear what he was playing. She tried to explain the Nintendo games, which could be attached to the television set, but she got confused. With a little help from his mother, Manuel figured out the games for himself. He played the game in which Mario and Luigi make their way toward the castle, past hostile beasts and other obstacles, and got as far as the waterfalls that the brothers have to cross. But then he shut the game off, and he wouldn't play it again that day. He knew something about waterfalls.

Mrs. Fisher was surprised to see him give up the Nintendo so soon. But she was very impressed when she watched him making high scores in Tetris, by quickly fitting different shapes into the right places. "I couldn't do that!" she said.

He bet Pepe couldn't either, Manuel thought smugly. He'd be too impatient to watch and plan. Though Pepe knew so much more than he, his hands and feet didn't obey his mind. He was no good at *futbol* either. Recently he had started to sneer at the game's popularity in their own country. "Bread and circuses for the masses!" he had said, without explaining what he meant — though Manuel recalled that his brother had applauded in the village when *he* made a goal.

How had Pepe managed to throw the brick so straight? At least his brother could act, while everyone else only talked and waved signs. He had got away, too. Poor Andrew — his brick had only bounced off, but he was still in jail. And his guitar was smashed, too. No one was sure what would happen to him.

Mrs. Fisher's gardener, Felipe, who also looked after the garden at the church, lived in an apartment behind her garage. Felipe didn't try to make Manuel talk. After asking his name the first day, he understood that the boy preferred to be silent.

Felipe did seem glad of Manuel's company, though. He often invited him to watch while he prepared the soil for a new bed or weeded an old one. Manuel helped him, reaching into places where Felipe's broad hands wouldn't fit. "Good!" the gardener had said, nodding approvingly. "A garden brings peace to all. Even those too lazy to help their father." He looked fondly at his own son, Marcos, who was sitting in the shade of a fence, strumming his guitar.

Marcos wasn't really lazy. He usually lived in town, in an apartment beside the garage where he was learning to be an auto mechanic. Marcos could fix anything on wheels, his father said. He just had to whistle at them and parts of the engine would come together. Marcos had come to his father's apartment at the same time as Manuel and his mother had come to stay with Mrs. Fisher. Mrs. Fisher had said to Manuel's mother, "Greta Pearl arranged for Marcos to stay for a while, Sonia. She thought people should see both your sons here with you."

She hadn't explained further, and Manuel's mother hadn't questioned her. In fact, Manuel noted, Marcos was Pepe's age and build; he looked much like him, except that he was trying to grow a mustache.

Felipe pulled out the garden hose and began to wet down the leaves of the orange tree he had persuaded to grow in this dry climate. "All living things need water, you know," he told his new helper. "You mustn't be afraid of water."

Felipe said this because he had watched Manuel's reaction the first time he turned on the sprinkling system, and its wide heads sprayed the rows of flowers between the garage and the house. It wasn't the actual spray that had frightened the boy, Felipe decided. Manuel liked to watch the little rainbows that formed in the mist. But more water was sprayed than even the dry earth could swallow. After a time some flowed back in a tiny river behind the garage, and disappeared into a hole in the earth at the far corner of the shed.

Felipe had thought it would amuse Manuel if he sailed twigs down this stream. At first Manuel had been terrified, until he saw that they really were only twigs. They had bark, and ribs, and branches; some of them had thorns. They could only be twigs. Now, though Manuel still avoided the sight of the tiny rushing river, its sound no longer disturbed him. As Felipe had said, all growing things needed water, and the water had to run somewhere.

His mother was staying in Mrs. Fisher's house too, but she

continued to work in the church basement. This gave her a chance to visit Pepe, who never left the sanctuary of the church. The grocer, Mr. Wemyss, often came to the church, she said. He always brought groceries, and he spent time talking to the two American ladies, and to her and Pepe as well. Hubert never came with him. Once, when Hubert tried to enter the church with a box of oranges, Mrs. Pearl told him firmly that she hadn't ordered them, and refused to let him in.

Pepe had to stay in the church, Mrs. Pearl had explained. The authorities didn't know who had smashed the van's window with the brick. All they had was a picture of Pepe's back as he ran away, a picture of a young man wearing the same prison-barred T-shirt as many others. No one had identified him to the authorities, who had been asking everyone Mrs. Fisher knew. "I lied like a trooper!" she said cheerfully. "I was sure Pepe had done something when he came running back inside the church that day; and some of our friends told me later what had happened. But none of them will talk."

"I wish we could be sure of that," said Mrs. Pearl.

They were all sitting in Mrs. Fisher's back yard, between the house and the garage, in an area shaded by a redwood fence and Felipe's orange tree. Mrs. Pearl had taken a number of papers from her briefcase and was running over a list of names with the tip of a ballpoint pen.

Mrs. Fisher looked uneasily at Manuel. He knew she would like it better if he began to practice with his soccer ball again; but it was more important to hear what the adults were saying. He took the ball into the shade below a redwood table and began to roll it gently back and forth between his foot and the blue-gray gravel. Maybe Mrs. Fisher would think this motion had some relation to a real game. Whenever she looked down at him, from the blue knitted sweater whose parts she was now sewing together, she smiled approvingly.

"So many people saw him!" Manuel's mother said. "How can they all keep a secret?"

"They can't," Mrs. Pearl said. "But fortunately we're the only ones who know who Pepe really is. The police probably suspect he's in the church, though. They may be watching it."

———

Someone *was* watching the church, Manuel knew. He had heard Felipe talking to Rosa, the cook. "You're right. I've seen one. He doesn't sit there long. But then he goes to the park behind the church and reads a newspaper. It would be hard for anyone to leave without him seeing."

"A *migra?*" Rosa had asked.

"No. But I've seen him talking to the *migras*. The other one is the barber who sings in the church choir. He's always in front of his shop now, looking at the church over the top of a newspaper, even though he doesn't like the heat and his shop is air-conditioned. He lets his assistant cut everyone's hair, even his favorite customers."

"Will you tell the señora?" Rosa nodded toward the front room, where Mrs. Fisher was playing the piano and singing. Her voice wasn't quite in tune, and Manuel was glad that Ricardo was keeping away.

"Not Mrs. Fisher!" Felipe said. "I'll tell Mrs. Pearl — she has more discretion. But I'm sure she already knows about the watchers."

———

In the garden, Mrs. Pearl rattled her papers. "We really have to keep Pepe out of sight. There wasn't much chance before that you could stay in this country as refugees, and now there's practically none. But if they catch Pepe and show that he threw the brick, they'll shut him up, and probably you too, until they've arranged to ship you all back."

"But do you think they'd actually go inside the church to get him?" Mrs. Fisher asked. "Even though we've declared it a sanctuary? They haven't desecrated any sanctuaries yet."

"Let's hope they don't start here. This time they have the excuse that Pepe committed a crime. . . ."

"What crime?" Mrs. Fisher demanded. "Trying to save those poor people from being sent back to the butchers they'd escaped from?"

"They'd call it obstructing justice; also assault, since that man was cut by flying glass. They're very angry about that."

"Well, they'd better not break into the sanctuary!"

"They probably won't. They wouldn't like the bad publicity. All the same, we'd better get Pepe and the two of you out of here as soon as we can."

Mrs. Fisher sighed. "I'm sorry to say, Sonia, that Pepe does present some problems, though I can well understand how he lost control of himself."

"Were all those people in the van sent back?" Manuel's mother asked quietly.

"They certainly were. The airplane took off right on time. At least that one family's together. I don't know what we would have done if the little girl had escaped."

"That would have been another problem, which we don't need right now." Then Mrs. Pearl's crisp voice softened. "Those poor people — they haven't much hope of getting up here again. The Security Police down there watch the main airports for anybody the U.S. sends back on commercial flights. We've asked our government to send people back on private planes, through private airports. That would at least give the returnees a chance to avoid arrest when they get home."

"I didn't know that," Mrs. Fisher said.

"We didn't want to draw attention to the idea. Anyway, our government refused. They said they knew nothing about private airports, and they don't want to help fugitives avoid justice in their own countries."

"You mean they didn't want to give the poor victims a chance to live!" Mrs. Fisher cried.

Manuel's mother coughed. "Manuel, what are you doing here?"

Mrs. Fisher looked down. "My goodness, I didn't realize! Do you think he understood what we were saying?" She stood up and looked around the garden. "Felipe," she called. "Shouldn't we water the flowers again? It's so dry!"

The gardener's head appeared from behind the garage. He yawned and looked at the ground. "Not today, señora," he said firmly, and withdrew.

"Oh dear," Mrs. Fisher said, "I interrupted his nap. But he must know. I'm always afraid the flowers will wither.

"It must seem strange to you, such a dry climate," she added to Manuel's mother.

"Not after the desert. But there was much rain in the village. It rained when we left, and before."

———

Much rain, Manuel remembered. He could never forget that rain; sometimes it was still raining in his head. It had rained on and off all day, a few weeks before they left. Then there was a hard rain all night. And after that came some days of bright sun. On the first day, the wet earth steamed.

But during that day and night of rain, the earth filled with water and hundreds of streams ran down the hillside. He could see one wetting the feet of the grove of bamboos in their back yard, sweeping down bits of newspaper and strips of lottery tickets that he had to clear off the bamboo stalks the next day — because it was so important to remove all traces of the wicked rain.

That was the morning after the rain, when his mother

called out, "Why are you doing that? Did your father tell you to do that? Have you seen him?"

Manuel didn't answer. Because he hadn't decided if his father *had* told him to clean up the bamboo stalks. He wouldn't speak to anyone until he could ask his father about it. There had been such a cleansing all through the village, with the water sweeping everything away. Garbage collectors were out working, too. He had seen them the day before, on the terrace beside the bus stop — four men dressed in green, standing beside a black van, tossing what must be logs into it, logs fresh from the forest, all covered with red flowers. The logs were spread out along the road, near the stream. They had been laid there so carelessly that the water of the stream, which had already overflowed its banks, was washing over two of them. The green men drew one of the logs back, but the water seized the second one and pulled it into the current. Manuel heard the green men shout and curse, so angry were they to lose that log, which was part of the garbage they were collecting. Then three of them ran after it.

Manuel ran too, to the window overlooking the church. Soon the log swam by, with the three green men helplessly looking on from above as it glided past into the still pond. Surely they were going to rescue it — or were they waiting for him to do it? But he couldn't move.

Manuel saw now that the pond was only calm in the dry season. In the rain, the stream that entered it was full. The water coursed across in a swollen current that didn't wait to pass under the walkway, but poured right over the top.

Of course, the stream had always carried bits of dead wood from the forest. The village boys, who often came to fish in this pond (though they were keeping out of sight now), used to bet on the time it would take pieces to pass over the dam. But those were only small scraps of wood. The log that the current was carrying now was as large as a man. The water was so high that the log came to rest against the walkway, while the current piled up behind it. With such high, strong water it would have been very dangerous for anyone to go out on the walkway and retrieve the log.

Even the men in green uniforms waited at the pond's edge. They were wearing dark glasses, like so many of the men in green — to protect their vision from the clear light of the sun. These men were much too cautious to approach the log more closely. The log clung to the top of the walkway for some time, as if it wanted to return to its place on the hillside with the other trees. But it didn't struggle long. No, in the end it went over the lip of the dam, curving down with the stream — which, with so much rain behind it, was now a beautiful, smooth waterfall.

The three green men, all in a row, looked over the water-fall, standing as close as they dared, and then walked down the path that followed the streambed. They must have wanted to collect the log farther downstream, when it finally came to rest.

Manuel had wanted to call to the green men to leave the log alone. Now that it had finally found its way back to the forest, why should they trouble it any more? But this might anger the green men, and his father had warned him never to do that. He did open his mouth once, but no words would come out.

Besides, how could he speak of such a little thing as a log washing over the top of the dam, when he should be out there looking for his father? If he said nothing to anyone, it would be as if nothing had happened — as if no log, as if nothing, had floated across the pond and escaped from the green men. He wouldn't speak until he had quite forgotten that such a thing had ever happened.

———————

"Manuel, what is it?" his mother cried. "What bad dream is with you now?"

Mrs. Fisher reached under the redwood table and laid her hand on Manuel's head. "He has no fever. But our talk did upset him. He must be tired here in the sun. He'd better have a nap too." And Manuel let himself be led off to his new room.

He closed his eyes so that they would leave him alone, and only opened them after his mother and Mrs. Fisher had tiptoed out. The faces of the rock stars on the wall stared angrily at him from behind the dark glasses. It was too dark to see if any of *them* were dressed in green. "I said nothing," he whispered, but they didn't answer, nor did their angry expressions change. He looked around for his father, who would assure these angry men that he, Manuel, had been silent; but his wise father was keeping well away. The figures on the wall trembled, as if they were ready to jump down to the floor.

A telephone rang in the kitchen. Mrs. Fisher answered it. "Wonderful!" she said after a time, then again, "Wonderful!" Her voice sounded happy through the bedroom door, and she hung up with a brisk clatter.

"Pepe may have done some good with his brick, after all!" she declared. "It got the story of the demonstration onto national television. Word reached your country, Sonia, and some people there really got organized. Fortunately, the national soccer team was landing at the same time, after a big win in Mexico. Our friends arranged a giant welcoming party for the soccer players. They packed the airport with people, and distracted the police so much that all those people from the van were able to mix with the crowd and get away."

"So Manuel's game is still being useful," his mother said.

"What? Oh, you mean the game of soccer. Greta," she called to Mrs. Pearl, "did you hear the news?" And Mrs. Fisher's footsteps returned to the garden.

Manuel glanced at the rock stars' posters on the wall. Sunlight had slipped in between the slats of a blind, and now he could see that none of the stars wore green uniforms. Why should they? *They* weren't garbage collectors. He knew their names; he knew that some of them could attract crowds almost as large as the ones that went to *futbol* games — noisy, friendly crowds. The figures on the posters, who now trembled in a breeze from somewhere, must be thinking only of their concerts and their eager public.

Manuel found that he couldn't sleep; he didn't need to. He slipped quietly out of bed and turned the television to the game of Tetris. By watching the beautiful forms that fell from the top of the screen and moving the controls smoothly and precisely, he managed to fit each one into its proper place. He made order in this way, over and over again, until he was so relaxed that he fell asleep during the game. Later, he discovered that someone had picked him up and put him to bed.

EIGHT

Choices of Borders

Mrs. Pearl returned to Mrs. Fisher's house two days later, on Sunday afternoon, when Marcos, the gardener's son, didn't go to the garage. For some reason he had shaved off his mustache, and he resembled Pepe a little more than before. At first, Manuel thought that even Mrs. Pearl had mistaken Marcos for his brother, when she introduced the man sitting in her passenger seat. "This is Jesús Mendoza," she told his mother. "A new recruit for our movement."

A jolly, smiling man got out of her car. "Only a beginning recruit," he said. "And this is your fine son." He put out a hand toward Manuel, who backed away, waiting to see what this stranger would do next.

"Mrs. Cárdenas has two fine sons," Mrs. Pearl said. "Mr. Mendoza has just volunteered to find lodgings for some of our clients."

"And food as well." The new recruit smiled proudly.

"Yes. Mr. Mendoza owns a fine small restaurant on the highway."

"My takeouts are famous," Mr. Mendoza said. "Both

Mexican and American cuisine. Refugees, especially, are usually hungry. Eventually I hope to transport more than food."

"You mean people?" Mrs. Pearl asked kindly.

"Exactly, señora. When you consider me worthy." He looked down modestly, but Manuel saw a gleam in his eye. What was this man up to? Why did he have such a smug, satisfied look on his face? Manuel tried to mimic Mr. Mendoza's face, but what was the point of just looking stupid? He stuck out his tongue at the visitor's back. His mother was watching him. He saw her smile, more happily than in a long time.

Mrs. Pearl had walked into the house; now she returned. She laughed apologetically — a strange sound coming from her, Manuel thought. "For the moment, we have to talk to Mrs. Fisher about delivering food," she said. "But I seem to have brought you on a fool's errand — she's apparently away. I'm sure we'll find her at the church. I do apologize for wasting your time."

"My time is entirely at your disposal," Mr. Mendoza assured her. "And it is no waste of time to meet this charming family."

"Yes," Mrs. Pearl said. "I'm glad you can do that. Oh look, there's the second son." She nodded to Marcos, who was plucking his guitar at the farthest corner of the wall, and he waved to her. "Isn't it nice that they're all home."

Manuel's mother opened her mouth to say something, then stopped at the look in Mrs. Pearl's eye. Mr. Mendoza hadn't noticed her slip, Manuel thought.

"I'm sure we can catch Mrs. Fisher at the church if we hurry," Mrs. Pearl said.

"*Hola*, Felipe!" Mr. Mendoza called. The gardener, who had just looked into the yard, turned his head and spat.

"He's a good friend," Mr. Mendoza explained. Felipe retreated behind the garage. "Oh," Mr. Mendoza added, "before we go, could I just step inside and use the telephone?"

"That won't be necessary," Mrs. Pearl told him. "Here's Mrs. Fisher's new cordless phone right out here. She has all the latest gadgets." She handed the telephone to Mr. Mendoza and waited for him to dial. His smile faded and he fumbled in his pocket. Finally he said, "I have forgotten the number. I must have it in the restaurant."

"We'll take you there right after you talk to Mrs. Fisher at the church. We'd better hurry." Then Mrs. Pearl and the jolly visitor, who suddenly seemed reluctant to leave, were gone. Marcos played some triumphant chords on his guitar as they left.

Felipe came out to watch them drive off. "My good friend!" he exclaimed. "I've never spoken to him. I don't want to. He's as good a friend as the devil!" He busied himself in sweeping the driveway, as if to remove all the dust where the visitor had stepped. Manuel found another broom and helped him. They had hardly finished when Mrs. Pearl returned, without her recent passenger, and smiling.

"The timing was perfect, Sonia," she told Manuel's mother. "Elizabeth was waiting at the filling station. The idiot thinks we met her there by chance. I got Chester, the mechanic, to keep the public phone busy until they drove off to the church. Mendoza didn't dare make a fuss about using the phone then, either."

"And why is that man helping you, señora?" Felipe demanded. He looked at Manuel, who had been watching Mrs. Pearl, very puzzled. How could she trust such a man?

Mrs. Pearl stopped rubbing her hands to look at Felipe and Manuel. "Don't you think I know he's a police informer? He'll telephone his bosses at the police station as soon as he can."

"Why?" Manuel's mother cried. "To tell them what?"

"To tell them that your son is here — the one who threw the brick."

"But he's not!"

"We want them to think he's here now; and to think, in an hour or so, that he's crossed back into Mexico. Marcos!"

"Yes, señora." The gardener's son was grinning broadly.

"Why aren't you in your costume already?"

"Sorry. In two seconds." And in a very short time Marcos had changed his shirt for a yellow LIBERTAD T-shirt and put on a straw hat with a red ribbon. "The very same ones, señora," he said happily.

Manuel's mother stared. "*He's* supposed to be my son?"

"At a distance. Which is the only way they'll see him."

The cordless telephone on the wooden table rang. "Yes. All right," Mrs. Pearl said. "We'll move. Can you keep Mendoza away from the telephone for ten more minutes? Let Penelope have a *very* long talk with her boyfriend."

She hung up, stepped to the driveway, and opened her car's trunk. "In you go, Marcos. No, you can't take the guitar."

Marcos looked sadly at the black case, painted with green and blue flowers. "But I have a girlfriend on the Mexican side."

"Let her do without music tonight. But don't tell her the real reason you left the guitar behind."

Marcos shrugged. "Okay. I'll say I'm trading it in for a better one. Goodbye, Papá. Put the guitar away for me."

Felipe hugged him. "You be careful now. This is no joke! You're sure there's no danger, señora?"

"If they call for him to stop, he will," Mrs. Pearl said. "But they won't have the chance. Besides, they aren't expecting Pepe to go to Mexico."

"I'll call you from the garage tomorrow, Papá." Marcos grinned. "Adiós, Mamá!" He blew a kiss to Manuel's mother. Despite herself, she smiled.

Then the car was gone. After the sound of its wheels had faded, the afternoon air became very quiet.

Cars kept passing on the highway. After half an hour another car passed, and stopped just out of sight. Felipe, who had been watching through the back fence, beckoned to Manuel and his mother. "Someone is there," he whispered. "Someone with binoculars. There, behind the little Joshua tree between the two tall ones. Is he coming here? No, he's waiting in case anyone tries to leave." He put his hand on Manuel's shoulder. "He's hiding, but do you see his shadow?"

Manuel did see it. The watcher wasn't really keeping still. His shadow trembled. Manuel thought he could hear the scratches and rustles as the lizards ran for cover. This one wouldn't be able to catch them!

———

Fifteen minutes later, Mrs. Fisher drove in. "That horrible man!" She glared at three paper bags on the back seat. "He insisted on giving me some of his frozen burritos when I took him to his restaurant — after he finally made his phone call, of course. I would have thrown these in the ditch, but I think I was followed."

A car passed on the road. "Yes, that's the one that followed me," she said. "He's stopping now. No, he's going on. I saw the other car along the road, waiting behind a tree, and there's one parked by the turnoff." She opened the back seat and took out the paper bags. "What do I do with these?"

"We keep them, señora," Rosa said firmly. "Mendoza, that Judas, has a very good cook. It's a sin to waste food."

"You're right. Let's not add to his other sins. Oh, I need a shower after all that running around! Call me if anyone comes."

For a time, no one came. After Mrs. Fisher had her shower, Felipe turned on the sprinkler system, which made its beautiful small rainbows. Manuel saw the watcher behind the middle Joshua tree walk away. Shortly after, the two cars parked down the road drove off.

Mrs. Fisher came out of the house in a loose blue gown; Rosa set a tray with ice and glasses on the table. Then Mrs. Pearl arrived, almost purring with satisfaction, Manuel thought. Just after her, Mr. Wemyss's van pulled into the driveway. Manuel had heard it slow almost to a stop just before it came in sight of the house.

The grocer was chuckling. "We have something to celebrate," he told Mrs. Pearl, who was touching the neck of a whiskey bottle to his glass. "Just a small one; I have to drive soon. Ah!" He set the glass down. "The operation went very smoothly. A truly professional job!" He winked at Manuel.

"Did you get a good view from the church tower?" Mrs. Pearl asked him.

"As good as a seat by the goal! I saw where you let Marcos out, in that sheltered part of the church parking lot. Naturally, when they saw him later, the watchers figured he'd come out of the church. But at the same time," Mr. Wemyss said to Manuel's mother, "that scum-bag Mendoza must have got word to his masters that your son was hiding here, in this house. They didn't know *where* to look for him."

"They had the house surrounded, señor," Felipe said. "Manuel and I were keeping watch."

Mr. Wemyss nodded. "That was the idea, to scatter their forces. I saw the man who was watching the alley talking on his cellular phone, trying to figure out what to do. Meanwhile, your son" — he turned to Felipe — "big as life in his yellow shirt and straw hat, had disappeared down an alley. Halfway down the alley someone opened a side door and pulled him inside. The watchers were running up and down like so many frantic hounds, trying to find the boy in the yellow shirt.

"But Marcos and his guide must have gotten into the old storm-sewer system. They stayed hidden until they came out of the old culvert halfway across the river, just as a church procession was passing on the Mexican side. They splashed across the river, mixed with the crowd, and disappeared. Of course, everyone saw them cross."

"Into Mexico?" Manuel's mother asked.

"That's right. Well, didn't *that* throw the *migras* off! They're used to watching folk trying to cross the other way. Only I'd have thought the culvert would be locked on this side, so people couldn't use it to cross *from* Mexico."

"The exit was locked," Mrs. Pearl told him. "But it appears that Mr. López is a skilled locksmith, among other things."

"Mr. López!" Manuel's mother cried.

"Yes, the man who brought you across the border," Mrs. Pearl told her. "He seems to move easily in both directions. It's been a pleasure to work with him. By the way, he sends you his best wishes. I think he wants to see you." She turned back to Mr. Wemyss. "So they got away clear into Mexico, Archie?"

"Clear as can be."

"But how will your son come back?" Manuel's mother asked Felipe.

"Why shouldn't he visit Mexico and come back here? He was born in this country. He has a passport to prove it."

"Marcos has made a number of crossings for us," Mrs. Pearl said.

"So then," Manuel's mother said, "those who are looking for my son are now sure that he has crossed back into Mexico. What do we say if they ask us?"

"Why," Mrs. Pearl told her, "that he's away and you don't know where. Who can keep track of such a wild young person? Only we won't give them a chance to ask you. We have to move you too."

"But where *is* Pepe? We can't leave him!"

"He's down the road," Mr. Wemyss said. "In the weeds behind a billboard. I brought him from the church after his look-alike crossed the border, as soon as I was sure the way was clear. We'll pick him up now, on the way out."

Manuel would not have believed that Mrs. Fisher and the members of her household could act with such energy as they now displayed. Mrs. Fisher called his mother into the bedroom and produced an old suitcase for their clothes. She added some new pants, shirts, and running shoes that, Manuel found out later, fitted him perfectly. She had new clothes for his mother as well, including a very sober black dress and some skirts from her daughter. "I hope Joan won't be mad at me," she said. "I'd give you some of mine, but they'd be too big, and we don't have time to take them in." She hesitated, then brought out the blue woolen sweater she had just finished. "I was making this for Joan, but you'll be seeing colder weather than she will."

Rosa brought a large bag of apples and grapes and some of her special chocolate-pecan cookies. Mrs. Fisher pointed out that they'd be going to a place with plenty of food; Rosa sniffed. "Not like mine!"

Rosa kissed Manuel and his mother as they were getting into the back of the grocery van, leaving the crumbs from a cookie she'd been munching on Manuel's cheek. Felipe, who had been watering the grass, squirted Manuel with the hose and winked at him. Manuel jumped at the touch of the water, then timidly smiled back. Surely no harm could come to him from this man who knew so well how to bring life from the earth. He looked back, wanting to touch Felipe's hand, but Mr. Wemyss was waiting to shut the back door of the van.

The inside of the van smelled of oranges, melons, and strange spices. Manuel and his mother sat on a narrow bench below a rack of bottles that clanked as they set off. In a minute they stopped in the shade of a billboard, and Mr. Wemyss opened the back door. Pepe leaped in; the grocer closed the door without saying a word. "We're on the road again," Pepe said cheerfully.

Manuel and his mother both hugged Pepe. Manuel hadn't been permitted to see him since the day of the demonstration. His brother looked tired and pale, he thought. How could he sleep in that church basement, with its smell of damp cement?

Their mother let Pepe go, then seized him and shook him. He gasped, surprised at her strength. "So you still think you can change the world?" she demanded.

Pepe looked down. "It almost worked," he muttered. "One of them nearly got away."

"And you nearly got caught. Now they're really after us. We all have to get away from here, and find somewhere else. Just keep your head down from now on, do you understand? Let the world look after itself."

Pepe's mouth tightened, then he nodded. "I wasn't trying to hit anyone."

"I know that. And the *migra* wasn't badly hurt."

"Good."

"It *is* good. But this isn't a game. The *migras* are very angry. They'll be hunting us like real criminals."

The van stopped. Mr. Wemyss had backed it into the carport of his house, one of a row of small bungalows on the outskirts of town. He opened the van's rear doors so that no one on the street could see his kitchen door, and his passengers slipped into the house.

The grocer pointed out the bathroom and their bedrooms, and made some telephone calls. "You'll spend the night here," he said presently. "Then I'm afraid you'll have to be on your way again."

Where to? Manuel wondered. He had grown used to the pattern of life in Mrs. Fisher's house: to Rosa making breakfast pancakes and standing behind him so he'd eat; to Felipe's care with the flowers; to Marcos plucking the guitar, lazily but with every note in the right place.

Once, only once, he had seen Ricardo at a distance among the Joshua trees, playing along with Marcos. It had almost seemed that Marcos could hear the sound of the flute, for he smiled and nodded as if to a partner.

That was strange, Manuel thought suddenly; with all the activity in Mrs. Fisher's house, he had almost forgotten his other, secret companions — or had they forgotten him? Would they follow, now that he, his mother, and Pepe had to leave all their new friends here?

It was all Pepe's fault, he thought angrily, that they had to be hiding and running again. But was it? No one had said they could stay in this town. If they had to leave, they might as well do so early as late. Kind as their hosts were, he had never really felt at home here. Tomorrow they would be somewhere else. Tonight they would have beds, with sheets on them; they wouldn't have to sleep in their clothes on bare mattresses, or on the ground, as they had done often enough before. But they hadn't hung up their new clothes and they had taken from the suitcase only what they needed for the night.

It was dark now. Before supper, Mr. Wemyss had closed all the blinds so that no one could see inside. The house was clean and bare; the wooden floors were highly polished, and the furniture was also wooden, with bright cushions on the chairs and couches. One wall was full of books. "History of the Southwest," Mr. Wemyss said. "I've learned something about it in this stay." He shook his head. "There'll be a lot to pack, though, when I have to move."

"Are you leaving too?" Manuel's mother asked him.

"It could happen."

The grocer took Manuel aside and showed him a shelf of trophies in the living room, and an old cracked soccer ball mounted on a wooden stand. "I made the winning goal with that against the Bradford Boozers, as we called them." He winked. "It was the high point of my career."

A photograph of a soccer team hung behind the trophy. Manuel pointed his finger at one of the players. "Yes, that was me back then," Mr. Wemyss said. "Somewhat lighter, and a lot more carefree." He cleared his throat. "But we have some other business to discuss." He called them all back to the kitchen and nodded for them to sit down around the table, then spoke to Pepe. "Lost your temper, laddy, didn't you? I mean the day of the demonstration, when you chucked that brick."

Pepe made a sour face and stared at the table. "Why didn't *you* lose your temper?" he asked at last. "I didn't see you on the picket line. What did *you* do to help?"

"Pepe!" his mother cried.

Mr. Wemyss raised a hand to still her. He nodded. "You're right. I wasn't there. I've been in enough such lines in the past, and they have their uses. Here, I keep out of the spotlight."

"I bet! You have your groceries to deliver."

"Not only groceries. I was able to deliver you and your family here, and I should be able to deliver you somewhere else tomorrow."

"Where will you take us?" Manuel's mother asked.

"All in good time." Mr. Wemyss turned back to Pepe. "You shouldn't be so snooty about my role as a greengrocer. Everyone has to eat, the good and the bad both. Don't you agree?"

Pepe shrugged.

"Mine is a very respectable trade." Mr. Wemyss was trying not to smile. "You'd hardly expect a businessman like me to carry signs and stomp around in demonstrations now, would you?"

"I sure wouldn't."

"No one would. And no one would expect a businessman like me to transport folk like you to where the *migras* won't find them. At least, I hope no one would," he added to himself.

Pepe looked more thoughtful, then suddenly grinned. "That's right. They wouldn't. *I* wouldn't have."

Mr. Wemyss nodded. "There's some hope for you yet. Now, the people I've transported so far have managed to keep quiet about me and my secret trips. Can you? All of you?"

"Yes, I can," Pepe said firmly. Manuel knew that the grocer needn't worry now. His brother always kept his word. Their mother nodded, and Manuel nodded too.

"Good." Mr. Wemyss smiled. "Sorry if I was a bit rough with you, young fellow. There's a reason. I had to be sure of your future behavior; I'm reasonably sure now. I envy you," he added, "going to one of my favorite places."

"Where are you sending us?" their mother asked.

"I'll show you." The grocer chuckled. "I enjoy talking about it. My sister married a Canadian studying in England, and moved back with him. They settled in Kingston at first; in Ontario, on the shore of the St. Lawrence." He turned to Manuel. "That's a very wide river between Canada and the United States, in the east," he explained. "Then a few years ago they bought a small resort hotel, Owl Point Lodge, on the St. Lawrence, in the Thousand Islands region, a big vacation area. My sister imagined it would almost run itself while she carried on making pottery; she's very keen on pottery. But her husband died suddenly last year, and she finds it hard to manage, and lonely. She can give you a job there, Mrs. Cárdenas, and a place for you and the boys."

"You're sending us to your own sister?" Manuel's mother asked in amazement.

"I'll explain why. But here, let me show you the place." Mr. Wemyss opened a drawer, pulled out a large manila envelope, and began drawing photographs and papers from it. "Here's the brochure."

Manuel squeezed between his mother and Pepe to study

the brochure, which showed a bedroom with wide twin beds, another large room with a fireplace and couches, and the corner of a dock.

"Here's a picture I took, too," Mr. Wemyss said. Manuel fixed his eyes on the large, glossy photograph of three small wooded islands in a wide, bright river. A canoe was tied to the nearest island. An eddy showed that the current was flowing from right to left. He drew back, but perhaps there was nothing to fear. The water must be full of life, it shone so. Could anything wicked have swum in such waters?

Manuel placed his finger on a tall, slanting straight line at the very edge of the picture and looked up at the grocer inquiringly. "That's a shadow," Mr. Wemyss said. "It must be from one of the lake freighters going down from the Great Lakes to the Atlantic. Here, this is the channel."

He pointed to a map on the table, all brown and blue. Manuel had been so busy watching the picture of clean, moving water that he hadn't even noticed the map.

"It's from the Geological Survey," Mr. Wemyss said. "The lodge is on this little point here, Owl Point, which my sister says has a story connected with it. Something about the Indians who used to live nearby."

Manuel looked at the brown dot on the map. Could they really cross the border and stay there, without running any more? He looked back at the photograph. The canoe was red; it couldn't be made of tree bark, like real Indian canoes. What were they called in English? Birchbark — that was it!

His mother must have been asking Mr. Wemyss about these Indians. "Not now," he said. "Some live on reservations, farther down the river."

Maybe they weren't too far away, Manuel thought. Maybe he could visit them, and spend the night in a lodge, and paddle a real birchbark canoe.

His mother touched his arm. "What do you see there?"

"It must be something good," Mr. Wemyss said. "You look so fascinated."

Meanwhile, Pepe was tracing the line on the map that marked the Canada–U.S. border, in the middle of the river. "Why are most of the islands on the U.S. side?" he demanded.

"Pepe," his mother warned him.

"That's only on this part of the map," Mr Wemyss said. "There are more than a thousand islands, counting all the little ones. Enough to go around." He ran his finger along the border. "The main thing is, once you've been accepted by Canadian immigration, you're safe. They won't send you back.

"Now for some practical details. The local school and high school are just over a mile away, no more than a good walk; though I believe there's a school bus for the cold weather. My sister says the school has a good reputation."

"Why?" Manuel's mother asked.

"Why does the school have a good reputation?"

"No, sir. Why are you doing this? You seem to be a kind man, but to send us to your sister! You hardly know us."

"Not as well as I'd like," Mr. Wemyss said warmly, then looked down. Why was he so shy? Manuel wondered. When he spoke again, his voice was more practical. "I do consider myself a good judge of character," and he smiled slowly. "Anyway, it's really as much for my sister's sake as yours. Her children are grown and gone; they want her to sell the lodge, but she still likes to live there. To keep it, she needs a good manager, and I hear that that's what you are." Mrs. Pearl said you got their office accounts in shape for the first time, and rearranged the furniture and the timetable to make everything run better — *and* had the volunteers eating out of your hand. Mrs. Fisher said, 'Why can't we keep her?'"

"Why indeed?" Their mother smiled briefly. "There was never much chance that we could stay in the United States, was there?"

"Not really. Of course, my sister knows about the refugee situation, and she helps out with a little money when she can, but I've never sent anyone to her before. Besides, I want to keep in touch with all of you. I have a soft spot for young Pelé here," and Mr. Wemyss tapped Manuel's shoulder. "Maybe he can even bring enough civilization to the shores of the St. Lawrence for them to start a proper soccer team."

"It doesn't look uncivilized now," said Manuel's mother, looking at the brochure again. Then she smiled warmly, which she hadn't done in a long time. "My husband was so interested in the game of soccer. Not that he was good at any sport. He didn't even watch it much on television. But he liked the idea that, for more than a thousand years, simple ball games could mean so much to so many people." She smiled again, wistfully this time.

Mr. Wemyss cleared his throat and looked back down at the map. "I think you'll like it there. I remember my visit last Christmas. It wasn't long after my sister's husband died. And it was a sad time for me too. I spent a lot of time outdoors, just walking, so as not to talk to anyone. The falling snow in the birches suited my mood, and the cold made me feel more alive."

"But why do you live here, so far away from your sister? Couldn't you have stayed?" Manuel's mother looked down. "Excuse me, it's a very personal thing to say, but I'm not sure you belong here."

"I don't mind your saying it, and you're right. I'm a stranger here, almost as much as you, and I had a better business back home in England. But my wife — my late wife — needed a dry climate."

"I'm sorry," Manuel's mother said. "Please forgive me."

"There's nothing to forgive. It's a natural question. Why did this Englishman end up in the dry American desert? Yes, I could have gone back to England or set up business in Canada.

Perhaps I will some day. I tell the locals I can't stand the cold, and that pleases them. But sometimes I do wonder how long I'll stay in this place, how long my work here will last."

A knock sounded on the kitchen door. Mr. Wemyss motioned them all away before he opened it. "No one is watching," Señor López said, closing the door silently behind him.

"You're sure, now?"

"Quite sure." At Mr. Wemyss's smile and nod, he sat at the kitchen table. The grocer poured him a large cup of coffee.

"How long were you watching?" Manuel's mother asked the Gray Coyote.

"Two hours." His voice sounded apologetic, as if he regretted waiting so long before coming in.

"Two hours!"

"I wanted to be really sure there was no danger for you. The *migras* and those who work for them can be patient. I can be more patient. I had a path of escape worked out in case the *migras* came here."

"You're good at that," Pepe said, grinning. "I hear you got me back across the river to Mexico."

Señor López rumpled his hair, then reached out and laid his hand on Manuel's head. "You could learn from Marcos," he told Pepe. "*He* can follow orders. He didn't want to do everything on his own."

Mr. Wemyss said, "I think Pepe's starting to understand. Now, we'd better all get to bed. Mr. López, do you want to stay here tonight?"

The Gray Coyote shook his head. "I have to cross the border again; I heard some news that I must investigate. I came to say goodbye for now."

He kissed Manuel and shook Pepe's hand. Then he stayed to drink his coffee with their mother and Mr. Wemyss while the boys went to bed.

Manuel went first, but he was still awake when Pepe came

in. "Well, we did some good after all," his brother whispered. "Mamá just told me about how all those people from the van snuck past the police at home, instead of being arrested in the airport. Did you know that?" Manuel nodded. Pepe lay down. "She said they didn't want to encourage me to try any more rescues. That's why they didn't talk about it when I was staying in the church." He sniffed. "They don't have to worry. I don't want to stay in a country that supports the government back home. I just want to get out of here."

Soon Manuel heard the grocer leave the kitchen. The other two voices went on speaking quietly for a long time, but in the morning Señor López was gone.

NINE

Shady Acres

Next morning, Mr. Wemyss cooked up a large spicy omelet, full of tomatoes, onions, and peppers. Manuel's mother raised her eyebrows. "Not exactly a proper English breakfast," the grocer remarked cheerfully. He opened the oven door. "But these are real scones. Eat them with butter and honey. It'll be some time before you can sit down again to a decent meal." He made a long telephone call. "Right," he said at the end, spoke to their mother, and retired to his bedroom. In a few minutes he came out dressed in a dark suit.

Their mother had changed into the black dress from Mrs. Fisher. She combed Manuel's hair and tied bands of black cloth round his and Pepe's arms.

Mr. Wemyss looked the boys over critically. "You'll do. We're going to a funeral, to find your next ride. It's a big affair, and not such a sad one. The man who died was ninety-five years old. His sons have grandsons already. But this man had lots of Mexican-born employees who will be there. You'll fit right in." He handed Manuel a black plastic bag. "Put this in your suitcase too. I thought you should have a real soccer ball. This one's leather, see? You probably won't get the chance to use it here, but I'm sure you'll find a team in Canada. It's all right," he added, for Manuel was holding the grocer's hand very tightly. Gently, Mr. Wemyss disengaged his hand. "But we should say goodbye now. There may not be time when I pass you on to your next guide."

"But you will come to Canada too, won't you?" Manuel's mother asked. "To see your sister?"

The grocer nodded. "Indeed. I will. But first I must try to find a decent assistant to mind the shop while I'm away." He frowned. "From Hubert's activities, I think I may come north sooner than planned."

This time, as they all traveled in the back of the van, Pepe had time to examine the racks of jars and bottles, and he pointed out some of the price tags. "You could feed a poor family for two days for the cost of one of those bottles," he said indignantly. "Hennesey VSOP, Château Rothschild — of course! Plums in brandy! Mango chutney!" He took the lid off the chutney jar.

"Pepe!" their mother exclaimed. "Stop that!"

Pepe closed the jar again. "He wouldn't notice if I just took a taste."

"It's just what he would notice."

Pepe shrugged, then grinned. "Well, maybe."

The van slowed down and stopped, and Mr. Wemyss opened the door. "All out!" he whispered. They were parked in a narrow lane with a high, grassy bank on one side. On the other was an iron fence that led to a wide gate ornamented with iron flowers and stars. A sign over the gate spelled out, in iron letters, "Shady Acres." From the fence the ground sloped down past a small grove of dry trees by a brick shed, then up to a ridge crowned with a row of solid, monumental tombs.

"I don't want anyone to see you leave the van," Mr.

Wemyss said. "I'll drive on to park behind the other cars. If you go through the fence here where the bars are bent, and up the hill, you'll find the funeral party. The driver of the hearse will get your suitcase from me and take you to the next stage — he's the one in the chauffeur's cap and the big white mustache. Mix with the crowd until he's ready to leave, but keep your eyes on each other." The grocer touched Manuel's head and Pepe's hand again, made as if to kiss their mother's cheek, then drew back. She smiled and pressed his hand warmly. Mr. Wemyss reddened, got in the van, and drove through the gate.

Pepe led the way downhill; their mother came last, watching carefully before she let Manuel follow his brother. They all waited out of sight in the trees until they were sure no one was watching. Then, in single file, they climbed the hill and took shelter behind separate monuments. Pepe's tomb was surmounted by a life-size concrete crucifixion with two women at the foot of the cross. Manuel's had a sorrowful angel. Their mother's was more modern, with a tall shaft of polished green stone.

The space beyond these monuments was filled with orderly rows of smaller tombstones. Farther on was the new grave, with people around it. Some had already drifted away. A boy Manuel's age stood close to the angel, watching a small bird on its head. When he saw Manuel he joined him, looking up at the angel's feet.

"Geraldo!" a woman's voice called. The boy winked at Manuel, then followed the voice. Manuel saw that Pepe and his mother had already left their hiding places and mixed with others around the grave. In a moment, he did so too.

It had been like this at his grandmother's funeral, he remembered. A group of men, all as old as his own grandfather, were leaning over, each dropping a handful of earth into the grave. Some were serious, but no one seemed really sad. Some were even smiling. Away from the grave, the smaller children had started to play hide-and-seek among the tombstones. Those of Manuel's age stayed near their parents, watching the small ones uneasily. They must be afraid, Manuel thought. At his grandmother's funeral, he certainly hadn't wanted to play among the headstones. He didn't want to do so now, in "Shady Acres," but he wasn't afraid.

The grass was carefully mown and the flower beds were weeded. As he looked at the people standing calmly here and there, Manuel half expected to see his father. But his father had no business here — graveyards were for dead people. Still, it was a very peaceful place. Look at those little boys, he thought, pretending to be scared and hiding behind the gravestones to say "Boo!" to each other. They watched Manuel curiously; did they expect him to be frightened too? He almost laughed at the thought.

To keep from laughing, he began to read the names and dates on the different stones: Cartwright, Laplante, Zimmerman, O'Neill. These must all be American names. One woman had lived to be a hundred and one — even older than the man they were burying today.

Pepe passed behind him and whispered, "You won't find any Mexicans buried here! It's pure white ground." But as Mr. Wemyss had said, there were plenty of Mexicans among the mourners, people with darker skin and glossy black hair, also dressed quietly in black.

Manuel's friends were there too. The flute boy sat in the lap of an angel's statue on one of the biggest monuments. As he played his melody, he looked up critically at the angel's long trumpet. The beggar-girl sat at the base of the same monument, her fingers in her mouth, motionless so that the boy would go on playing as long as possible.

And there was his father, looking over the names of soldiers on a monument to those who had fallen in two world wars. Naturally, Manuel thought, his father would find this place and its history interesting. He'd say, there's no point in traveling without looking around — and after all, they were here for only a short time. Elena had left the angel monument to join his father; in a moment, Ricardo followed her.

Manuel joined them. They were in a quieter part of the cemetery. One or two people were standing before tombstones, reading the inscriptions thoughtfully. A woman and a little girl were laying a bunch of wildflowers at the foot of a new stone. The woman was wiping her eyes while the girl whispered to her.

A caretaker in green overalls was raking the gravel around one of the older graves near the angel monument, talking to himself as he worked. He looked up suddenly and winked at Ricardo and Elena. Manuel drew in his breath sharply. How could the man see them? Who was he? Then he looked at the broad, foolish face more closely. Of course — it was Sergeant Confusión again. The Lord of Xibalba, dressed this time as a cemetery caretaker! That High Command of his must keep him busy.

The sergeant read from the nearest gravestone, a large, plain one. " 'Richard and Helen, our Beloved Angels. Gone to a Better Place.' They were a brother and sister, twelve and eight years old, who drowned on the same day fifty years ago. The foolish boy was trying to save his sister. But look how clean the lettering still is in the dry air. A beautiful monument!"

The woman and little girl walked by without noticing the caretaker, who continued to address Manuel's friends. "Richard and Helen. Why, those are your names! There's a place for you right here. The children who are already there wouldn't mind; they'd like the company." He smiled. "And if they didn't, so what?"

Ricardo smiled for a moment at the thought of this "Richard's" discomfort, but when he saw Elena shrink from the caretaker-sergeant he said, "No, why should we bother them? They never bothered us."

"Did you worry so much about others before?" Sergeant Confusión demanded.

"I didn't have the chance to," Ricardo told him. "I had to look out for myself."

How displeased the sergeant looked! "I see your freedom is going to your head. The sooner you come down to Xibalba and learn proper discipline, the better. But wait here for now, while I attend to some business."

The sergeant walked away backwards, carefully raking the ground, and stopped behind a stout man in a white suit and black armband, a man of comfortable, jolly aspect. Sergeant Confusión whispered in the ear of this man, who didn't turn his head. Though he couldn't have heard, he began to look around as if he had received *some* message.

The sergeant raked his way back to the children. "What, still up here? Why haven't you gone home?" He tapped the ground firmly with his foot.

"Excuse me, sir," Ricardo said, "but we're traveling now."

Sergeant Confusión winced. "Traveling! Who wants to travel? Home is best. You don't realize the sacrifice I made when I left Xibalba to look into your case. But I'm a soldier, I go where I'm told. And so should you."

"Our case?" Ricardo asked.

"It's well documented," Sergeant Confusión said. "We know all about you. And we have excellent means of communication." He smiled down at his collar. A snake extended its head and hissed in his ear. "Aha!" the sergeant said. The snake whispered again. "Well!" He smirked at Ricardo. "You weren't really deprived. It appears that you had a perfectly good chance for an education. Sergeant Duarte of the Seguridad made all the arrangements for you to go to school. Why didn't you go?"

"I wasn't sure what I'd learn there, sir."

"Learn! You'd have learned what the other students were saying about the government. You could have told the sergeant, and he could have dealt properly with the trouble-makers. He could have sent them down to us, where they belong."

"Let them do their own spying!" Ricardo said angrily. He added, more calmly, "Besides, it was too dangerous. Sergeant Duarte didn't like people who got information for him, because they got to know too much."

The Lord of Xibalba laughed. "I doubt you told the army that!"

"I sure didn't. I'm not stupid!"

The snake whispered again. "You weren't so smart, either," the sergeant told Ricardo. "The officers had you figured for a traitor. They were going to ask Sergeant Duarte to give you some of his 'special treatment.' Only he kicked your head harder than he meant to, so he never got to play his little games on you."

"Lucky me," Ricardo said.

"Don't press your luck. Even in your new state, you didn't do a thing to help recapture that silly little girl who ran away from the van. And you, young miss," he said to Elena, who cowered behind Ricardo, "you were actually trying to help her escape. But you're both young. Come down to Xibalba and you'll soon find your place. If you serve us well, we'll take good care of you. You won't have to run any more.

"Let me tell you about our land," the sergeant continued, shouldering his rake in military fashion. "About beautiful Xibalba, where the sun never shines; where the dim light casts no shadows; where everything is as it should be, and everything stays as it is. Where those who were made to rule do so, and all the others serve their lords." He frowned. "Not like that chaotic land you come from, all rebels and malcontents and Communists — where teachers coach their students in treason, and priests make excuses for the lazy poor, and people waste everybody's time in a stupid, pointless search for their disappeared relatives — disappeared? No, down in Xibalba, where they belong!"

Ricardo was listening with open mouth, and Manuel wondered if Sergeant Confusión really thought he could tempt him with such talk. But the sergeant hadn't finished. "Can you imagine the dangers you face if you don't join us?" he demanded. Elena sidled even closer to Ricardo, looking at his face for reassurance. Sergeant Confusión pointed a long finger at both of them and scowled at Manuel. "How long can you stay on this earth? Only until they catch that boy and his family. Then you'll go wandering off forever into the sky, into empty space! You'll go to — who knows where you'll end up? But you'll never get to Xibalba."

In a sudden burst of courage, Ricardo said, "What about the schoolteacher? Is he going to Xibalba?"

The sergeant snorted. "Schoolteacher! I don't know any schoolteacher. Schoolteachers work for the government, and teach what they're told to teach; they don't go running off to villages in the hills." But even as he spoke, his gaze wandered across the cemetery, as though he'd been reminded to look for someone. "Stay here," he said, "I'll be right back." And he headed for a crowd of people, raking his path as he went.

Was he looking at Manuel's father? Manuel looked for his father himself. There he was, in front of the green stone monument, beckoning frantically. Then Manuel saw Pepe's head peeping out from behind the monument. He couldn't see his mother anywhere. Why were they hiding?

Pepe motioned to him to come forward and keep down. Then Manuel saw why: the jolly man the sergeant had spoken to earlier was Jesús Mendoza, the police informer! Whatever signal Mr. Mendoza had received from the sergeant, he was certainly keeping a sharp lookout now! He was walking around in the crowd, examining every face closely. And Manuel had let himself be distracted by the Lord of Xibalba. He had almost lost sight of his family!

As he dropped to his knees to crawl behind the nearest tombstones and join Pepe, he heard Elena say to Ricardo, "Let's go, quick, before that sergeant comes back. He scares me!"

Manuel reached Pepe's side unseen. Together they stole past the monument to their mother, who was hiding behind a thick-branched pine tree.

A few feet away, Mr. Mendoza was talking to Mr. Wemyss. "A beautiful day," he said.

"It was." Then Mr. Wemyss coughed, as if he had said too much. "A perfect day for such an occasion," he added.

"I wasn't aware you knew the dear departed."

"He was a very good customer."

"I didn't have the pleasure of seeing him in my restaurant," Mr. Mendoza said. "At his age, could he eat my fine, spicy food? But many of his children patronized me. He had so many friends. I thought I saw Mrs. Cárdenas among the mourners."

"Who?"

"Did she know the deceased's family? How could she, such a recent immigrant?"

"I'm sorry, who are you talking about?" Mr. Wemyss scratched his head.

"Mrs. Cárdenas, the charming lady with the two sons who was staying with our friend Mrs. Fisher. I believe you often make deliveries there."

"I make deliveries all over," said Mr. Wemyss. "I don't keep track of my customers' guests."

"Of course not! I wonder how Mrs. Cárdenas came here."

"Well, I certainly didn't bring her *in my van*."

"I'm sure you didn't." And Mr. Mendoza chuckled. "I was only wondering in case she needs a ride back, wherever she's going."

"Speaking of which, I must be going too," Mr. Wemyss said. He walked away quickly and mixed with the mourners. He spoke briefly to a young man who wore a black straw hat, then shook hands gravely with a white-haired woman. Mr. Mendoza followed him into the crowd and would have followed him out of it, but the man in the black straw hat hailed him, shook his hand, and held him in conversation.

Manuel saw Hubert, Mr. Wemyss's assistant, at the edge of the crowd. He wasn't dressed for the funeral, and he had just taken a small camera from the pocket of his jeans jacket.

Mr. Wemyss stopped to tie his shoe near Manuel and his family. "Mendoza thinks you're hiding in my van," he whispered loudly, without looking at them. "Just keep out of sight until we're both gone."

He straightened up and strode out the gate toward his van. In a moment, Mr. Mendoza followed him. The grocer turned his van around with some difficulty in the narrow road. Mr. Mendoza waited in his car until the van had driven out of the gate. Then he turned around very quickly, scraping the fender of the car behind him as he did so. A large man ran into the road and shouted. Gravel flew out behind Mr. Mendoza's rear wheels and sprayed the large man's legs as he drove off in pursuit of the grocer's van. The grocer's assistant stood in the middle of the road, taking pictures of the van and the car.

The young man with the black hat walked over near Manuel's mother, and glanced around to see that no one was watching. "He's in trouble, that Mendoza," he said happily. "That was Hank Putnam's new car he banged up. I wouldn't like to get on Hank's bad side; he settles things his own way.

I'm supposed to show you the way to your next ride. Just follow me, one at a time."

They followed him, one at a time, to the other side of the long black hearse. No one saw them go except Sergeant Confusión, who now had a complicated-looking camera around his neck. He took pictures of all of them, and waved urgently to the grocer's assistant, who didn't seem to notice him.

The driver was already waiting, in his black coat and hat and his splendid flowing mustache. He didn't look up as their guide opened the rear side door and waved his passengers into the back compartment, which had held the coffin and now held their suitcase and a pile of blankets. There was a perfumy smell, from the flowers of a hundred funerals, and a sharper chemical smell underneath that. The windows were dark and covered with black curtains, but the young man told them to hide under the blankets until they were on the highway.

"It's scratchy down here!" Pepe complained. "Say, what did they use these blankets for?"

The driver chuckled. "Just for padding, and to keep the boxes of flowers from spilling. You stay down. It won't be long."

The hearse drove away smoothly and picked up speed. Soon they passed Mr. Mendoza's car, which was keeping its distance from the grocer's van. As the hearse passed the van, Manuel saw the driver give Mr. Wemyss a thumbs-up sign. The grocer waved back at him. "You can come out now," the driver told them. "But duck down when we pass through towns. Somebody may see you through the curtains."

Half an hour later, when they stopped at a railroad crossing, the driver took off his black jacket and loosened his necktie. He turned the radio to a station of religious music and whistled along with the hymns as they drove along.

They were approaching the red rock hills that Manuel had seen from the motel. Soon, as the road curved and climbed, they were surrounded by their spires and spikes. This would be a good place for their enemies to watch them pass, Manuel thought. But beyond the sharp rock points he saw nothing but empty blue sky. The road descended again, leaving the guardian rocks behind as they drove through a new landscape, which showed more and more patches of green as they headed north.

Their driver stopped whistling and turned off the radio. "You were so quiet I forgot you were there," he said. "I guess I missed the chance to talk to you. I'm not used to live passengers. You're the first illegal immigrants I've transported. In fact," and he smiled under his fine mustache as he half turned toward the back, "officially, I don't know anything about you. I'm just taking you on a trip for my friend, Mr. Wemyss. I wish you could sit up in front, but they told me to keep you hidden. No one suspects me yet. Wait."

They were driving into a shopping center on the highway. The driver parked and entered a convenience store. The window directly in front of them had a sign, "Native American Artwork," over a display of turquoise and silver chains and brooches. Manuel looked eagerly for living Indians, but saw only a crude wooden profile of one, with a painted feather headdress, standing by the door.

The driver was back. He leaned over the front seat of the hearse and handed them a box with three ice-cream cones and three cans of soda. "I hope you like chocolate. We'll be there soon."

"Thank you," Manuel's mother said. "Where is *there*?"

"Where you get your next ride. I don't even know who's coming for you. They don't want any of us to know too much, for when the police start asking questions."

"They aren't asking already?" Manuel's mother asked.

"They may be."

They drove on. Manuel was so busy watching the road for

Indians that his ice cream dripped onto his hand; he had to lick it off. He saw a chocolate smudge on his nose mirrored in the glass, and hastily wiped it away.

They were turning off the highway to another town, about the size of the one on the border. "Keep down, now," the driver called back, and they all huddled down. After a time he said, "It's all right; no one's around." He was driving along a street with yellow school buses parked on either side. He stopped before a garage where other school buses were parked.

He opened the back door and picked up their suitcase. "They said they'd leave the garage door open. I hope they did."

The back door was indeed open. The driver pointed to two couches covered with sleeping bags. "The bus driver knows you're coming with her tomorrow, but she'll pretend you're just two new students with their mother. She'll knock on the back door first, then you wait here until she starts the bus. Listen," he added, "I'm really sorry to leave you here. I'd take tomorrow off and drive you up to where you get the Greyhound bus for Albuquerque if it was up to me. But I'm on call tomorrow, and Mr. Wemyss told me not to make any change in my routine. They're really watching everyone this close to the border.

"The john's around the corner and there's some sandwiches in that little refrigerator. You'd better leave the light off; try to get as much sleep as you can. You'll be traveling for a long time after this. I'll lock the door. Good luck!"

The driver closed the door carefully. They ate the sandwiches in twilight, then stretched out on the sleeping bags; it was much too warm to cover up. A large fan in another part of the building drew a current of air over them.

Before it grew quite dark, Pepe and their mother sorted through the suitcase. She took out a black leather purse with a shoulder strap, and tugged on the strap. "It's strong. I'll keep the money here."

"Is it safe?" Pepe whispered.

"No one had better try to take it! I can't stand wearing that money belt next to my skin any more. I'm getting a rash."

"I can carry the money," Pepe said.

She looked at him. "No thanks. But you'd better have some money too." There was a rustle of paper in the dark. "Shh!" she whispered.

Someone was walking outside. Their mother stayed completely still, and they all held their breath. Pepe put his finger to his lips, which almost made Manuel laugh. Did his brother think he would speak *now*?

The footsteps passed without stopping. Then a bus door opened. Through the dusty slats of a blind, Manuel could see the row of yellow school buses and their shadows under the streetlight. A man in a blue uniform passed along the buses, testing each door. Could he be another policeman? One bus door was open. The man climbed in, then came out carrying a paper sack. Would he come to the garage now? Manuel's mother joined him at the window. Pepe had stretched out, yawning, on a sleeping bag; he must have decided it was time to rest. They should all do that, Manuel thought, and let whatever was going to happen do so. The man in the wide cap, who must have been a bus driver, walked off the lot and away.

It grew dark; the sound of the fan was louder. Now it seemed to have a voice of its own. "Where you going, going, going?" it said, over and over again. Both Pepe and his mother were sleeping. Manuel rose very quietly and looked into the back room. It was darker there. The light that entered the front room between the blinds stopped just past the threshold, between a high set of steel shelves full of boxes, and a high row of hooks on which dark uniform coats hung. The coat closest to him swayed back and forth in the fan's wind, and the empty sleeves swung out as if to point the way to somewhere. For a moment Manuel felt fear rising in him. What if they were caught? What if they were sent back to the hands of their enemies — and from them to the Lords of Xibalba? Then he pulled himself together, and left the dark, swaying shapes to ask their own questions. Tomorrow they would be far away from Shady Acres and its stones and whatever lay beneath them. They would be traveling not in a hearse, with its odor of funerals, but in a normal school bus, and then the regular Greyhound bus to Albuquerque. How dangerous could that be? He lay down on the sleeping bag beside Pepe, and was soon fast asleep.

TEN

Wayside Watchers

The driver of the school bus the next morning was a serious middle-aged woman. Manuel and his family all sat near the back, apart from everyone else. The other children stared at them at first, then were politely silent when the driver told them that Manuel and Pepe were on their way to register at a school in the next district, with their mother. Apart from that she didn't speak to them or about them at all.

Had the others been able to follow? Then Manuel saw his father sitting in the last row of seats, beneath the rear window. The beggar-girl was perched on a single seat near the driver, eagerly watching the scenery pass. The flute boy sat by the aisle a few seats behind her, playing a soft accompaniment to the tune coming out of the driver's radio. Could the driver hear him? From time to time she fiddled with the radio dial, as if puzzled by an extra sound.

The bus slowed down and stopped. The front door opened and a *migra*'s tall hat appeared. Manuel seized the armrest, and sneaked a look at his mother. She seemed calm, but he could see worry in her eyes. The beggar-girl kept looking calmly out the window; the flute boy went on playing.

"That's a pretty tune," the *migra* said to the driver, nodding at the radio.

"It is," said the bus driver. "I don't know who's playing it. They haven't announced it yet. So you're being mother today, Tom?"

Two young girls climbed on past the *migra* and walked down the aisle.

"Carole's gone to write the civil service exam," the *migra* said. "She didn't have time to get the kids to the bus. Goodbye, little darlings," he called loudly.

His daughters looked down, embarrassed. A boy called out in a squeaky voice, "Goodbye, Daddy!"

The *migra* smiled, stepped down from the bus, and waved it on. Manuel began to breathe again. His mother reached over and gave his hand a little squeeze.

The bus let off half the children in a schoolyard and the rest under a tree opposite a second school. The tree had rich green leaves, and the houses had lush green lawns. They were leaving the dry land, Manuel thought. "I wish we could stop here for a little," his mother whispered, but of course she made no move to leave the bus.

After all the other children had left, the driver closed the doors and drove on through back streets to a shopping plaza where a Greyhound bus was just pulling in. The driver motioned them out with a nod. Then, as they passed her, she squeezed their mother's arm and called, "God bless you!"

A young man in a bright red jacket came out of a restaurant, beckoned to them, and led them to the Greyhound bus. He handed the bus driver three tickets and followed them into the bus.

A young woman was sitting near the back of the bus, with a large paper shopping bag on the seat beside her. The two seats across the aisle were covered with a backpack, and the seats behind her with two windbreakers.

"Wonderful!" she called loudly. "You've all made it!"

The young man put his fingers to his lips, then hissed, "Don't advertise them, Jill!"

Jill blushed a beautiful pink, then began to clear the seats around her for Manuel's family. The young man joined her and promptly fell asleep, his head on her shoulder. "Darryl was so worried that something would go wrong," Jill said to Manuel's mother, who had taken the seat across the aisle from her. "He couldn't sleep all night."

They traveled all day, through alternating stretches of sand and green. The highway was so smooth that it seemed as if the bus weren't moving at all — as if the scenery were just flowing past them. They were cozy and safe in the bus, Manuel thought. Maybe it wouldn't have to stop anywhere. Maybe they'd go all the way to Albuquerque without anyone noticing them. Their guides were sleeping, Jill with her head on Darryl's shoulder now. Manuel was sitting on the left side of the bus. Blue mountains appeared in the distance, moving slowly past them, which showed how big and far away they were. The bus was passing huge fenced-in fields, with brown-and-black cows looking on without interest. Then, by a gravel road leading off to some low, dry hills, Manuel saw a sign, "To the Reservation."

That must mean Indians! A sharp-faced man in blue jeans and a denim shirt, standing beside a pickup truck, watched the bus roll by. Was he an Indian? Manuel thought back to the pictures he'd seen in books, but he wasn't sure. He was a little disappointed that the man's clothes were so ordinary.

Now they were working their way through the great blue mountains. The late afternoon sun was low behind them, and off to the left. As they passed into the shade of a red cliff, Manuel saw his own face reflected in the window. It looked so worried! A woman across the aisle was watching him with concern. He had better pretend to sleep before she started asking questions.

Toward midnight the bus drove into a grimy terminal in a large city. "You can go on alone now," Darryl said. "But we'll wait here to put you on the right bus. Here are the tickets. Do you have enough money?"

Manuel's mother put the tickets into her purse. "We were given enough for the next few days."

"That's all you need. You still have to change buses a couple of times, but I've written down all the details. Someone will meet you in Buffalo. I've jotted down some telephone numbers too, of friends who will help you if you run into trouble. But whatever happens, *please* don't let the police find those numbers."

Jill had been reading the bus schedule posted on one wall. "Oh no! We *can't* wait, Darryl. We have to catch our own bus in ten minutes, to meet those people in Texarkana."

Darryl looked quickly at the board. "They aren't going to get there till noon. We can catch the next bus."

Jill looked around the station and shuddered. "And wait in this place till five in the morning? No thanks! Besides, Harry and Jonas will give us a bed in Texarkana, so at least we'll get a little sleep. They won't care what time we get in."

"I guess you're right," Darryl said. "Listen," he told Manuel's mother, "if you're sure you can get yourselves on your bus, we'll leave you now. You only have an hour to wait. I don't think anyone's following you. We hope they'll forget you once you're a long way north of the Mexican border." Then Jill kissed them all; she left lipstick on Pepe's face, Manuel saw, and he rubbed his own cheek where her lips had touched. Hand in hand, their guides walked away to find their bus.

"Come on, boys," said Manuel's mother. "Let's see if we can find a place to lie down, or sit down, at least."

They found the station waiting room, which was long and

narrow. A high, dirty window at one end was open, and five pigeons perched on an inside ledge were cooing in sequence. A black bat had also come in. It swooped along the length of the ceiling, then hung from a light bracket at the far end.

Pepe went to sleep at once. He lay snoring on a bench opposite Manuel, his head pillowed on their suitcase. Their mother sat by Pepe's feet, dozing and waking again, over and over. The strap of her purse dangled from her shoulder, and the purse lay loose on the bench. She must be very tired, Manuel thought. She had clutched the purse to her side till now, even though it hurt her to do so. That purse held their tickets and money; it held all the rest of their voyage. It would get them all the way to Canada, where they would be safe and free, where the Indians lived in the cold forests.

Many of the other passengers slept, but not all. Two men sat alone on a bench against a side wall. Though other benches were crowded, no one else sat with these two, and in a moment Manuel understood why. One of the men was enormous; he bulged out of his wide trousers and floppy shirt, and his arms swelled the sleeves of his big blue denim jacket. He sat between two large paper bags, one of which seemed filled with sandwiches, the other with beer cans. While one hand was kept busy feeding himself sandwiches and beer, the other was somewhere inside his shirt, scratching.

His companion, a tall, dry, leathery man in a black suit and black hat, watched him sourly. "Just what are you looking for in there, Bubba?" he asked at last.

Bubba kept on scratching. "No tellin' what critters I might find, Clyde," he said. "But I guess we got enough of 'em in here already." He poked the bag of sandwiches with an elbow; it rocked, then settled back rustling, as if something were moving inside it.

Clyde scowled. "I don't know why you bring such filthy beasts with you."

"They're company." Then Bubba looked at the bench on the right and snickered. "Those two finally got your message, Clyde," he said.

Two young men, hardly older than Pepe, whispered together by the water fountain. Then they separated, the dark-haired one strolling by the door to the men's room, the blond one taking a seat an aisle away from Manuel and his family. He shifted his seat again, so that he was sitting right opposite their mother. His eyes closed, but Manuel saw that he wasn't really sleeping; he was watching through a slit under his eyelids.

The dark-haired man now sat on the next bench over, looking idly at the ceiling, whistling silently.

Ricardo and Elena were sitting beside Manuel. "They're going to use the snatch-and-stumble trick," the flute boy whispered.

"What's that?" the beggar-girl asked. Whatever it was, Manuel didn't like the sound of it.

Ricardo said to Manuel, "You see blondie there? His feet are flat on the floor, but he's raised his heels. He's getting ready to grab your mother's purse. She's not even sitting on it. And she's got all the money in there now, because the money belt hurt her side. She'll be sorry!" he added scornfully.

"What will the other one do?" Elena asked, before Manuel could.

"He'll pretend to chase blondie, but he'll make sure he gets in the way of anyone who's really chasing him. I've seen them do the trick lots of times in the stations at home."

"Did you do it too?" Elena asked.

"Did *I* do it? I went there to play music for the rich passengers. I couldn't carry my flute and snatch bags at the same time. But you" — and the flute boy turned to Manuel — "will you speak to your mother now? Will you warn her?"

He wouldn't have to speak, Manuel thought. If he just moved forward between his mother and the snatcher, he could save their journey. But would he be fast enough? The blond man was close to his mother, and had such long arms and legs. Manuel put his feet down too, ready to leap forward. But suddenly the snatcher settled down. Why? Manuel heard Elena giggle, and followed the direction of her eyes.

A large German shepherd had just run into the station. It was followed by Manuel's father, then by a policeman. "Winston!" the policeman called. "Come back here! What made you run off like that?" The dog gave Manuel's father a surprised look, then sidled to the policeman's leg.

The policeman patted the dog; then he realized that some passengers were watching him, drew himself up, and started to walk along the benches. He laid his hand on the shoulder of one man, who woke up. The policeman spoke to him, and the man took a ticket from his pocket and waved it sleepily in the air. The policeman nodded and moved down the aisle. He spoke to a black man who was already holding his ticket out. Clyde held out two tickets. The policeman took a look at Bubba and kept his distance. Maybe he didn't want to get too close to whatever "critters" might be in the bag, Manuel thought. He heard Bubba say, "Some tricks don't work," and Clyde answer, "There'll always be another chance."

Blondie had risen while the policeman's back was turned. He strolled toward the water fountain, drank, then turned toward the men's room, but vanished around a corner. His companion was already halfway to the street door. The policeman called to him but he kept going. The policeman just shook his head.

"Can I see your tickets, ma'am?" the policeman asked. Their mother opened her eyes, blinked, then reached for her purse and started to pull out the tickets. "That's fine, thanks," the policeman said. "But if I were you, I'd hang onto that purse a little tighter, or keep it in your suitcase till your bus is called. Thieves like to hang around here to see what they can take from tired passengers. I'd planned to check the station later, but it's just as well my dog here took a notion to run in now. Funny how dogs have a nose for these things." He patted Winston, who licked his hand.

His mother looked at the purse, gasped, and drew it close to her side. "I was so careless! How could I have been so careless? Thank you both for warning me."

"We're glad to help." The policeman looked around the station one last time, then he and Winston walked out. Manuel settled down again. The purse and their journey were safe, but he should have been the one to save them. He would have been, too, if his father hadn't acted first.

The station became quiet again. An old man swept the floor with a long broom, muttering to himself, leaving dust beneath the benches. A young woman with stringy hair stood by an instant-photo booth, waiting for her pictures. When the strip of four came out, she scowled at them and showed them to a man sitting beside two suitcases; he shrugged.

Someone turned on a tape player, and Ricardo's face twisted at the loud rock music. Elena watched the people sleeping on the benches with a mischievous smile. She clicked her castanets by the ears of one man, who jerked awake and looked around. "Zat the phone?" he mumbled. "Some'ne calling me?" Then he fell asleep again.

A calico cat with a lean body and a suspicious face was walking arrogantly along the dirty marble floor. It looked in Elena's direction with wide yellow eyes, then glanced at Clyde and Bubba and scooted under a bench.

A few minutes later, Manuel's mother told him their bus had come. Another bus, Manuel thought wearily; first the grocer's van, then the hearse, then the Greyhound; and now they had to move again. Still, it would be safer on the bus than out here under everyone's eyes. And now they were farther from the *migras*.

But Darryl had been wrong when he said no one was following them. As they approached the door of their bus, Manuel saw Clyde and Bubba waiting by the head of the line. Then Bubba shook one of the bags in his arms; a bat's head peered out, then another. And these weren't bats of this world, like the one by the ceiling, which was now swooping over to investigate. No, their fierce heads and gaping maws showed that these two bats had come from Xibalba. His father had told him that the bats of Xibalba could grow to enormous sizes; that their eyes could freeze the blood in your heart; that their chisel-sharp teeth could tear off your head in a single bite, as one of them had done so long ago to Hunahpu. Even at their present size they frightened him. There were serpents' heads poking out of the bag too. So "Clyde" and "Bubba" must really be Lords of Xibalba, though Manuel had no idea what their real names were. People in the station could see them, so they must have borrowed these bodies from real people, just as Sergeant Confusión had borrowed the body of Fred in the immigration office.

His mother's voice reached him from outside: "Manuel, what is it?"

"He's seeing things again," Pepe's voice said.

Ricardo and Elena had followed Manuel. "Where are you all going?" Bubba asked them.

"They're not going anywhere for a while," said Clyde.

Manuel tried to walk past the lords and found he couldn't move. "We have to get on the bus," he said.

"No hurry!" Bubba laughed.

"You may not have noticed it, but time has stopped." Clyde's weary voice seemed to say that time would probably never start again, and that he hoped it wouldn't.

It was true that time had stopped. The line to the bus had come to a halt. The bat of this world was suspended in the air above. The driver's outstretched hand was frozen in time, as was that of the man giving him a ticket. "So we can have a nice, cozy talk," Bubba said.

Time might have stopped, but Manuel's companions could still move. Ricardo and Elena lined up near him; his father, who had kept out of his sight in the station, appeared silently a few feet behind them.

"What are you doing here, up in this world?" Clyde said to the two musical children. "Do you think you can raise the spirits of these passengers with your tricks? Will they pay to hear your flute and drum?" He nodded toward the motionless passengers. The old man who had been sweeping was stalled in his hunched position. The woman who had taken the snapshots looked blankly toward them, frozen in mid-yawn. Clyde waved a hand at the tape player, which again filled the air with rock music; after a moment he waved it off again. "Do you want to make music in *this* world?"

The flute boy looked around the bus station with great distaste, as he had done many times since they first arrived. He shrugged his shoulders, and turned his eyes away from the people frozen in time. Bubba laughed, and Clyde smiled, or tried to. The slit of his mouth was like an open wound. But he spoke very quietly and nodded toward the frozen line of bus passengers. "Why go on their bus at all?" he asked Ricardo and Elena.

A second bus pulled in behind theirs. A bus? No, it was a van painted with a desert scene of sand and Joshua trees, just like the van the *migras* had rented from the country music group to carry away the people in the cage. There was new glass in the rear window. "That's where you want to go," Clyde said to the two children.

"Sure," said Bubba, "it was just made for musicians."

Manuel saw Ricardo's eyes light up with curiosity, but Elena hung back. "You can stay here," Manuel said.

"Stay here!" Clyde sneered. He looked around the bus station. "What a place to stay!"

"It sure ain't the Las Vegas Hilton!" Bubba tossed away one beer can and took out another.

"But we'll be taking the real bus somewhere else," Manuel said.

"Somewhere else?" Clyde asked, and the slit in his mouth widened. "In this world, one place is very much like another."

"We're going to Canada," Manuel said proudly. He was pleased to see Elena smile. Maybe he shouldn't have said this in front of the lords, but he figured they knew already.

Bubba hooted. "Canada! That froze-up place!"

"Why do you bother with them?" Clyde asked Manuel, nodding toward the children. "Why do you keep them with you?"

"I don't keep them," Manuel said. "They followed us on their own."

"So why don't you send them back where they belong?"

"How?" Manuel asked. Then he realized he should have been more careful; he should first have asked *where* the children "belonged," and why he should send them back.

"You gotta speak out, little buddy," Bubba said. "Not just say no to your ma when she wants to dig you a make-believe pond."

"That *was* a pond." Clyde really smiled for the first time.

"Look, fella," Bubba said, "why don't you open your mouth and make your mother happy for once? So she won't have to keep pretending to smile. And what about your brother? Remember how you always argued with him?"

Manuel did remember. Back in the city and in the village, he had never minded asking Pepe about his crazy ideas — some of which had turned out not to be so crazy after all.

"Just speak up," Clyde said. "Or can't you speak? Have you forgotten how? Has the cat got your tongue?" He sneered and nodded toward the cat, which was now frozen motionless under the bench.

Manuel wasn't going to give in to this sarcasm. "I have to keep my secret," he said firmly.

Bubba laughed. "You got a secret, little buddy? What kind of secret?"

But of course Manuel didn't answer. He wouldn't tell these evil lords about that terrible rainy day at the pond, when he had seen the swimming log.

Clyde sneered. "A little boy like you with important secrets! You'd do better playing little games with your little soccer ball. What could you have seen?"

But Manuel wasn't going to tell his secret to any Lord of Xibalba. They knew too much already. Despite their modern clothes, he thought these two were older than the world itself. Clyde's next words showed him that he at least suspected something. "You think that at your age you can understand miracles, do you? Do you think you know when flesh is turned into wood, or blood into flowers? The Old Ones, the Creators, were wiser than that! They made the early people of wood, and very poor material it was. Then later they made the others, such as they are." Clyde waved his hand over the motionless passengers.

"What a bunch!" Bubba chortled.

But Manuel heard voices from the outside. "Shall I carry him?" Pepe was saying.

"Not yet," his mother was answering. "He'll be all right."

Clyde said, "There are no more miracles. That was no log you saw floating in the pond and washing over the waterfall, it was someone's body — wasn't it?"

Such nonsense! Manuel thought. As if he didn't know a log when he saw one! He didn't have to answer such a foolish question. "No," he said firmly. "Now leave us alone!" Clyde's face twitched with anger, but a buzz of noise slowly overcame the silence of the station, and Manuel found he could move again. He felt his feet shift on the floor and saw Pepe start forward to catch him if he fell. But he didn't fall. He walked right to the bus, and saw that Ricardo and Elena were following him. He knew his father would follow too.

But instead of leaving, Clyde and Bubba joined the line of passengers and handed their tickets to the driver. Well, Manuel thought, if the High Command was sending such foolish lords along on the next part of the trip, it shouldn't be hard to deal with them.

ELEVEN

Filth-Maker and Bringer of Misery

Many of the seats in the Greyhound bus were empty. Pepe and their mother sat halfway toward the front, Manuel a few seats behind them, and Ricardo and Elena behind him, with his father alone, farther back still. The two Lords of Xibalba in human form entered the bus after them. Clyde sat across the aisle from Ricardo and Elena; Bubba and his paper bags took the seat behind Clyde.

No one spoke as the bus started or while they were driving through city streets to the thruway. From the rustle of the bags, Bubba seemed to be drinking more beer and eating more sandwiches. Manuel wondered how he could stick his hand in those bags without being bitten. But probably the snakes and bats wouldn't touch him.

These two lords weren't the only ones following them. As they turned a corner, Manuel saw the musicians' van behind them, ready to make the turn too. Was it really the same van the *migras* had used at the jail? Or was it some trick of Xibalba — a Bus of Death from the Land of Death? When the lords were around, nothing was what it seemed to be. He lost sight of the van for a time on the thruway; then, on a long curve, he saw that it was still there, always keeping the same distance.

Most passengers were already asleep. Manuel knew he must stay awake to learn what the lords were up to, but time passed very slowly. Whenever their bus passed a large truck, its headlights shone across the faces of the two lords. They seemed asleep, but Manuel was sure they were just waiting for him to close his eyes. The dim light inside the bus also showed his own face, mirrored in the window, watching them anxiously.

Bubba gave up pretending to sleep. He reached into his bags for more beer and sandwiches, and for the next few minutes the sounds of slurping and swallowing rose around him. Manuel could smell the yeasty odor of the beer. He wasn't the only one to smell it — soon the heads of thirsty snakes stretched out of their paper sack toward the beer can, but they couldn't reach it. The two bats flew up out of the sack and chirped angrily.

"You want some, my little pets?" Bubba crooned. He opened a new beer can, undid his shirt buttons, poured some foamy beer into the folds of his belly, and giggled happily as the bats lapped it up. One adventurous snake slithered out toward this quivering pond.

"I certainly wouldn't like to clean up after you," Clyde remarked acidly.

"Don't worry," Bubba replied. "You won't have to." He belched and turned to Ricardo. "Any time, little buddy, you can get on *our* bus." He nodded back at the van.

"I imagine you want to leave this messy place," Clyde added. "Both of you."

But Elena didn't wait to hear him say more. She slipped from her seat and ran back to the seat behind Manuel's father, and Manuel heard them whispering together. He'll speak to her but not to me, he thought jealously. He tried to make out their conversation, but their voices were too low.

"Where's that brat gone?" Bubba demanded.

"Let her be," said Clyde. "She can't get off the bus without us. Besides, we have to have a serious talk with this young man." He nodded to Ricardo, who sat up and saluted. "Now, don't be smart," Clyde said in a weary voice. "Listen to what we have to say."

"He better," said Bubba.

"No, no," Clyde said. "I'm sure he'll want to. We have an old friend of yours with us — Sergeant Duarte of the Security Police. He came down to Xibalba just recently."

"No kidding!" said Ricardo, smiling broadly. "How did you catch him?"

"Catch?" Clyde asked. "We don't 'catch' anyone."

"Let's give ourselves some credit, though," Bubba said. "We're around when our friends in the Security Police — or the others, the ones people call 'the gentlemen of the night' — catch thick ones and turn 'em into thin ones. We even sing while they do it." And suddenly he sang:

We'll be there in the evening,
We'll be there in the morn.
You won't know when we come to you,
You can't know when we're gone.

His voice was surprisingly true, and Ricardo looked at him with respect for the first time. Manuel was trying to figure out what he meant by "thick ones" and "thin ones." Ricardo and Elena must be thin ones, he decided — so thin that most people looked right through them. His mother and Pepe were thick ones. And he and his father?

"Sergeant Duarte caught himself," Clyde said, with grim pleasure.

Bubba chortled. "He was drinkin' at a party and he tried to make off with the girlfriend of Corporal Delgado, from the hills. He didn't know the corporal was so good with a knife. We watched the fight; funniest dang thing I ever seen."

Clyde said, "He came directly to us. His past life made him a natural recruit for Xibalba. But it turns out he's become a hero back in his own land. No one else saw the fight, so the Security Police say Sergeant Duarte is another valiant victim of the rebels."

"Pity there ain't more of 'em," said Bubba. "We could use the help."

Ricardo's smile had faded. "Is Sergeant Duarte in charge of a squad in your land, in Xibalba?" he asked.

Bubba laughed in derision, and Clyde said scornfully, "Of course not! He has a long way to go before that. At present, he's cleaning out the House of Jaguars."

"An' they know what to do with him!" Bubba chuckled. "A nip here and a nip there; they keep him hoppin'! When he's done with that, we'll have him work on the House of Knives. He'll be a fine man with a blade before he's done."

"And you want us to go down there?" Ricardo asked. "What would we have to clean? Do you have a House of Electricity?"

"We sure do! We got all the modern appliances!" Bubba's tone was jubilant, but Clyde's was smoother.

"Why, you wouldn't have to clean anything. We'd put you in charge of Sergeant Duarte."

"Yeah," Bubba said. "So you could order him around."

"No kidding!" Ricardo really seemed to believe them, Manuel thought.

"You could play your flute and make him dance to your tune in the House of Knives," Bubba crowed, "and pay him back for when he kicked you in the head."

"Or," Clyde said, "you could pretend to be his friend. You could make his tasks a little easier. He's managed to keep his mouth shut so far, but if he thought you were a friend, he'd

start to complain. Then you could tell us what he said."
Ricardo made a sour face, and Clyde added craftily, "But that
would be dangerous work. Maybe you're afraid."

"I'm not afraid!" Ricardo asserted.

"I'm sure you're not," said Clyde.

"We know you're not, little buddy," Bubba added. "What
say we all make a transfer to our own bus back there?"

Ricardo didn't answer immediately. In the silence, Manuel
heard his father and Elena whispering together. He's still
talking to her! Manuel thought. When will he talk to me?

But when his father spoke, it was to the two lords from
Xibalba. He rose and said, "And what about the little girl?"

The lords' heads jerked. "Did someone say somethin'?"
Bubba demanded. "Say, Clyde, did you hear anyone talkin'?"

"Not a word," Clyde replied. "Who'd be talking to us? No
one's there. What is there to ask, anyway?"

But of course Ricardo had heard. "What about Elena?" he
asked. "Would you have dangerous work for her too?"

"Rest your mind, little buddy," said Bubba.

"Of course her work wouldn't be dangerous," Clyde said.

"No," said Bubba, "she'd just have to beat on a special little
drum we'd give her and click her little castanets."

"That's all she'd have to do?" Ricardo asked suspiciously.

Clyde said, "A child like that can go anywhere in Xibalba,
mix with the crowds, she'd never be noticed. People would
talk as freely as if she weren't there."

"But we'd know where she went and what they said," Bubba
whispered exultantly. "We'd pick up every word. And if anybody said anything disloyal, we'd know what to do about it."

"As my friend said, we do have all the modern appliances,"
said Clyde. He turned toward Elena. "Come along, child. You
don't want your friend to go off without you, do you?"

Those were almost the same words, Manuel thought, that
the *migra* had used to lure the escaped child into the van.

"If you don't both watch out, you'll go flyin' off alone into the empty air," Bubba added. "You sure don't want that!"

Elena drew a breath in fear. Would she go? But now she was whispering with his father again. She turned to the lords. "The schoolteacher says no."

"A schoolteacher, did you say? I don't see any school-teacher! Where are his diploma and his classroom? I'll bet he was a schoolteacher!" Clyde's voice was angry for the first time. "Do you see any schoolteacher?" he asked Bubba.

Bubba looked back toward Manuel's father. "I sure don't."

Both lords glared at Manuel's father. Of course they could see him, Manuel thought. Fortunately their words hadn't moved Elena. "The schoolteacher says no," she repeated firmly.

"I guess you're right," Ricardo said, shamefaced. "We'll stick around with this bunch for a while." He nodded toward Manuel and his family.

There was something in the tone of both children's voices that made the two lords stop trying to persuade them. Clyde was silent, pursing his thin lips. "We'll see how long *this bunch* sticks around," he said finally.

"Why, they're headin' up to Canada, ain't you heard?" Bubba asked.

"To *Canada!*" Clyde shook his head. "Why would anyone want to go there?"

"I sure wouldn't," Bubba said. "I can't stand freezin' weather."

"They won't be able to either," Clyde asserted. He turned to Ricardo. "Why, back home you could sleep out on the street all year round."

"Sometimes I had to," Ricardo said.

"I did too," said Elena, from where she sat with Manuel's father. "It was so cold sometimes. I hate the cold."

"Well, little girl," Bubba said, "now you're showin' some sense. Just think how cold you'll be in Canada!"

"They have polar bears in the streets there," Clyde observed. "Savage brutes, half the size of this bus, with teeth like butcher knives."

"That's right," said Bubba. "And everybody lives in igloos — they're just blocks of ice. And all they have to eat is . . . is . . ."

"Flies," Clyde filled in. "Big fat black flies. If the people don't eat the flies, then the flies eat the people."

Elena whispered together with Manuel's father. "The schoolteacher says that's not true," she announced. "He says you're just making that up."

Bubba giggled. "That line don't seem to be workin' either, Clyde. You got any more of those snatch-and-stumblers around? Maybe we could just grab the little brats."

Clyde glared at Bubba, and at the mess that surrounded him. "Be still, you filthy creature!"

Bubba unwrapped another sandwich, and dunked it in the beer beneath his open shirt. "That's what I am," he said proudly. "Filthy. But I enjoy it. Only thing you ever enjoy is misery."

His words woke a memory in Manuel — what was it? Something his father had told him. Something about Xibalba. But before he could catch the thought, Bubba announced, "Now, let me show you how to stop these here 'refugees.' We'll just get the police to come; they'll do our work for us!" He sat upright, brushing crumbs and beer from his belly, and began to sing loudly, slurring all the words. Clyde looked at him in disgust, then reluctantly joined in, shaking his head. "Quiet it down!" some of the passengers called, which only made them sing more loudly. Manuel caught the words of one verse:

> We'll hunt the critters in the hollow,
> They can't run where we can't follow.
> We'll stick real close, and when they fall,
> We'll nail their skins to the outhouse wall!

The bus slowed and pulled off beside the road, and the driver walked back. "You're disturbing everyone," he said sternly.

"You may not like the way we sing," Clyde retorted, "but we're within our rights. I believe it's a free country."

Bubba said, "Ain't it the land of the free and the home of the brave?" He belched noisily.

More passengers called, "Can't you shut those idiots up?"

"I'll need a little help," the driver said. He walked to the front of the bus and talked into a radio before driving on. In a short time the bus turned off the highway and into a nearby shopping mall, and drew up by a police car. The van from Xibalba followed the bus, and stopped at the edge of the parking lot. The bus door opened, and two policemen climbed aboard and stopped to speak to the driver. As the first of them, a tall, gray-haired man, started down the aisle, the two lords paused in their song, then started a new one:

> *A hunting we will go,*
> *A hunting we will go.*
> *We'll catch a soul and put it in the hole*
> *And never let it go!*

Bubba sang with gusto, but though Clyde's voice was strong, he didn't seem to enjoy singing. Bubba's right, thought Manuel, he doesn't enjoy anything.

The driver said, "See what I mean? They keep singing that gibberish, and they won't stop."

The second policeman, a short, dark-skinned man, had joined the first, and the two exchanged glances. Then the first policeman looked at the lords calmly until they stopped. Bubba opened another beer can. "You gents are causing quite a disturbance here," said the policeman. "The driver says you wouldn't stop when he asked you politely. Is that correct?"

Bubba belched and Clyde gave out a mean laugh. "Well, I suppose those are answers of a kind," the policeman said. "I think you'd both better get off the bus. You can wait here for the next bus, in two hours. We'll drop by to see if you're quiet enough to get on it."

"Well, listen to that!" Clyde barked. "Telling *us* to get off the bus. *We're* American citizens. You're letting these foreigners stay on it — who knows how *they* came into the country?" He nodded toward Manuel's mother, who sat without turning around. Manuel could see that she was holding tightly to Pepe's arm, keeping him in his seat. "Ask to see their papers!" Clyde said.

The first policeman looked at Manuel's mother, scratching his chin. She stayed very still. Then Bubba added, "They're just a bunch of dirty wetbacks! You gonna let 'em stay on a white man's bus?"

The first policeman relaxed and turned to his black-haired partner. "Hector, these men object to 'wetbacks' on the bus."

"Do they, now?" Hector asked. "They shouldn't say so in front of the lady. *Buenas tardes, señora,*" he said to Manuel's mother.

"*Buenas tardes, señor.*"

"Have these men been annoying you, ma'am? Harassing you in any way?"

"No sir. Not us especially."

The driver said, "They've been annoying everyone on the bus."

"We can see that," the dark-haired policeman said. "Let's take it easy now, gentlemen. You have to get off here and quiet down. We have a good place for you to do that."

The gray-haired officer looked at Bubba with distaste. "We'd better air this one out a little before he gets in the squad car," he said to his partner, in a lower voice. "Talk about filth!" Turning to Clyde and Bubba, he said, "Officer

Pérez isn't fond of remarks about wetbacks. Neither am I. You come along, both of you. And bring all those cans with you; the sign says no drinking on the bus."

Manuel was relieved to see them leaving, but he wondered how soon they would catch up with him again. And then — in a flash of understanding — he suddenly realized that they had no power over him. And that they couldn't hurt his family. *He knew their names!* He knew them from his father's reading him the *Popul Vuh!* "Bubba" could only be Filth-Maker, and "Clyde" must be Bringer of Misery.

He couldn't bear to let them leave the bus without telling them that their secret had been discovered. "Oh, Mr. Filth-Maker!" he called.

Behind him, his father cried, "No! No!" So he's talking to me now, Manuel thought. But he doesn't have to worry. I can look after myself. I was the one who figured out their names.

Bubba turned around and staggered back. "Huh? Wazzat?"

Manuel heard his father's voice again, calling, "Go back!"

But Manuel hadn't finished. "And Mr. Bringer of Misery," he said to Clyde. "Have a nice rest!"

Clyde smiled, but the look in his eyes was poisonous. "Oh, we will, boy, we will." He shoved Bubba's arm so that the fat lord stumbled toward Manuel. A snake's long body reached out of the paper bag, its head curved around Manuel's back. He felt it touch his back. It couldn't have bitten him, for he felt no sting, but there was a dull ache.

Bubba had regained his balance and was moving toward the bus's door. Clyde stepped aside to let him pass, and turned back to Manuel. "You know our names, do you? Then you should learn one of the sayings of our land: 'Courage and skill come and go, but malice lasts forever.'"

"Come on, you two, stop mumbling and get off!" the first policeman called. Without any more talk, the lords left the bus.

Manuel rubbed his back; it still ached. He felt beneath his shirt but he couldn't find any teeth marks. He couldn't have been bitten — could he?

"Sorry, folks," the second policeman called. "Get back to sleep now." He followed the lords off the bus, smiling warmly at Manuel's family before he left.

As their bus started, Manuel saw the van from Xibalba drive away. He wondered if the two men being escorted to the squad car were the real Filth-Maker and Bringer of Misery — or were the real lords on the van, together with the bats and snakes? Had they slipped out of their borrowed bodies and left the original owners to explain themselves? And what could they say? That they couldn't remember a thing? That they'd been sitting quietly in a bus station, and had fallen asleep only to wake up in the hands of the police? Who would believe them?

The bus was moving again, and the passengers tried to get to sleep, muttering and grumbling about the kind of travelers who rode buses nowadays. But Manuel couldn't sleep. The ache seemed to be spreading up his back. He was sure the skin hadn't been broken, but somehow the serpent from Xibalba had bitten him deeply.

Two hours later, as they waited in an almost empty station for the next bus, he felt the ache spreading around his waist. His insides were weak and cold. He saw his father watching him, his face full of concern.

The flute boy and the beggar-girl didn't seem to notice anything, though. At first they hadn't liked any of the bus rides. Now, as they boarded a new bus, they seemed to be looking forward to the journey. Elena even whispered, "It goes so slowly!" Ricardo told her, "We'll travel faster soon." They smiled, as if sharing a secret.

Their songs, as the bus rolled along, seemed to be about travel, about going to very distant places. Manuel couldn't exactly catch the words. He felt deeply weary and oddly cold. For a time, his mother sat with her arm round his shoulder and sang old songs that he hadn't realized she knew. They weren't about travel at all. He was glad that no one expected him to speak now.

Somehow he had become very weak. He stumbled when he had to use the smelly toilet in the back of the bus, and Pepe had to walk with him and wait to bring him back. As they returned to his seat, he felt his big brother stroke the back of his neck. At the next bus station, his mother urged him to eat a sandwich, but he couldn't swallow it. She made him lie down on the hard bench, and covered him with a shawl.

She filled a jar with cool water and wiped his head with a dampened handkerchief when it became too hot. When he shivered, she kept him covered with a shawl and with Mrs. Fisher's sweater.

They were driving along a wide river with thick trees on the opposite bank. Many of the leaves had turned brown and gold; it was autumn here in Indiana, Pepe told him. Indiana? Could this be the land of the Indians? But he was too sleepy to sit up and look out.

He tried to keep their journey clear in his mind, and to recall the map of the United States in the atlas that Pepe had consulted in the library. But all their travel seemed the same now: at night he saw lights of shopping centers and service centers pass; in daylight they floated along, carried by the swift current of traffic, along wide thruways with high fences that stopped the bus from escaping into the forest. At every stop Pepe offered him juice, but it only made him feel sick. Dimly he heard and remembered names of cities, though he wasn't sure when one began and another ended: Dodge City, Kansas City, St. Louis, Indianapolis, Columbus, Pittsburgh. Pittsburgh — that was close to the border. They must be almost there. Manuel wanted to pass on this news to Ricardo and Elena, but they were paying little attention to him. They watched the scenery pass by, whispering together. He heard Elena say, "So slow! So slow!" and Ricardo agreed with her. Would they be content to stay in Canada when they all got there? It was so close now!

But a tall, thin man with a thin beard approached them in one of the bus stations. After glancing around nervously, he spoke to their mother. "Señora Cárdenas, I'm afraid we'll have to change your travel arrangements. We were planning for you to cross into Canada at Buffalo, but now they're looking for your oldest son there."

"But I got back across to Mexico, didn't I?" Pepe asked him.

"They don't believe that impersonation any more. Someone's really watching La Casa, our safe house in Buffalo. All the sanctuary locations are being watched. Some of the workers on the Mexican border will probably be arrested soon; maybe some of us too. But we won't be sent out of the country, the way you would be. We'll ship you up through Syracuse to the Thousand Islands; it's easy enough to cross into Canada there, if you have to go secretly. We've found a place for you." Then the man gave them some instructions, which Manuel was too sleepy to understand.

Later, after another — or was it two? — more bus stations, a short, gray-haired woman met them. Her eyes fixed on Manuel immediately. "That child doesn't look at all well!" She picked him up easily, and felt his forehead. "He has a high fever," she announced. "Has he been eating and drinking?"

"Only a little water," Manuel's mother said.

"What would they have in those bus stations, anyway? Nothing but junk food! We'll get some proper food inside you, young man. How long has he had this fever?"

"For the last two days," his mother said.

"And you went on traveling?"

"Where could we stop?"

The woman shook her head. "No, you're right — you couldn't stop. I'll examine you properly at home," she told Manuel. "You'll feel better when you can rest, won't you? My goodness!" she added. "He's so worn out that he can't talk!"

"He can but he won't," Pepe told her.

"Nonsense!" said the short woman. "I'm Dr. Hildebrand," she added as she led the way to her station wagon, carrying Manuel. "You'll be staying at my house."

"Are we across the border yet?" Pepe asked.

"You know we're not," their mother said sharply.

"Sorry. I'm tired of traveling too. I wish this was over."

"Crossing into Canada is not quite as easy as that," said Dr. Hildebrand. "But we should be able to get you across the river one way or another. I only hope we can wait until your brother is well."

TWELVE

The Fisher-Folk

D r. Hildebrand's house was low and wide, of gray and red stone, with windows overlooking the fast-moving St. Lawrence River. Manuel grew uneasy when he had to sit indoors. He wanted to be as close to Canada as possible. On days when his fever had gone down, Manuel went with Dr. Hildebrand to her favorite "thinking place" beside the water. This was a semicircular grove of old spruce trees sheltering a wooden armchair with cracked green paint. The chair had been there so long that it seemed planted in a carpet of brown needles. A spicy breeze passed through the branches and over the chair, which Dr. Hildebrand had padded with thick cushions and a blanket.

She had told Manuel that there were *migras* on this river too, though here they were called the Border Patrol. They were looking for people trying to cross into the United States *from* Canada, not those going the other way. Still, there was a chance that they were looking for Manuel's family. She described their boats, and said they were all well marked and official-looking. "If you see one, just move back into the trees, without being too obvious about it — can you?" Manuel nodded.

He knew that the spruce trees were "evergreens" and would keep their needles however long he stayed; they'd provide good cover for him. But the other trees on the river would soon lose all their leaves; they were changing color quickly, some to a dark red. He knew that many leaves changed color in the fall in this northern country. Pepe had explained the chemical changes that took place, but he had forgotten what they were.

Dr. Hildebrand didn't have to warn him not to be frightened of the excursion boats that passed every hour. He could see that they were full of passengers who had come to admire the beautiful border. There was plenty to see, too. The river was a whole world in itself. He couldn't tell how wide it was, because he couldn't see the far shore; wherever he looked, he could only see islands. A small rocky one a hundred yards from shore, a large wooded one at twice that distance, then a somewhat smaller one to the left, and another behind that. All the islands but the small rocky one had large houses on them — some as big as castles. Most had boats that were already drawn up for the winter, on docks or in boathouses. It seemed funny to him that boats should have their own little houses, as if they were people.

When the wind was quiet he could hear the tour guides on the excursion boats. They talked about the famous owners of the big houses: movie and stage stars, hotel owners and sausage manufacturers. Most talked about the St. Lawrence River, too, saying that it carried one-quarter of the world's fresh water from the Great Lakes to the sea, and formed part of "the longest undefended border in the world." The passengers waved hats and bright scarves at anyone on the shore, and there was probably no danger if Manuel waved back.

Once he woke up in the armchair and realized that one of the Border Patrol boats had passed while he slept. He could just see its stern, and a *migra* sitting there, not watching him. He looked around, frightened, at Dr. Hildebrand, who sat beside him on a hard straight chair, reading from a shiny medical journal. The fishing rod in its stand beside her chair was upright, the line from it to the river was slack. She paid no attention to the Border Patrol boat.

Dr. Hildebrand often read a journal or one of her big books beside him, after she had cast out a fishing line with a red float and a baited hook. She always let the float drift while she read, never watching it carefully. Sometimes it bobbed up and down a dozen times while a fish nibbled at the bait, then stopped moving. The doctor seemed to know when this happened. She would reel the line in and bait the hook again. "I don't know why I do this," she remarked to Manuel. "Ilsa hopes I'll catch a carp one day. She knows fifteen ways to cook carp. I keep telling her this isn't the right water — we'd need a quieter stretch. There's a place downriver, but then she'd soon be after me to get another carp, and another.

"Besides," she sniffed, "they're such dull fish. They don't put up a real fight."

Ilsa was Dr. Hildebrand's housekeeper and gardener. When she raked the rose beds on the other side of the wharf, she watched for the excursion boats and glared at them. "Holiday-makers!" she muttered. "The doctor hasn't had a holiday in years!" She had told Manuel that Dr. Hildebrand was in charge of the unit that dealt with premature babies at the nearest hospital, and was usually on call. "When babies are born too soon, they need a lot of special care," Ilsa explained. "Some make it and some don't."

Though Dr. Hildebrand didn't want to catch a big carp, Manuel noticed that she wasn't really interested in small fish either. She measured the ones she caught, then carefully unhooked most of them and threw them back. When she felt a tug on the line and reeled it in to find an empty hook, she seemed pleased. "Another one that got away," she remarked to Manuel. "I wish they all could, but I promised Ilsa fish for supper at least once this week." Then she added, while she put fresh bait on the hook, "I wish all the small ones in the hospital could get away from that big fisherman who's after them. Anyway, I save more of them than he keeps."

Fish, and the people who caught them, were much on Dr. Hildebrand's mind. When Pepe and his mother came out and asked about her luck, she said, "Nothing so far. But people have been catching fish in this river forever. There was a settlement of Indians just upriver. We don't know what tribe they were; everyone called them the Fisher-Folk. They had been living peacefully on the river as long as anyone could remember, fishing and trapping and selling their catch to the white settlers on both sides of the river. I found a book about them written at the beginning of the last century by a Canadian minister's wife, Felicity Chandler. She was a real artist in watercolors. The Indians used to paddle their canoes in close order, in a line; that's how she painted them. I'll be able to show you the book soon; I've just lent it to a friend. She wrote that both Canadian and American settlers were proud of themselves for tolerating these 'gentle savages,' as she called them. But I can't find any account of the Fisher-Folk after 1810. Something seems to have happened to them."

"Maybe they tried to take their land back from the settlers!" Pepe said, ignoring his mother's frown.

"No," Dr. Hildebrand said, "there's no story of an uprising. This author wrote that she had never seen people so lacking in malice. My friend — the one who borrowed the book — may know more about them. He's on the Canadian side, and he's trying to get access to some other papers from the minister's rectory. He's very interested in history."

"Do you have any books on Canadian history?" Pepe asked.

"Of course. I'll lend you some," Dr. Hildebrand said. "What are you looking at?" she asked Manuel. "Oh, those logs are pulpwood from the booms upriver. There's still some logging on the Canadian side. They cut the logs to size before they float them down the little rivers to the St. Lawrence, and then they collect them in booms for the paper mills. Some logs get away. Small boats pick them up if it seems worthwhile." Dr. Hildebrand stepped forward and touched Manuel's shoulder. "You've grown cold all over. Is it the wind from the river? No, it's a still day." She pulled Manuel's blankets tightly around him.

Manuel closed his eyes and pretended to be asleep so they wouldn't carry him inside, away from the border. Soon he felt himself growing warm again, but not hot with fever. He wanted to think of those calm, friendly Fisher-Folk. Somehow, their presence on the river partly made up for any logs floating by.

The next day he heard Dr. Hildebrand tell his mother that they should cross the river soon, by a private way that she knew.

Most immigrants at this part of the border crossed into Canada at the big Thousand Island Bridge upstream from her house. She didn't think the bridge or the roads to it were being watched, but they shouldn't take any chances. The government was cracking down on members of the sanctuary movement in the southern United States, and some of the members who had transported illegal immigrants had been arrested. "I haven't heard of any arrests in the northern groups yet," she told Manuel's mother, "but they may still be on the lookout for Pepe."

"Have they heard about him in Canada too?" Manuel's mother asked.

"Not officially." Dr. Hildebrand explained that there was a small customs and immigration office a few miles downstream, on the Canadian side. It was used to admit visitors from the American side to a historic church and rectory. Dr. Hildebrand winked. "I know the senior immigration officer from the Thousand Islands station who'll be across the river most of next week."

"Is this officer your friend?" Manuel's mother asked.

"He sometimes fishes on this side of the river. He's a retired army officer who had quite a distinguished career in the war. We compare notes about the history of the border." She sniffed. "He claims to know more than I do about these islands, but never mind that. You should be able to convince him to let you stay in Canada. You've convinced me, and I certainly don't believe all the stories I hear. Besides, he saw the news last night too. He won't forget that soon." She lowered her voice when she said this, as she saw Manuel watching her, but he heard her anyway.

What was Dr. Hildebrand talking about? Why should the senior immigration officer care about all those logs? Last night, Pepe had come to visit him on the couch in Dr. Hildebrand's study, where he slept under the shelves of brown and green books, and had left the door partly open. There was no harm in this: Manuel could see the television screen that the others were watching in the next room, and he had often fallen asleep watching it. Some sort of comedy with the sound turned low came to an end; then he saw a news announcer at a desk. Dr. Hildebrand said dryly, "This news item seems to be from your country."

Then the announcer was replaced by a forest scene, with trees beside a road and a roadside ditch in which many logs were lying.

"Oh!" Ilsa cried. She ran over and tried to shut Manuel's door, but the carpet curled up under it and blocked it. Pepe had run forward to hide the forest scene with his body — though Manuel could still see logs peeping out on either side of the screen. Pepe seemed to be looking for the switch, and having trouble finding it; his hands scrabbled furiously around the face of the television set. Ilsa ran forward to help him, but they only got in each other's way. Then Dr. Hildebrand reached behind the set and pulled the plug from the wall socket.

Manuel only wanted to sleep, and when the others looked into the room he closed his eyes and pretended he had seen nothing. In a moment the rug was straightened and the door was closed.

Dr. Hildebrand had planned to wait two days, but after only one day had passed, on a cold, rainy morning, she decided to take them across. "I'm off duty now. And I heard someone was asking questions in town. I thought of taking you at night, but that would look suspicious if we met a patrol boat. And Manuel would have to be out in the cold until the office opened. This is the best plan."

The doctor drove her motorboat, while Manuel's family kept out of sight in the forward cabin. His mother had covered him with a tan blanket. Ilsa sat behind, in full view of the river, trolling out a long line from a large fishing rod. "There's plenty of fisher-folk on the river," Dr. Hildebrand said. Ilsa sat there stoically, though rain and cold spray sprinkled her. "You keep him covered," she called back to Manuel's mother, and almost rose to pull the blankets over him.

That wasn't necessary, Manuel thought. His head wasn't hot and his mind was clear. Now they were really on the way! The rain stopped. Drops sparkled on the island trees and on the roofs and windows of the castles. Manuel sniffed the clean wind that blew across the water. It was cooler air than any he had yet known, smelling of cool green life, and there was a touch of cold behind it. He looked up; the clouds had parted to reveal the hardest-looking sky he had ever seen. Winter would be coming soon, the long, sleepy Canadian winter Mr. Wemyss had talked about. Then they would be able to rest at last, and stop running.

But would they be all alone? In the worry and excitement of the last few days, Manuel had lost sight of his father. Were this clear, cold blue river and sky going to separate them forever? He couldn't believe it — his father would have said goodbye. But he couldn't imagine that either. No, his father — and probably his other secret friends — must be coming along too. He wanted to crawl to the back of the boat to look for them, but this might give their presence away, especially since his red lifejacket would show above the sides of the boat. Dr. Hildebrand had insisted that they all wear lifejackets. The water was so cold, she said, that even experienced swimmers would be in trouble in it. Pepe had accepted the jacket with bad grace, partly because, Manuel was sure, he didn't want to admit that he could hardly swim at all. Somehow, he had always been too busy to learn.

"That's the Canadian side," Pepe whispered. Manuel saw a wide dock with a house behind it, over which the red Maple Leaf flag flew. "We're almost there," Pepe said. "Oh-oh!"

One of the American *migra* boats was tied up at the Canadian dock. "What does he want there?" Pepe demanded. "Can't they leave us alone?" He stood up in the cabin to glare at the intruders.

"You stay down!" Dr. Hildebrand whispered sharply. "The immigration people keep in touch with each other at these border stations. It may be just a friendly visit. We'll wait. Cast out your line again, Ilsa."

As Ilsa did this, Dr. Hildebrand slowed the boat and passed the Canadian border station. She nodded to the sailor in charge of the *migras'* boat, who waved back. They proceeded, without haste, to the foot of the next island downstream, and circled behind it, just as Ilsa hooked a fish. "We'll get close to shore and drift," Dr. Hildebrand said. "If I see them coming back, I'll pull into that little cove. You can hide in the bushes behind that house." She nodded toward a three-story house crowned with a high, pointed green roof. At one end was a tall, round tower with small, round windows.

"They call that the French Château," Ilsa remarked. "No one's home there now." She had reeled in her fish. "It's a big one, a lake trout."

Dr. Hildebrand looked back. "Keep it for supper." She turned the bow of her boat outward, to watch for the *migras'* boat coming from either side of the island.

Manuel's mother watched him anxiously. Did she think he couldn't run into the bush, so close to the border? He could run and hide forever if he had to. He could easily conceal himself in the shelter of the French Château, behind the thick evergreen bushes that hugged the near side.

He knew that "château" meant "castle." Perhaps the houses along this river were true castles, he thought, and would protect them from their evil pursuers. In the old days, castles had been set up along frontiers to guard a land from its enemies. Would these castles do the same thing here, now?

The French Château had glass windows and sliding glass doors at ground level, leading to a wide lawn. This castle didn't need strong walls or soldiers to guard it, Manuel decided. If the river was part of an "undefended border," as the guides on the tour boats said, it must not need defending; it must be a barrier all by itself. On the other side the Indians, the Fisher-Folk, would be living their busy, peaceful lives. He would soon be well; they could all go and visit them.

"There they go!" Dr. Hildebrand exclaimed. They had all heard the *migras'* boat start up. Now they saw its stern as it headed upstream past their island; no one looked their way. Dr. Hildebrand waited until the boat was out of sight, then turned back by the foot of their island and aimed for the Canadian shore.

———

While the immigration officer was speaking to his mother and Pepe, Manuel sat with Dr. Hildebrand on the wide dock outside the small office. Ilsa sat in the boat. She had a rod with a spinning reel now, and kept casting out a large shiny lure. Past her head, they could see the church tower and its high, open belfry, which attracted boat tours to this shore; the next one would arrive in two hours.

Manuel couldn't hear exactly what was being said inside the office, but the tone of the voices was calm and measured. The immigration officer was letting Manuel's mother answer his questions at her own speed. Dr. Hildebrand, who seemed to have very sharp ears, was listening intently. "Yes," she said to herself, "he saw the news too."

The door to the dock opened, and Pepe beckoned Manuel inside. A guard was sitting by the other door, near a black wood stove, yawning over a newspaper. The senior officer, a thin man with sparse gray hair and a thick gray mustache, smiled at Manuel and pointed to a straight wooden chair. Manuel sat down.

"Well, young man," he said, "your mother and brother have made quite clear statements about your past history." Manuel looked quickly at Pepe, who started to wink but stopped in time.

The officer coughed. "Your past history in your own country," he said mildly, which made Manuel think he might know more than he was willing to say. "I have only one or two questions for you. But your mother says that at present you don't want to speak. Is that correct?"

Manuel nodded.

"But you do understand me, I see," the officer said. "We probably won't need a translator. Your mother can translate if necessary. Just nod if you understand what I've said so far."

Manuel nodded again.

"Good. If I need a more detailed answer, can you write it

down?" Manuel tried to steady his hand, which was trembling on the chair. "It may not be necessary," the officer said. "Now, I understand that on May tenth of this year your father did not come home when you expected him to. Had you seen him in his school?"

Manuel shook his head.

The officer said, "That agrees with what I was told. Your father was not at the regular school that day, I understand. He had to go to a school in the next valley, a small one that had been damaged." The officer looked at his note pad. "I believe it was damaged by a hand grenade. Had he discussed that?"

This was getting dangerous. Of course his father had spoken of the destroyed school, mainly asking the sky above who could have brought himself to do such a thing. But if he, Manuel, nodded yes, the officer might somehow trick him into speaking his father's words — which he must never do. He shook his head.

"You know he talked about it!" his mother cried.

"Please, Mrs. Cárdenas," the officer said. "I have to ask these questions." Then he looked even more closely at Manuel. "His face is flushed. Does he have a fever?"

Manuel's mother placed a hand on his forehead. "No," she lied. Of course, she knew better than to tell the officer how Manuel's head was burning. They wouldn't want to let sick people into Canada! But would the officer be fooled?

Maybe he was. He looked carefully at Manuel's mother, then continued his questions. "Now, I understand that your father left for that damaged school early in the morning, because it had been raining overnight and more rain was expected. He hoped to reach the damaged school between two periods of rain. Do you think he did, sonny? Was there enough time after your father left home for him to reach that school before the rain started again?" The immigration officer turned a kindly, alert smile toward Manuel. "Just nod yes or no."

But Manuel wasn't going to admit that he knew what time his father had left home. He shrugged his shoulders and raised his hands, palms up.

"I understand that means you don't know. But surely you saw him leave? Your mother says you were very close to your father."

Manuel shook his head.

"You didn't see him leave that morning?"

He shook his head again.

"You saw nothing all that day, then? You didn't see your father return? You didn't see him at all?"

Manuel shook his head so violently that his chair scraped the floor.

The officer wrote something on a pad of paper and read what he had written. He frowned thoughtfully. "Just a few more questions, but I don't insist that you answer. Two nights ago there was a news item on television about your country. I wonder if you saw it?"

Manuel's mother turned so suddenly to glare at the officer that her chair legs also scraped the floor. The officer didn't turn his eyes from Manuel's face. "Did you see it?" he asked softly.

Manuel thought quickly. Should he deny what he'd seen? But his mother might have already told the officer that he had been watching. If this man caught him in a lie, even an unspoken one, they might all be sent back. And then what would happen? He nodded.

"Yes," the officer said, and wrote on his pad. "Had you seen such things before?"

Seen such things? What a foolish question, from a man who had seemed intelligent! The television had only shown a forest scene with lots of logs. As he turned his head away from the officer's searching gaze, Manuel saw a pile of logs outside the window. These were quite short ones, cut into fire-wood for the winter. In fact, he now saw that some of the logs had been brought inside and lay by the wood stove, next to the feet of the guard, who had put down his newspaper to watch Manuel.

Manuel pointed out the window, then to the logs beside the stove. The officer looked puzzled. "Logs?" he asked. Manuel nodded. "What you saw was . . ." The officer paused, and looked quickly at Manuel's mother. "All right," he said. "All you saw was logs." Manuel nodded again. "Logs on the ground," the officer added. After a time he added, "Don't worry. Where you'll be going, you'll see fine trees growing tall, like these trees around us." He gestured out the window. "I hope they'll help you forget those other logs." He looked over his notes. "Now, I'll ask you and your brother to wait outside for a little while."

Pepe held Manuel's arm, but he found he could walk without difficulty. Had they really got through? Suddenly he felt cold again. Dr Hildebrand saw him shiver and draped the blanket around him again. Pepe watched him, very con-cerned. "Don't be angry with the man. He's no fool. He told us that he had to talk to you as well."

They heard the officer's voice indoors, and their mother answering it without the sharp tone she slipped into with people who *were* fools.

Finally the door opened and their mother walked out. She smiled and said softly, "It's all right." He is letting us into Canada for now. He has telephoned Mr. Wemyss's sister, and she is coming to pick us up. We'll have a new home, very soon."

For a moment Manuel thought she was going to cry. Pepe had been waiting to go to the bathroom; he just took time to kiss her, then knocked at the door and walked into the office.

The officer came out to the dock. "Ingrid," he said to Dr. Hildebrand, "it was good of you to come."

"I'm glad I had the time. Did you find the rectory papers yet?" She nodded toward the church steeple.

The officer shook his head. "The family that owns all the papers is still dickering with the Queen's University Library. They have an exaggerated idea of their archives' value. But I did find something else in the military archives in the museum. I'm afraid it deals with your — what did Mrs. Chandler call them? 'Gentle savages'?"

"Not the Fisher-Folk?"

"Yes. Oh, excuse me, Mrs. Cárdenas," the officer said. "Dr. Hildebrand and I are both amateur historians of the river and the islands. Until now she's been well ahead of me, with this wonderful journal that she found in the back shelves of a second-hand bookstore."

He was holding a small black-bound book, which he now handed to Dr. Hildebrand. "The color photocopies came out pretty well, and I photographed the paintings, to make sure."

"I'm glad to have it back," Dr. Hildebrand said. "Look at this line of canoes!" She held the book open with two hands, toward Manuel and his mother. Facing a page of fine, regular handwriting was a small painting of three white canoes, each with several Indian paddlers. The canoes were passing one of the islands in the river, evenly distanced from each other. The blue water around the prows seemed fresh and alive.

"I found the passage in the book you mentioned, about the Peaceable Kingdom," the officer added.

"I was telling Mrs. Cárdenas about the Fisher-Folk," Dr. Hildebrand said. "What is it that you found in the military archives?"

"Nothing you'll like to hear," the officer said. "When the war broke out between Canada and the Americans in 1812, a troop of soldiers was sent here from Fort York, in Toronto. Some of them were involved in the battle of Beecher's Point, as it was called then. That's where you'll be going," he added to Manuel's mother, "though it's called Owl Point now. The Kingston archives say, 'Hostile Indians were also encountered, but a concerted military action drove them off without loss.' Meaning without loss to the Canadian soldiers. But I've found a letter that one of the soldiers wrote to his brother and never sent." He looked at his watch. "Since your employer still hasn't come, Mrs. Cárdenas, perhaps you'd like to hear the story too." Manuel's head began to swim. How long would the officer keep talking? Though he tried to focus on the sound of the water slapping against the dock, Manuel soon found himself listening to the letter from the long-dead soldier:

Dear Brother Charles, my heart is sick at what I have seen, and done. After arriving here, we rested in the "barracks" — really a derelict farm building on which little effort has been spent to render it habitable — for our first two weeks, not knowing what was expected of us or what awaited us. The men were uneasy, angry at being closed up in this mean place, tormented by enterprising mosquitoes, forbidden even to go to Malloryville, the hamlet down the road. Still, we kept good order, and when we were told to take positions along the river the hopes and fears of some action at last lifted our spirits. We were stationed along Beecher's Point, an island rather than a peninsula, but very close to the mainland, and attached to it by a small wooden footbridge. There we had only to wait. Sgt. Grimes's strict discipline hushed the voices of some of the soldiers, but enough of us spoke to make the American troops across the river — for here the islands were sufficiently apart for us to see the far shore — well aware of our presence. We heard the sounds of drums and bugles; then, from all appearances, the Yankees withdrew. General disappointment was evident. If Sgt. Grimes had not been keeping his eye on us, I fully believe some of the younger troops would have fired across the wide river, though it was far beyond rifle range.

A low green boat had drawn near the dock, so quietly that its movement made no waves and only Manuel saw it. The boat's captain, in a green uniform and peaked gold cap, stood on the deck. Beside him were other officers and sailors, also dressed in green. They were all listening to the soldier's letter with close attention. Some of the sailors pointed at Manuel, and nudged each other, laughing silently.

The immigration officer continued reading:

But a nearer, quite unexpected target presented itself. Around the bend of the nearest island, which was a wide, almost bare rocky protrusion crowned at one end by a few windblown pines, a canoe appeared. It was followed by another canoe, and yet another. Finally there were six large vessels, each with four or five Indian men. They kept an excellent discipline, so that their vessels were exactly evenly spaced one from the other. They had clearly not seen us, but when our men began to murmur among themselves, the Indians took no alarm from our presence. One or two nodded their heads gravely and politely at us, which caused more fear than a frankly hostile gesture would have done. What were they doing there? The question was whispered from one soldier to another. They could be up to no good. My neighbor, Pvt. Bowles, whispered that these must be diabolical allies of the Yankees.

All such speculations were brought to an end by Sgt. Grimes's order to aim and fire. The men set to with a will, and so did I. A sudden madness had seized us all. Cries and yells rose from the canoes, but to our great surprise not one of the Indians fired back. The neat formation of their canoes was broken up in an instant. Three were overturned immediately; one paddler rose in a foam of blood, then sank; another never surfaced. Two swimmers made for shore, being joined by swimmers from the other canoes — six in all. The rest died in their vessels, or in the water beside them. Those who reached the near island found that its bare stony slopes offered no protection. The last swimmer had almost reached the trees at the island's crest when he too was shot down.

On the green boat, the captain and officers chuckled with satisfaction at this tale of slaughter. The sailors poked each other in the ribs and snickered, and one of them hoisted an imaginary rifle and mimicked the attack — "kapow, kapow, kapow!"

The immigration officer coughed before he read the next paragraph:

> I have since learned that the stony island is called Refuge Island, since the time, ten years ago, when it provided shelter for a picnic party from a nearby church, capsized in a sudden storm.
>
> Charles, in the excitement of this engagement none of us realized — nor did I — that the "warriors" we were attacking were quite unarmed: terrified, peaceful fishermen flying for their lives from those they had never before considered their enemies. Two of their canoes drifted within our reach, and proved to be plentifully stocked with river trout. We dined well on these, since the "battle" had sharpened our appetites. I have since wondered how such senseless, evil doings can provoke so great a hunger.
>
> There were a few fine furs in the canoe as well, but

the Lieutenant and Sgt. Grimes laid claim to these.

I will write no more for the present, Charles, but will add to this — and, I hope, in a happier vein — when I have learned from your own letter that you have reached the trading port in Newfoundland and that your new enterprise has begun.

"He signed it, 'Your loving brother, Percival Pomeroy,'" the officer said. "For some reason, the letter was never sent. Perhaps his brother didn't reach Newfoundland, or the writer may have had second thoughts, and felt too ashamed to admit what they'd done."

"I should hope he would be ashamed!" Dr. Hildebrand said.

The officer looked over the letter again, shaking his head. "You have to excuse me, Mrs. Cárdenas," he said. "This letter is really a find for us." He glanced at Manuel. "Isn't your son feeling well?"

Manuel's eyes were fixed on the green boat, where an officer with a megaphone was addressing the sailors. "Fellow warriors! The time for joking is past. We wish we could personally thank the reader of that account of the wonderful events that took place along the 'longest undefended border in the world.' Alas, Percival Pomeroy chose not to join us and is now floating in the upper air, lost and homeless." (At these words, a disappointed mutter arose among the sailors.) "But who could have defended any border against us? Some of us were there —" and here several sailors nodded. "We implanted fear of an unknown enemy into the empty hearts of those untrained soldiers until, as the chronicler wrote, a sudden madness seized them.

"Think of our splendid work at that time, as we go back to our present heavy task of collecting logs along this river, under the hostile sun." Some of the sailors, who had been cowering beneath the open sky, straightened up bravely at these words. The green boat sailed away; the captain's eyes mocked Manuel.

"What is it, Manuel?" Dr. Hildebrand demanded. She stepped forward and laid her hand on his forehead. "The fever has come back since this morning," she whispered to his mother. "We must have said too much."

They heard wheels on gravel in the parking lot, then new voices in the room. The guard opened the door to the dock. "Mrs. Dorset's here." In the room was a small, active-looking woman, her gray-brown hair in a long braid. Pepe, who had been talking with the guard about some of the "wanted" notices on the walls, joined them.

The officer sat down at his desk again. "It was good of you to come," he said. "I won't keep you now." He looked uneasily at Manuel and exchanged a quick glance with Dr. Hildebrand. "I've explained to Mrs. Cárdenas that she and her sons have permission to stay and work, especially since you have a job for her. They'll have to have a regular immigration hearing at a later date, to decide if they can stay permanently. With the backlog at the Kingston office, that'll be at least six months. We'll send her the forms and the information at your address, and we're counting on her and her sons to attend the hearing."

"They'll be there," Mrs. Dorset said.

"I'm sure they will." Then the officer shook all their hands, and nodded to the guard by the door to let them through.

Dr. Hildebrand accompanied them to a blue van with "Owl Point Lodge" written on the side. They put Manuel in the back seat of the van, covered again with blankets. He wanted to protest, but looked at his mother's face and decided not to. Dr. Hildebrand was standing beside the driver's door and talking through the window to Mrs. Dorset. "Why is it called Owl Point now?" she asked in a louder voice.

The van had started to roll forward; Mrs. Dorset stopped it. "I suppose because it has so many owls. Sometimes they

keep me awake, but I don't mind. I think they find good
hunting in the woods and on the bare island just across. I've
hardly seen a rabbit or a squirrel around the place.

"But there's a story about the point, too," she added.
"Some Indian legend. They call it 'the place of the sorrowing
owls.' The owls, being hunters themselves, are mourning a
tragedy, some shameful thing that happened long ago to some
quite innocent hunters."

"Ah!" Dr. Hildebrand said. "I won't keep you now, but I'd
like to hear more about that story later. I'm off duty one day next
week, and I should be able to drop by and learn how our
friends are doing. Who's your doctor?" she asked, and nodded
at Mrs. Dorset's answer. "Yes, he's good. I'll be in touch with him
too. You get better now, Manuel," she called, as they drove off.

Manuel knew he should lie down, but after a time he sat
up high enough to look out the window. They were still
driving along the wide river with its many islands, and its
grand homes and castles. But the castles had not been strong
enough to keep the evil lords away. He remembered their
faces as they laughed at the story of the Fisher-Folk, gunned
down for no reason at all. The Lords of Xibalba had been
behind the terrible, senseless slaughter along the river. Or so
they claimed. Should he believe them? And what had their
officer said about "collecting logs"? Which logs?

But what was that in the river? A little white boat, slipping
along the edge of the water. It was a canoe — a *birchbark*
canoe — and look who was in it! His father was paddling in
the stern, Ricardo in the bow. Elena sat between them, beating
her drum to the time of their strokes. All three were watching the water flow past with pleasure, and the children kept
raising their heads to sniff the air.

Manuel knew the canoe couldn't possibly travel as fast as
Mrs. Dorset's van. But somehow, whenever he looked out the
window, it was still there.

THIRTEEN

On Owl Point

D r. Friesen was a small, bearded man who knew Dr. Hildebrand well. She had called him the same day that Manuel and his family crossed the Canadian border. "A bad kidney infection," he said. "He must have been sickening for some time. Where did he pick that up? Were the buses air-conditioned? A chill on his back could start it."

"I kept him warm," Manuel's mother said.

"I'm sure you did, but in his condition, after whatever shock he had, anything could have set him off. He shouldn't have been traveling."

"We had to travel."

The doctor nodded. "Of course; he's one of Ingrid Hildebrand's chickens. At least he can rest now."

That was the only thing to do, really, the doctor added: to rest. There was no point taking Manuel to the hospital now. "It would upset him too much to be separated from the rest of you. Besides, there are some pretty nasty drug-resistant bacteria developing in our hospital. I don't send my patients there unless it's strictly necessary. Can you keep him on his antibiotics, Mrs. Cárdenas?" Manuel's mother, of course, said she would.

She and Manuel shared a room on the ground floor. One of its doors led to the reception desk, so she could take care of any guests who arrived late. She always spoke softly, which made the guests speak softly too. Manuel thought, though, that she wasn't trying to keep from waking him up, since he slept most of the day.

Opposite his bed was a calendar from a company that sold Mrs. Dorset the clay she used for her pots. On the calendar was a picture of a large, shiny urn. The moving sun made its image travel along the opposite wall. By the door to the office were two lists — one of buses that stopped at a shelter on the highway, and one of trains that stopped in the next town, six miles away. His mother consulted these lists until she knew them by heart. Manuel learned them too, but had difficulty remembering them. Perhaps their travels had ended here. He already thought of Canada as a land of snow, although no snow had yet fallen outside. His bedsheets made him think of snow, because they were almost always fresh and white; he sweated so that they had to be changed every day. He had thought his mother would be more pleased than she was to see him lie so clean and comfortable.

He didn't want her to worry so much about him. She had to concentrate on her new job. Whenever Mrs. Dorset looked into the office and the bedroom behind it, she asked about Manuel, but mainly she seemed pleased that his mother was taking charge of the office. This was the slack season, Mrs. Dorset said, after the summer crowd and before those who came for the cross-country skiing. It was wonderful that Sonia Cárdenas could put the books in shape. She herself could get back to her pots, which had been so neglected recently. Her workshop was at the back of the lodge, looking over the river, but Sonia could call her at any time.

Such words proved that they were expected to stay, not to run any more. His mother and Pepe could settle down and make the most of their new lives. Pepe had started school, and had brought a number of new books into the bedroom behind the office. He told Manuel that he was almost ashamed that his classes were so easy. Some of his teachers were all right, he said. They were teaching chemistry at a very elementary level, but so far they hadn't made any major mistakes. There was a good mathematics teacher, who had set some problems that even he had trouble answering. Math was all right — they couldn't really change that — but you had to be careful with the other courses, especially the Canadian version of history.

At times, when it didn't seem to make his brother too tired, Pepe sat beside him, sponging his forehead to cool him, and talked about going on to university to study chemistry or physics, he still wasn't sure which. He had not yet found a branch of science he didn't like. It was early to make plans, but Mrs. Dorset had mentioned that there might be a scholarship to help support his university studies in Kingston or Toronto. But was he being selfish, he asked Manuel, to study what he liked, when the world was in such a bad state? Manuel thought about that a long time before he finally shook his head. "You're right," Pepe said. "We still have to learn about the world, no matter how many things are wrong with it."

Often, his old companions called — at least, the two children did. They tapped on the window when no one was in the room, and beckoned to him to come out. But of course he couldn't get up and pass through the window — as he supposed they could. He saw his father, too, watching sadly from a distance — always from a distance. Why didn't his father come closer now? Was he still keeping watch against the Lords of Xibalba? He didn't have to: they always announced their coming, by serpents, or bats, or uniforms, and now by boats.

After some cold gray days, the weather became so warm that Mrs. Dorset and his mother agreed he would do better outdoors. They carried him out and across a wooden footbridge to a small island called Owl Point. There they laid him, well covered, on a reclining chair within the red granite walls that Mrs. Dorset called her "castle keep."

It was all in the lodge's brochure, she said. These three walls which opened out onto the river had been the beginnings of a tower. The owner of a long stretch of the river had planned to build a castle there, modeled after one he had seen in Germany, as a gift for his new bride. But the tower's three walls had only risen six feet when she died. The husband stopped the work and never set foot on the property again.

Despite its sad story, this was Manuel's favorite spot. The stones reflected the sun throughout the day, so that it was warm inside the walls well into autumn. The open side of the tower base was situated so that Manuel's mother could see him lying there from her office. Some years before, Mrs. Dorset's husband had set up a grape arbor over the top of the walls. The grapes weren't the usual purple Concord ones, which didn't mind a cold climate, but a pale yellow strain that her husband had ordered from France. Most had been picked by now, but a few had been left on the vines to dry to a shriveled gold. On still days a faint scent from the dried grapes spread inside the enclosure.

Manuel had taken to watching these vines, and the ivy that climbed between the stones. If he looked very carefully he could follow a single vine up from the ground, between the leaves, to the highest stones, where it spread out into a delta of delicate twigs.

"I used to look at the vines like that," Mrs. Dorset told

him. "I'd say to myself that if I followed one vine all the way to the top, I'd get through whatever problems I had. Is that how you see it, too?"

Manuel thought gravely for a time, nodded his head, then shook it immediately after. "More complicated than that, is it?" Mrs. Dorset asked. He nodded again. To him, the vines were in such a tangle that each strand blocked the others. The branches that reached the top had escaped, had made it through the dense tangle that contained so many dark holes and corners — places where the Lords of Xibalba might be lying in wait.

But if he had turned his eyes away, he could see things that were less complicated than these tangled vines. By the river-bank was a large maple tree whose leaves had all turned red. That was the owls' tree; he thought there were four owls, though he could usually only see two at once. Or he could look back at the lodge, at the windows of Mrs. Dorset's work-shop, with shelves at the back where red and brown pots were displayed, and at the big gray barn near the highway. Nearer, to his left, some of the lodge's red canoes were tied. After school Pepe would be out learning to use one, under Mrs. Dorset's direction. She had gone with him a few times, but now she let him paddle alone, as long as he stayed within the small bay between Owl Point and the mainland. Manuel had heard her explaining that the canoe was harder to handle with just one person in it, since it rode higher in the water and was blown about more by gusts of wind. Of course, she insisted that Pepe wear a lifejacket, though he complained that it interfered with his paddling. Even good swimmers wore lifejackets, Manuel heard her say, especially now that the water was becoming colder.

Someone had gotten out the soccer ball that Mr. Wemyss had given Manuel, and blown it up and laid it by the foot of his chair. He had heard Pepe whisper, "It'll be a long time before he plays with that again." But Mrs. Dorset had whispered back, "Shh! We want to encourage him to get well."

In time he stopped trying to listen to them, because it seemed more important to watch the river. As the trees lost their leaves, he could even see how far it was across; the shore of the American side appeared beyond the large, bare island in front of him, the one called Refuge Island. When the Americans and Canadians were at war over 170 years ago, the soldiers' rifles couldn't reach all the way from Canada across the river to the far side. But they could reach Refuge Island, and cover every part of its smooth stone slopes. To get away from those rifles, you would have to run up to the trees on top — and who could reach those in time? Some of the Fisher-Folk had tried — but it was too far, and the guns were too fast.

There were other islands in the river: a wooded island on his right would have provided more shelter, even without the two houses that were on it now. He thought of the refuge that it might have given, one morning as he drifted into sleep in his chair. When he opened his eyes he saw some sticks — one a whole tree branch with a few leaves still on it — floating past at a slow, steady pace. A small motorboat heading upstream cut its engine, and two men began to fish from either side as the boat started to drift down the river.

Four birchbark canoes appeared at one end of Refuge Island. The paddlers kept perfect rhythm, but one of the Fisher-Folk in the middle looked at Manuel, then smiled and waved to him. He poked the man in front of him, who also waved. Some of the people in the other canoes noticed and waved too.

Then one of the tour boats appeared upstream, around a bend in the river. The guide's voice boomed out over the loudspeaker, "No, madam, there has been no fighting along this river for more than a hundred and fifty years. It's part of the longest undefended border in the world, the border between the United States and Canada."

The tour boat spread waves as it passed. The small motorboat with the two fishermen rocked, and one of them looked up, annoyed. Waves washed the stone slopes of Refuge Island too. But the birchbark canoes glided on as smoothly as before.

People talked about this undefended river, Manuel thought, as if it didn't need to be defended. What did they know? Did they really think these wide waters and tall trees were any protection against the evil Lords of Xibalba?

The river was becoming cluttered with logs now; they must be coming from the sawmill up the river, where the tall trees were sliced into short logs, later to be ground into paper pulp. The logs moved slowly, languidly, in the current.

The low green boat had come back from somewhere. The captain and the officers beside him stood sternly at attention, ready for action. A tarpaulin was spread over a pile of something on the rear deck, and beside it a sailor sat at a long black machine-gun with gold trim. He swung this weapon from side to side, looking fiercely for enemies or victims.

Now three more sailors, also in green with green sailor hats, rose up from below deck and joined the captain and the other lords. The sailors walked to the stern of the boat and let out a long net that was attached to metal bars sticking out from either side of the boat. The net was weighted so that most of it sank below the water surface, except for a kind of lip that gathered things on the surface as it swept along.

It was a very unusual net, Manuel saw, for it only caught logs; a fish jumped right through it. But it caught logs very well, and when they were within grasp the sailors thrust out poles with long hooks, and dragged the logs into the boat. They had drawn back the tarpaulin now, revealing a small heap of logs they had already trapped.

The Fisher-Folk in their birchbark canoes watched the green boat, shaking their heads sadly at each log it caught. They didn't seem afraid of the boat, though it was so much

larger than their own. But the captain had been watching these
fishers and hunters with increasing anger, and now he barked
out a command. The helmsman turned the boat's prow toward
the canoes, gunned the motor, and tried to ram them.

It was wonderful, Manuel marveled, how easily the Fisher-
Folk evaded the green boat. With nimble flicks of their
paddles they turned their graceful craft aside. They easily
kept away from the boat's sweeping net; when one of the
canoes seemed to be trapped, the paddlers quickly and
cleanly reversed direction and drew it clear.

The green boat passed so close to one of the canoes that
it overturned and dumped its occupants into the cold water.
Manuel gasped — even if they could swim, what if they were
caught in the net? While one of the paddlers surfaced and
grasped the canoe, strongly pushing it away, the others sank
beneath the surface. Manuel held his breath in dismay, scan-
ning the dark waters where they had vanished. But they
weren't there — instead they burst to the surface beside the
green boat, and started climbing up its sides. They must have
planned the whole thing! Before the sailors could stop them,
they started throwing the logs overboard. The machine-
gunner swung his weapon around and fired at them, but they
only laughed and flipped backwards into the river.

By this time Fisher-Folk from the other canoes were in the
water too, catching the logs with friendly hands and pushing
them on their way. Some of the Fisher-Folk climbed back into
their canoes again; others had run up the shore of Refuge
Island, where they danced together on the smooth slopes. The
machine-gunner turned his terrible weapon toward Refuge
Island, but his bullets missed all the triumphant dancers.

The logs that had been thrown back in the river didn't just
float along near the green boat, Manuel noticed. They sailed
away — and how quickly! But they had names written on
them, he realized now — names like Carlos Centeno

Gonzáles, 26, and Oracio Gomes Miranal, 53, and Miranda María Cardenal, 27, and Luis Álvarez, 34. And they were moving in the current as if they were still able to swim by themselves. They raced past Refuge Island and the wooded island beside it, where Manuel's father waved them on their way. They sped past the motorboat, in which one of the men seemed to have hooked a fish.

Then Manuel saw that the logs weren't traveling alone. The flute boy and the beggar-girl were riding them, dancing along the tops so that their feet seemed to dance over the water's surface. They danced so vigorously that Manuel could see the logs spin underneath them, and they leaped from log to log, too, laughing at the danger.

His father, who had watched everything closely, now crossed over, walking on the water, and stood by Manuel's chair. He applauded the Fisher-Folk, who waved at him.

The green boat landed at Owl Point and the captain came ashore. But instead of approaching them, he stepped to one side and bowed deeply. Another figure swept past him. This was clearly a Lord of Xibalba, tall and forbidding, with a high forehead, a jutting nose, and a wide, severe mouth. He wore a long green cape, on whose front panels were large number sevens that glittered in the setting sun. He was Lord Seven Death himself, Manuel realized — one of the most fearsome of all the Lords of Xibalba, and so proud of his name that he scorned to conceal it. No disguises for him, and no borrowed human bodies!

Seven Death looked his father up and down, curiously, as if to take in all his nature. "So, you are still here, school-teacher?" he said at last.

"I've always been with my family," his father said.

"So I've been informed."

"Some of you didn't admit I was there."

"Our lower ranks were told you were of no importance," Seven Death said disdainfully. "Besides, it makes them uncomfortable to admit that anyone 'disappears.' They'd prefer trouble-makers to be dealt with through proper official channels, as they are in Xibalba. Up here a simple 'disappearance' is usually easier."

"I didn't find it so easy," Manuel's father said.

"No, you wouldn't have. But now you're to be congratulated. We admit that once you did exist."

"I'm honored, Your Excellency."

"It *is* an honor to be recognized by us. And now we have a place for you."

Manuel's father shook his head. "I think not. My place is still with my family."

Slowly, sparks of rage grew and crackled around the green lord's head. He controlled himself, then folded his long arms and half closed his hooded eyes. "You have no place here, neither you nor those street brats. Let's be quite clear on that! Except that you might have one last function as a schoolteacher." He turned to glare at Ricardo and Elena, who had walked to the shore and were now whispering together by the riverbank. "You can talk some sense into those two. Tell them to come with us now!"

Manuel's father said, "They don't need a schoolteacher any more. They know how to look after themselves."

"You think so, do you?" Seven Death glanced angrily at the Fisher-Folk in the water, who splashed and waved to him. "They've been talking to those foolish, naked savages."

"Who also know how to look after themselves."

Seven Death ignored this. "The savages have been telling those urchins tales of some 'land above the sky'! Surely you don't believe such a place exists."

"I'll keep an open mind, till I find out."

Seven Death drew himself up so that his shadow spread over the island. "The time for open minds is past! You all belong in our Land of Death now."

"No," Manuel's father said. "The children didn't serve you before; they don't have to do so now. I've finally learned that only those who choose to do so, go to your land. You have no power over those who turn away from you."

"You've *learned*! How can a schoolteacher learn?" Seven Death stood motionless, but a trickle of green flame licked around his head. "Who *told you* such a thing?"

Manuel's father glanced up at the maple, on whose branch all four owls were perched, watching intently. Seven Death followed his gaze and hissed, "The *owls*! Those traitors who defied the wishes of Lord Gathered Blood and spared the life of his vile daughter, Ixquic!" He shook his head mockingly. "Oh, schoolteacher, how foolish you have become to listen to teachers like those!"

"Very foolish," said Manuel's father, "but I'm starting to learn."

Lord Seven Death shook his head pityingly. "None of you is worth wasting my time on." His narrow lips twisted into what might have been meant for a smile. "Ixquic had two sons — do you know that, schoolteacher? Though she defied us, her two sons grew up. Not everyone is so lucky. And your younger son's new friends will want a companion." He spun on his heel and stalked back to the boat, his cape swirling around his ankles.

Ricardo and Elena stood before Manuel's father. "You scared him away," Ricardo said.

Manuel's father shrugged. "In any case, he left us." Manuel wondered why he wasn't more pleased.

"You really did!" Elena cried happily. "Come on, Manuel, let's dance!"

But Manuel didn't want to dance, only to rest. If the

children wanted to play, let them go off and play alone. But why was his father so sad and so worried?

Elena was leaning over him. "You're lazy!" Elena said. There was a fresh light in her eyes, he thought; she had never seemed so strong before.

"Yes, you are," Ricardo added. "You just lie there."

Manuel knew they were wrong; he wasn't lazy, he was just resting. "I'll get up soon," he told them. "I have to practice my *futbol.*"

The flute boy laughed. "That's hard work! Why don't you play with us instead?" He played a new tune whose words Manuel knew, though he couldn't quite recall them.

But Elena seemed to know them; at least, she spoke as if she were singing. "Come with us, out to the water," she urged him. "If you get out of this chair — just take our hands, you can do it — you can walk along the logs the same way we do."

"But I have to take my *futbol* along," Manuel told her.

"That old thing!" The beggar-girl's scorn surprised him. "It's part of *this* world, the old world. You don't need it any more." Where had she learned to talk this way, with such authority? "We've left all that behind," Elena continued. "Come with us and leave all this behind too."

And the flute boy played a new, sprightly tune that seemed to leap from wave to ripple on the flowing blue river.

"We play with music!" said the beggar-girl, and she clicked her castanets in a new rhythm which also seemed to leap across the water. "Not with dirty old toys like that!" she added.

But his ball was much more than a toy, Manuel thought, and she shouldn't talk about it that way. He wanted to hold it again, to remember how it felt in his hands. He leaned forward to reach for it. But the effort was such a great one! His body had become so heavy that he could barely lift one hand, and he heard a curious sound, like an engine trying to push a too-heavy load. That was his heart thumping, he realized after a time, and the noise of his breathing, as his lungs fought to get enough air.

The flute boy stopped playing and leaned forward, watching Manuel with interest. The beggar-girl only smiled. "So much effort! And all for a dirty toy! When you come with us, you'll find lots of better toys. And balls that you don't have to kick or throw — you only have to think of what you want to make it so!" And she beamed more kindly at Manuel, who was lying back again, exhausted.

Down in the river, the lords in the green boat had given up collecting logs. It was possible to escape their net, after all.

His father stood in front of him, looking at him over the heads of the children. Does he want me to go with them or stay here? Manuel wondered. Why doesn't he say?

"You see, he's watching too," the beggar-girl told Manuel. "He doesn't look happy, does he? Because he's waiting for you, so we can all make our journey together. First down the river to where it grows wide and mixes with the sea, where the seals and the small whales play. And then past great cliffs, until the shores on either side disappear, and there's only water everywhere. But you won't mind the open sea; none of us will. We won't even mind the cold. We can climb the icebergs and slide down again as often as we like. And that's only the beginning of our voyage."

And the beggar-girl's eyes shone as she thought of leaving behind the sad bus stations, and the dull sleeping passengers, and the barren deserts, and the village street where she had lived, and the stinking heap of rags from which she had first joined them.

Ricardo and Elena walked to the river's edge and waited for him. Was it true that his father would follow them? He might stay with those owls of his. But Manuel could go part way down the river with the children and then come back.

He'd be so light then that it would be no problem to go wherever he chose. He could walk on the logs and play with them as well as the children did. He could help the logs escape from the green boat — which was just vanishing round the head of a distant island, perhaps in search of some poor logs that had gone astray. But neither the children nor his father nor he would ever be afraid of those stupid green boatmen again.

And the others, Manuel thought, the ones who would stay behind? His mother must be near the office, though when he turned his eyes in that direction he couldn't see her. And Pepe? Would his brother be back from school yet? He must just be home. He was coming toward Manuel, still carrying his schoolbooks. Manuel shut his eyes, and kept them shut while Pepe stood in front of him, speaking softly, until Pepe decided he really was asleep, and walked away. He set his books down on the picnic table near the footbridge, and disappeared from Manuel's view.

Manuel heard owls hooting in the maple tree, four of them now. In a few minutes Pepe glided into view again, sitting in the red canoe. No one was there to watch him this time, and no one had made him put on his lifejacket. Still, surely he would be careful out on the cold water.

And Pepe was careful. He stayed close to shore, within the little bay between Owl Point and the lodge. He couldn't keep a straight course at first, unless he kept switching the paddle from one side to the other. Then he got the knack of controlling the canoe from one side only. He crossed the little bay, still sitting on the rear thwart. As his confidence grew, he headed out into the river. The winds caught him and pushed the canoe sideways, but Pepe knew what to do about that. He knelt in front of the thwart and began paddling again. Now he had the canoe under control, and he headed farther out on the river.

The Fisher-Folk on the shore of Refuge Island watched with concern. The two fishermen in the motorboat didn't look up, but started their motor and headed away upstream.

Pepe was handling the canoe well, Manuel thought. His brother looked up at him and waved. But then the owls called out in alarm. His father must have heard them: he had left Manuel's side and was staring at his other son. Out on the water, a gust of wind and a wave came together and tipped the canoe toward the left. Pepe leaned to the other side to right it. But he leaned too far, and the canoe suddenly tipped and threw him into the river. He disappeared, then came up again, paddling with his hands near the canoe; his blue denim jacket seemed to be holding his arms back as he tried to grab the canoe.

He wouldn't be able to reach it, Manuel thought. And there was no one to help him! His father leaned over him, staring into his eyes. Would he forgive him if he called for help? Would something terrible happen if he spoke? His father touched his shoulder. "Speak!" he said. "You must speak, you must choose your brother!"

It would be all right. "Help! Help Pepe!" Manuel called loudly. The owls in the maple tree echoed him.

His brother's head was still above the water. "Help him! He's drowning!" Manuel cried. He saw his mother run toward the footbridge, with Mrs. Dorset right behind her. In the river, the fishermen's motorboat had turned toward the canoe. "Hold on to the canoe, kid!" one of the men shouted. "Don't try to swim, just hold on!" "Hold on, Pepe," echoed Manuel. "Please, try to hold on!"

Pepe's head went beneath the water, then appeared again. He made three strokes and managed to grab the canoe's submerged side. He clung to it as the motorboat drew alongside.

The man in front grabbed him under the arms and dragged him into the boat.

Mrs. Dorset stood by the shore. "Is he all right?" she called to the fishermen.

"Sure I'm all right!" Pepe called. "I was going to swim to shore."

"Just as well you didn't, sonny," the fisherman who had caught him said. "The way you swim, you never would have made it."

"I'll get a blanket," Mrs. Dorset called. She ran into the lodge and was back with the blanket before the motorboat reached the landing stage, towing the canoe behind it. Soon the fisherman who had caught Pepe was guiding him, protesting and covered with a blanket, toward the lodge.

Where was his mother? Manuel thought, and then realized that she was standing behind him. "So you spoke," she said softly. "You spoke. Oh, Manuel! I wondered what would make you speak again. I'm glad it was your brother. You spoke up for the living."

Mrs. Dorset came up beside her. "It's so lucky those men heard Pepe call," she said. His mother didn't correct her, and Manuel quickly shut his eyes. He felt exhausted, but in a good way, somehow.

"Is he sleeping?" Mrs. Dorset whispered.

"I think so."

"He's breathing better, isn't he?" Mrs. Dorset said after a time. "And his color is so much better. The sleep must be doing him a lot of good. Dr. Friesen will be pleased when he sees him this evening. He was afraid we'd have to take him to the hospital after all."

"Let's let him sleep," Manuel's mother said.

"Of course."

When he was quite sure they were gone, Manuel opened

his eyes again. His father was standing by his feet. "That was hard, wasn't it, to cry out so?" he said gently. "Much harder than to fly away down the river."

"Are you going away?" Manuel asked him.

"Because you spoke? Not yet. But for now I'll let you rest." His father walked off into the trees, and soon Manuel couldn't see him any more. He couldn't see the musical children either, at first. Then he caught a glimpse of them far off on the river, riding the logs. They waved to him as they disappeared around the bend. At least, he thought, they had waited to say goodbye, before taking their long journey to the open sea and the sky.

FOURTEEN

Ball Games

Now he could rest easily by the river, where the guides of the last tour boats of the year were still talking about the undefended border.

His brother was no worse for his dunking in the St. Lawrence River. Pepe had insisted on taking the canoe out again the next day — wearing a lifejacket this time, with Mrs. Dorset watching him from shore.

Mrs. Dorset was so pleased that Manuel's fever was down, that his strength was coming back, and that he was talking again — though of course she didn't press him to do so — that she volunteered to look after the office herself, while her pots were firing in the kiln, and let his mother sit with him by the river. On one warm night they stayed outside until the stars came out, and were then replaced by a display of Northern Lights. They looked up in wonder at the great shifting curtain of blue-green shimmer in the sky. Pepe explained that it came from rays from the sun hitting the earth's upper atmosphere. But neither Manuel nor his mother was convinced, and the next day she read to him a Canadian Indian story that said that the good spirits in the sky country used these lights to call people up to their kingdom, and that the lights showed that the sky spirits were looking after their land on earth.

"Did you like that story?" she asked.

Manuel nodded. "*Claro*. Those were good lords." He didn't explain, and his mother didn't ask him to.

One day an unusual number of pulpwood logs floated down the river past them. Manuel's mother watched him with concern. "One of the cages up the river, what they call 'log booms,' broke," she said. "The local radio was talking about it; they think someone was trying to steal the logs. That happens sometimes."

"They got away too." Manuel smiled as he said this, and his mother relaxed.

"You aren't afraid when you watch them now?"

Manuel thought. "No."

"You were before."

Manuel looked at her. She had seen and learned so much, why shouldn't she know the rest? "They turned Papá into a log."

"Ah!" His mother drew a long breath. "Who did?"

"The green men. The green lords, in the village. But he got away from them. He swam down the stream, across the pond, and over the waterfall."

His mother nodded. She got up quickly and walked away from him for a few minutes, by the river, her face turned away. Her cheeks were still wet when she came back. "Is that what you saw?"

Manuel nodded. His mother's eyes were brimming with tears. She wiped them and said, "Did you see something like that on television, before we crossed into Canada? Do you remember? The show that the Canadian immigration officer had seen? I'm sure that show helped convince him to let us in."

Manuel considered. "Something like that. But those logs

were on the ground. No, they weren't logs — they were people."

"Yes, they were people," his mother said.

To make her happier, Manuel said, "They tried to catch him, you know. They really did. But he got away. They'll never be able to get him now."

She wiped her eyes again. "Are you sure?"

"Oh yes. And afterwards, when we had left home, they kept trying to catch him. They tried to trick him, pretending he had to go with them." He laughed. "But Papá was too smart for them!"

"I'm sure he was." His mother looked at him closely. "You'd better rest now. We don't want you getting sick again."

Manuel was grateful that she hadn't asked him who *they* were, who his father had been too smart for. But before she left so that he could take a nap, she asked, "Where's Papá now?"

"I don't see him," Manuel said cleverly, without really looking. He thought he might be able to see his father if he looked hard enough, but that was one of his father's secrets that he should still keep.

His mother must have told Pepe what Manuel thought he'd seen the green men doing, but his brother didn't speak to him about it until he was almost well and they were sitting together on the sunny veranda that looked out on the highway.

"You couldn't really have seen that it was Papá," Pepe said. "Look, I remember how far it was from our house to the bus stop because I used to count my steps when I came home on weekends. It was four hundred and sixty steps — twice as far as it is to the road here. Look at that car passing. Can you tell who's driving, at that distance?"

Manuel looked at the car. He was pretty sure the driver was the electrician his mother had called the day before, to install outlets for block heaters in the parking lot. But why not let Pepe think that he, Manuel, had been mistaken? "Well," he said, "I'm not sure."

But now Pepe sighed and shook his head. "Who am I trying to fool? You saw what you saw. We would have heard from him if he was still alive." Abruptly, he walked away, head down, hugging himself with both arms.

Pepe was sure now too, Manuel thought. His brother might question him again, but only to get the scene clear in his mind, not to explain it away. Manuel hadn't told Pepe about seeing his father since that day; he thought he'd never tell him that, or how his father and the others had followed them on their journey.

He saw his father one evening, beneath the tree of owls. Three of the owls had been there when he arrived and had hooted at him like old friends; the fourth one came shortly afterward and hooted at him too.

But he hadn't seen his father by full daylight. Once or twice he thought he saw his shadow underneath the owl tree, but when he looked again it always proved to be the shadow of something else. He decided not to investigate further. If his father was spending all his time with those night birds, he probably wanted to be left alone. What was he saying to the owls? Or what were they saying to him? Was he learning more about the Land of Xibalba?

But Manuel had other things to think of; he'd be going to school after Christmas. He had missed too much of the first term to start sooner, the grown-ups said, and he'd need a little time to get used to the cold weather. But he should be able to enter the sixth grade, the right one for his age, if his mother and Pepe helped him study at home.

He and Pepe each had a room now; their mother kept the one behind the office so that she could let late arrivals in without awaking anyone.

One night Manuel woke up and found his father sitting

at his desk. His father was looking at a large jigsaw puzzle that Pepe had brought Manuel. The lid of the box showed a forest scene, tall trees and rocks and a rushing stream. Most of the trees were done, but Manuel was finding it hard to fit the pieces of foaming water together. His father started to put the pieces in place, almost without looking at them. "Water is difficult, isn't it? It has so many shapes — and it changes so fast. Like life."

His father was talking to him just as he had done in the old days! Manuel started to pinch himself to make sure he wasn't dreaming; then he thought he *might* be dreaming, and stopped. Why should he wake up? "What do you talk about with the owls, Papá?"

"Oh, about all kinds of things. Mainly about what they remember — and their memories go back a long way."

"To Xibalba, you mean?"

"And here, too. They've told me that not all the Fisher-Folk were drowned or shot. Some made it to shore, and their descendants are still living along the river. You may see them." His father was still putting pieces of the puzzle together, one after another. He chuckled. "The owls have a strange sense of time. I told them our own story. They're repeating it now as if it happened at the same time as events before they left Xibalba, or in the forest here before any white men came. I'm looking for the pattern in their stories. I *think* the only one that matters is whether or not the people in them obeyed the Lords of Xibalba."

His father looked down at the puzzle again. "Everything they remember is part of the picture. Just as this strange dark shape" — he held up a piece of the puzzle — "will make sense when it's fitted in. But the past and the present are so much more complicated than the puzzle. There are so many pieces to learn about, and nobody can understand them all. But I have time now to learn about all of our past: about here, about home, about Xibalba — and about places I haven't even thought of yet." He picked up another piece and examined it closely, turning it one way and another, then smiled as he slipped it into place.

For a time Manuel watched his father working on the puzzle. But his eyes grew heavier and heavier, and finally he fell asleep. When he woke up, his father was gone.

————

Manuel was well enough now to help his mother and Mrs. Dorset in the lodge. They cut back the rose bushes and covered them with wood chips to protect them during the winter. They fenced in the bushes and some of the shrubs with hinged green boards — little two-sided tepees, Manuel thought — to keep off the icy winds. Some of the guests had been complaining about drafts, and the pipes had frozen in a few bathrooms last winter, so Manuel's mother called in a carpenter to insulate the walls properly. Together, she and Manuel repainted these rooms, and did a good job of it.

By the time the snow began to fall in earnest, the lodge was warm and cozy. A large pile of firewood was stacked outside, around the corner from the door to the lounge — a room with leather couches and armchairs, a sad, glassy-eyed deer's head on the wall, and a wide fireplace. Manuel had the job of bringing in wood for the fire, and he always managed to keep the blaze going until the guests went to bed. There were fewer guests in winter, but some people put up for the night when they were driving between Toronto and Montreal. More would come later, for the cross-country skiing, and stay longer.

One evening Manuel went out to get more logs, and took a few minutes to stand in the cold air, looking out over the river and watching his breath turn to frost. When he returned, he saw a van with a dent on the rear left fender. He knew that van, even though it was now painted a solid dark green and had a Texas license plate. As he carried the logs into the lounge, he heard a familiar voice.

Mr. Wemyss was sitting on a couch before the fire, his sister at his side with her hand on his arm. Manuel's mother, sitting opposite them, called Manuel over to her.

Mr. Wemyss gave Manuel a warm smile. "I hear you had a tough time of it, youngster."

What had they been saying about him? He was all right now, and he didn't want Mr. Wemyss to think he wasn't. "Not so tough."

Mr. Wemyss raised his eyebrows at these first words. "I can see you're better now. You'll tell me about it soon."

Manuel's mother said, "Mr. Wemyss was telling us *his* story."

"Not such an exciting one." The grocer smiled. "I had to move, so I took advantage of my British citizenship and came here."

"What about your work on the border?" Manuel's mother asked.

"That seems to have disappeared, at least for the time being. Anyway, this is a border too. I may find some work here."

Pepe walked into the lounge, his knapsack of school-books still on his back. "Is that your van outside?"

Mr. Wemyss squeezed his shoulder.

"It's the same one he had before. He just painted it," Manuel said.

"The situation called for a change of color," Mr. Wemyss told Pepe.

"Were they chasing you?" Pepe asked.

"You might say so."

"Good."

"Pepe!" their mother said.

"Well, he didn't belong down there any more than we did."

"You talk too much," their mother said.

Over supper, the grown-ups discussed many things among themselves — mainly, it seemed, where Mr. Wemyss was to sleep and how long he could stay. He was in no hurry to leave, Manuel thought.

That evening, and over the next few days, they learned more about Mr. Wemyss's flight north. He had been very active in the sanctuary movement, helping refugees to safety. He had tried to keep his activities secret, but he was soon spotted by the immigration authorities. They had sent agents to observe and infiltrate the movement almost from the first. Some were as obvious as Jesús Mendoza, with his false friendliness and offers of help. Others, such as Mr. Wemyss's assistant, Hubert, never pretended to be part of the movement, but passed notes and photographs to the immigration authorities and the FBI. Still others were more subtle, and only became known when they testified at the trials of sanctuary members. No, he replied to Manuel's mother's anxious question, the ladies at the church were definitely not informers. In fact, it had even seemed for a time that Mrs. Fisher would be charged with aiding and transporting illegal aliens, but that hadn't happened. Others had been arrested on such charges and now faced the possibility of several years in jail. Manuel thought about the church ladies. Mrs. Pearl would likely have stood being in jail better than Mrs. Fisher — or would she? He hoped neither one would have to find out.

"They certainly would have arrested me," Mr. Wemyss added. "Some of the right-wing newspapers were describing me as a 'foreign agent.' It was high time to leave."

"What about your grocery store?" Manuel's mother asked.

"Well, Sonia, I have a lawyer friend there whose son is running it for the present, until it can be sold. I expect I'll do all right out of it."

Mrs. Dorset put her arm around her brother's shoulder.

"They need a good grocery in Mallorytown; that's only six miles away."

"We'll see. I'll look around." Mr. Wemyss nodded at Manuel's mother. "I wasn't really sorry to leave. It was time for me to be moving on."

"I'm glad you came here," Manuel said.

"We all are," his mother added.

———

Later that evening, when Manuel walked into the lounge to say good night to his mother, he found her talking quietly with Mr. Wemyss. "Did you hear any news of Señor López?" she was asking.

"Only a little," Mr. Wemyss said. "He went south again, to the Yucatán, to follow a rumor about his family. But it came to nothing. He's waiting in Mexico near the border again. We know how to reach him."

"I think he'll always be near that border," Manuel's mother said. "Always waiting."

"I think you're right. But this border suits me better."

"I'm glad," Manuel's mother said. "It suits me better too."

Mr. Wemyss seemed in no rush to start up a business, in Mallorytown or anywhere else. He helped the others finish getting the lodge ready for winter. Together with Pepe, he raised the canoe dock before the bay froze. Manuel's mother watched them anxiously, lest they freeze their hands. When Mr. Wemyss climbed a ladder to nail a shutter to an upper window of the barn, she called out, "The carpenter's coming tomorrow."

Mr. Wemyss smiled down at her. "He doesn't have a head for heights, so he'd be very slow at this. And he charges by the hour."

"Well, be careful." Manuel's mother walked inside to the kitchen, where Manuel had already retreated from the cold.

Mrs. Dorset was watching her brother through the window. "Archie never was afraid of heights. He took me rock-climbing once. Never again! He's almost forty-five now, and acting younger than ever. I think moving north has been good for him. He seemed so sad and old for a while, after his wife died. It's good to see him acting like himself again."

The kitchen door opened and Mr. Wemyss came in, rubbing his hands together. "I've got the last of the shutters up," he said. "They'll keep the snow out. It can come now, whenever it wants."

And the snow did come. First it covered the grass lightly, so that some blades stuck up out of the white blanket. Manuel thought the snow had killed the grass, but Mrs. Dorset assured him that it would grow up from its roots in the spring; all the plants would rise again in the spring, she said, provided enough snow fell to protect them from the winter's deep cold.

The tips of the grass blades disappeared quickly. In early December, three snowstorms followed each other within a week. The first covered the hydrangeas; after the last, only the top of the small blue spruce by the entrance of the office was still visible. Pepe had been walking to school, a mile away, by a wooded path along the highway. Now he began to take the school bus, but he practiced on cross-country skis on weekends, helping Mrs. Dorset clear the easy trails some visitors to the lodge would use. "I'll be able to ski to school next year," he said, shivering, as he stamped snow off his boots by the back door.

Mr. Wemyss used a snowplow attached to the pickup truck to clear the road from the lodge to the highway. The highway itself was kept clear by big clanking orange plows with blue lights flashing behind them.

The road to the barn became completely snowed in. The only marks on it were tracks and droppings of rabbits who came out of the woods to nibble at a clump of weeds that the swirling wind somehow kept clear.

During breakfast one morning, Manuel heard the sound of hammering from the big barn. A road had now been plowed there, and the pickup truck was parked beside the big door at one end. He put on his boots and warm jacket and walked out to the barn. Someone, probably Mr. Wemyss, had been working outside. The big door was closed tight, and sealed shut with plastic sheets held in place by boards nailed along the edges. How long had it taken the grocer to do this work? It was the coldest day Manuel had seen. Though he would have liked to stay outside longer, to enjoy the sparkle and shadows of the snow, the stinging air numbed his nose and lips; even in wool gloves, his fingers were freezing.

He followed the path to the smaller barn door, which was open. Inside, Mr. Wemyss was nailing a board over another piece of plastic sheeting that covered a wide gap in the wall. "That's about the last of them," he said, nodding at several similar patches around the wall. "That'll do for now. I've been talking to a carpenter in town about doing a proper insulation job on the walls, and then finishing them off with some rustic wood paneling."

Mr. Wemyss went on to describe his plans for the space inside the barn: a large main room with a stage at one end, smaller dressing rooms, bathrooms, a lobby by the entrance door. He was so enthusiastic that Manuel didn't want to ask him why, but Mr. Wemyss saw the question on his face.

"What's it for, you're wondering? I've been talking it over with my sister and your mother — she's got a lot of good ideas too. There's all this fine space." He waved his hand toward the high roof, the crossbeams with their dangling ropes, the rusty scythes and mildewed harnesses that hung from the walls. Along either side were rows of empty stalls. "This hasn't been used as a barn in years," he said. "But it would make a fine theater."

As he moved around the walls, finding new gaps that needed small patches, Mr. Wemyss talked of buying seats from a movie-house in Kingston that had recently closed down, and talking to theatrical groups in Kingston or Toronto or Montreal, who could find summer audiences among the many cottagers and visitors to the resort hotels along the river. He spoke of setting up his own gourmet food shop in the lobby, maybe even expanding the restaurant in the lodge — which, without wanting to criticize his sister, he considered little more than a snack bar. It seemed Mr. Wemyss was planning to stay.

Manuel and his family would be staying too. They had not yet had their hearing before the immigration board, but a counselor, a young lawyer from Kingston, had assured them that there was no real danger any of them would be sent back. Manuel was quite well now. Their mother had a responsible job. There was good reason to think that her husband had been murdered for political reasons, and that they all faced great danger if they returned home. It was "a classic case for refugee status," the counselor had said. "Especially," she'd added, "since Manuel is finally willing to describe what he saw after his father disappeared. You will do that, won't you?"

"Yes," Manuel had said. "I'll tell them." He wasn't looking forward to it, but he'd be able to go through with it.

Meanwhile, Mr. Wemyss was talking about new uses for the barn. "We can make a dance floor too. Your mother tells me there are some groups around here who need more room, for square dancing and Scottish dancing and that sort of thing."

Mr. Wemyss and his mother had been talking together a great deal recently, Manuel thought. They never seemed to discuss particularly private matters, but they appeared very comfortable with each other. He wondered what his father would think. Would he mind?

Pepe seemed to be getting on better with Mr. Wemyss

now. They had been spending a lot of time discussing the high school courses Pepe was taking. He was especially interested in Canadian history, even though he knew it had been written by the European conquerors. Once he had grinned, half ashamed, and admitted, "Still, they were the ones who let us stay here."

"Good boy!" Mr. Wemyss had said.

Now, in the barn, Mr. Wemyss had finally stopped sealing cracks and was starting to smooth the dirt floor with an old rake. "After we dig a basement, we'll put in a good hardwood floor. But this one still has its uses. I brought your ball along." He nodded toward the far wall. A short board with a metal hoop attached to it leaned against the wall; beneath it was the *futbol* he had given Manuel so long ago.

"Come on," Mr. Wemyss said, "let's have a game." He scooped the ball out with his foot.

"Good!" Manuel said, taking up a position opposite the grocer.

"So it is. I haven't seen that smile before. It suits you; you'd better keep it."

Manuel and Mr. Wemyss kicked the ball back and forth over the barn floor. Manuel was glad to see that he hadn't lost his skill, though he no longer thought that he would have to play a great game against the Lords of Xibalba. He hadn't thought of them for some time, he realized. And now the thought didn't frighten him.

Perhaps there would be a soccer team at school. Mr. Wemyss, who seemed to have become part of the life of the district, had talked of coaching such a team, if the school would set one up.

Manuel's mother walked into the barn. She was wearing a long brown parka that reached below her knees. "Isn't it too cold here?" She pointed to the cloud of her own breath.

"We're keeping warm with our ball game," Mr. Wemyss

assured her. "Look, there's a basketball hoop too. We'll set it up soon — why are you smiling?"

"I was wondering how you should set it up," she said. "My husband talked about the ball games they used to play in our country, very long ago. In the old ball courts the hoops are set in a vertical position, and a little lower down the sides of the court."

"Is that so? And you throw the ball through them? That doesn't sound hard."

"They didn't *throw* the ball in those old games," Manuel told him. "They had to hit it with their shoulders or their arms. It was really hard to get the ball through the hole."

"I imagine it was. Let's try it," Mr. Wemyss said. "We can hang the hoop over there."

Manuel helped him, handing the hoop up the ladder to him once he'd found a good place for it on the side wall. He nailed it so that the hoop was up and down rather than side to side. Manuel's mother watched them, not even warning her son to be careful. She seemed more worried about the way Mr. Wemyss was standing on the ladder, but said nothing.

"My husband used to talk about the most famous game of all," she said when they were both down. "It was when the young gods Hunahpu and Ixbalanque played against the wicked Lords of Xibalba, the Land of Death. It's described in the old book, the *Popul Vuh*. But I think Manuel knows more about it than I do."

Manuel looked down. He wouldn't tell even his mother just how much he knew.

"I read about the reason for the game," his mother said. "People played it to make the sun come up again. They thought the sun came right out of the earth. It's funny; they seemed to worry more about losing the sun in that hot green land than people up here do in their long dark winter. Here, people take it for granted that the sun will come back. But years ago, in our land, people thought they needed human sacrifices to make the sun rise again. They sometimes used ball games to select the sacrifice victim. If one team won by scoring goals at the end of the court, the captain of the losing side would lose his head.

"But if a team managed to drive the ball through the ring in the wall, which was very hard to do, they won the game immediately and no one had to die. When the ball went through the ring, they said the sun had already risen. Those rings were symbols of life."

"I didn't know that," Manuel said.

"You can't know everything," his mother reminded him.

Mr. Wemyss chuckled. "That wouldn't work with basketball, where there can be over a hundred goals in a game. The poor sun would be dizzy with so much rising and falling. Well," and he shook his head, "we'd better get back to the real world."

He and Manuel played opposite sides, each trying to get the ball through the vertical hoop. Mr. Wemyss handled the ball better than Manuel, striking it accurately with his head, arms, and shoulders, and several times he almost drove the ball through the hoop. But it was Manuel who first bounced the ball against the wall so that it went right through the hoop without even touching it.

The two adults applauded. "You've saved a life and brought back the sun! I'll try to do that too," Mr. Wemyss said. He did, but only after several efforts. "We've both done it now," he said. "The sun's sure to rise again tomorrow!"

"We really had better go in," Manuel's mother said. Now that they weren't moving, the players felt the chill of the cold air.

Before they left, Mr. Wemyss noticed another loose board. While he fastened a strip of plastic over it, and his mother stamped her feet impatiently, Manuel thought back over that old story. How did it end, after the ball game the divine twins won? His father, he remembered, had gone quickly over the last part of the story. Hunahpu and Ixbalanque had stayed for a long time in Xibalba and had finally "died" there. Then, being immortal, they had returned to life and tricked the lords, causing them to die in their turn.

But these lords must be immortal too, Manuel decided. They couldn't really die, even if you could defeat them in a game or make them disappear. He himself didn't expect to see them again, but that didn't mean they were gone. They could surely change their faces and reappear in other forms when they chose.

Mr. Wemyss and his mother were talking together, looking up at the barn roof. As he walked out of the barn behind them, Manuel saw three owls in the air, near the shores of Owl Point. Were they hunting in broad daylight? Ice had formed along the river's edge, but the water ran swiftly farther out, and some small chunks of ice were moving with it. Had some mice been stranded on these floes?

Then he remembered the dreams he'd had when he was sick, and even when he was getting well. He remembered his father putting the jigsaw puzzle together, seeing so quickly what the pieces were and how they fitted in. The rocks and trees were part of the picture. So was the water. So were the owls. And what else? Nobody can understand all the pieces, his father had said, but he wanted to learn about them, and how they fitted together. Perhaps the owls would give him all the pieces he could ever use.

As he followed the others into the lodge, Manuel twisted his head around for a moment to see if he could catch sight of his father, or of his shadow. But he could only see the snow-covered branches of the trees by the river, and the distant sky.

THE END

Afterword

This book is a work of fiction, but the sanctuary movement in the United States — which tried to protect political refugees from Central America, especially El Salvador and Guatemala, from being returned to their murderous governments and unofficial "death squads" — was quite real. Concerned Americans tried to persuade immigration authorities to permit such refugees to remain in the United States. The accounts in this book of pressure by immigration authorities to make refugees sign "Voluntary Departure Forms" (and the forced deportation of those who did so), as well as the temporary protection offered by G-28 forms, are based on actual incidents.

Refugees from Central American countries with right-wing governments were assumed to be left-wing or even Communist. Moreover, the U.S. generally supported these governments as a measure against the spread of Communism, and was unwilling to admit to the atrocities being practiced. As a result, such refugees' requests for political asylum were almost never granted, no matter how desperate the refugees might be. When this became clear, sympathetic Americans developed an "underground railroad" like that used over a century earlier for fugitive slaves. Churches all over the United States, involving an estimated seventy thousand citizens, offered sanctuary to illegal refugees. This sanctuary was seldom if ever violated by authorities. However, the sanctuary movement was soon infiltrated by government agents and informers. Much of the literature on the movement deals with the trials, convictions, and sentencing of the Americans involved in it.

This story is intended to take place in the early 1980s. At that time, the success rate for applications in the United States for refugee claimants from El Salvador and Guatemala was less than one percent. The rate in Canada was approximately seventy percent, and the Cárdenas family's entry to Canada could have been almost as simple as described here. In the last few years, however, the success rate in the United States has increased slightly; that in Canada has decreased.

Some of the Lords of Xibalba, the Land of Death — Gathered Blood, Seven Death, Filth-Maker, and Bringer of Misery — are listed in the *Popul Vuh*, a tale whose implications and symbolism go far beyond those hinted at here. Hunahpu, Ixbalanque, their father, mother, uncle, and the good owls are also found there. Sergeant Confusión is my invention.

The Fisher-Folk are my invention too, though there were incidents in Canada's treatment of its aboriginal people and others which make it clear that the Lords of Xibalba came into this country long ago.

Glossary

Adiós: "goodbye" (Spanish)

Adobe: built out of sun-dried bricks

Barrio: in Spanish, a neighborhood; in English, a neighborhood (often poor) where most people are of Spanish-speaking origin

Buenas tardes: "good afternoon" or "good evening" (Spanish)

Castanets: two concave pieces of wood held in the hand and clicked together, usually to accompany dancing

Claro: "yes!" "certainly!" "sure!" (Spanish)

Futbol: the game of soccer (Spanish)

Green card: a card from the United States Immigration Service, showing that someone has been allowed into the U.S. as a legal immigrant

Gringo: a contemptuous name for someone of English-speaking origin (Spanish)

Hola: "hello" (Spanish)

Jicaro tree: a Central American name for the calabash tree. The tree bears large, hard-shelled fruits called calabashes; the shells can be used for holding liquids, and even boiling them

Maya, an Amerindian people in Central America. The Maya had a highly developed civilization, with great cities and pyramids, before European explorers "discovered" America. The Quiché nation, one of the most powerful Maya nations, was conquered by the Spaniards in 1524

Migra: an immigration officer (Spanish)

Popul Vuh: the sacred book of the ancient Quiché Maya, copied into our alphabet from ancient Mayan hieroglyphic books around 1550, probably by surviving members of the Quiché royal family. However, most Mayan hieroglyphic books were burned by the Spanish

Sanctuary: a holy place near the altar of a church. Also a place of refuge; there is a custom (though not a law) that someone who flees into a church is not pursued and removed

Sanctuary movement: a loose organization of churches and synagogues in the United States in the 1980s, whose main purpose was to prevent Central American refugees from being sent back to persecution in their own countries

Seguridad: security (Spanish); also the government forces responsible for maintaining order and putting down dissent

Xibalba: [Shi-bal-ba]; the underworld, the Land of Death, in Mayan mythology. It is described in the *Popul Vuh*

Sources

BOOKS

The Complete Grimm's Fairy Tales. Margaret Hunt, translator; revised by James Stern. New York: Pantheon, 1972.

The Ground Is Holy: Church Sanctuary and Central American Refugees. Ignatius Bau. New York: Paulist Press, 1985.

Mexican and Central American Mythology. Irene Nicholson. London: Paul Hamlyn, 1967.

Popul Vuh: The Great Mythological Book of the Ancient Maya. Ralph Nelson, translator. Boston: Houghton Mifflin, 1976.

Popul Vuh: The Sacred Book of the Ancient Quiché Maya. Delia Goetz and Sylvanus Morley, from the translation of Adrian Recinos. Norman, Oklahoma: University of Oklahoma Press, 1950.

Sanctuary: A Story of American Conscience and the Law in Collision. Ann Crittenden. New York: Weidenfeld and Nicolson, 1988.

Sanctuary: The New Underground Railroad. Renny Golden and Michael McConnell. Maryknoll, New York: Orbis Books, 1986.

PERIODICALS

"The American Sanctuary Movement." Robert Tomso. *Texas Monthly Press* (Austin, Texas), 1987.

"The Symbolism and Ritual Function of the Middle Classic Ball Game in Mesoamerica." M. Cohodas. *American Indian Quarterly* 2 (2) 99–130, 1975.

Various articles in *Sojourner*, a magazine based in Washington, D.C.